THE CLOCKWORK QUIGLEY

CHRONICLES

MURDER AT THE WORLD'S FAIR

MJ LYONS

Renaissance.
Diverse Canadian Voices

Cover art by Alexander Barratin. Typesetting and interior design by Nathan Fréchette. Edited by Nathalie Cousineau, Meaghan Côté, Myryam Ladouceur, and Evan McKinley.
Legal deposit, Library and Archives Canada, 2019.
Paperback ISBN: 978-1-987963-54-0
Ebook ISBN: 978-1-987963-55-7
Renaissance Press
pressesrenaissancepress.ca

To Mom & Dad,

for making this whole adventure possible.

I write this in Toronto, aboard the steamboat, the *Algerian*, two o'clock p. m. We are off presently. The boat from Lewiston, New York, has just come in—the usual hurry with passengers and freight—as I write, I hear the pilot's bells, the thud of hawsers unloosened, and feel the boat squirming slowly from her ties, out into freedom. We are off, off into Toronto Bay (soon the wide expanse & cool breezes of Lake Ontario). As we steam out a mile or so, we get a pretty view of Toronto, from the blue foreground of the waters—the whole rising spread of the city—groupings of roofs, spires, trees, hills in the background. Good bye Toronto, with your memories of a very lively & agreeable visit.

-Walt Whitman, *Diary in Canada*, 1880

In tedious exile now too long detain'd,
Daedalus languish'd for his native land:
The sea foreclos'd his flight; yet thus he said:
Tho' earth and water in subjection laid,
O cruel Minos, thy dominion be,
We'll go thro' air; for sure the air is free.

-Ovid, *Metamorphoses, Book VIII*

PROLOGUE

IN WHICH OUR INTREPID HERO NORWOOD QUIGLEY BOTHERS A MAN WHO IS PROMPTLY MURDERED

I can still picture that evening, the opening of the New World Exhibition, perfectly in my mind, as if captured in a series of photographs.

The first picture would show an unassuming young man of British stock, fist raised to knock at door 902B on the deck of an enormous steamboat sitting on Lake Ontario, lit up by fireworks on the shore and novel electricity coursing through the ship.

The next, a portly Prussian man with an exaggerated walrus moustache, slightly mussed, in a plush robe standing in the door, only slightly ajar. The Prussian is surly; the aforementioned young man has interrupted something for a bare back is shown over the Prussian's shoulder, ducking into the water closet.

The next photograph illuminates the mistake: the young man had the wrong room for its neighbour, 902A, was the objective of his search. Although, just as he is about to knock, the young man's face contorts in horror as his attention is drawn back to 902B. He has heard a blood-curdling scream.

In the next picture, the young man is slamming into the door of the

Prussian's room, although another gentleman, taller, leaner and robust approaches. In the next the man's face is shown, proud, stern, statuesque, but not unkind. He places a hand gently on the young man's shoulder. He is an older man; there is a family resemblance. This is the young man's father. The next photograph depicts the father expertly kicking in the door to the Prussian's room. The young man, his father, and two steamboat sailors look in, shocked and horrified.

The perspective changes, the comfortable cabin is shown, a large, tall, ornate armoire, a compact writing desk, a bed with blankets and sheets dishevelled, and the body of the murdered Prussian in a pool of blood. Another young man stands above him. He is of Chinese ancestry and is wearing a comely, short silk robe. He clutches a bloody dagger awkwardly, eyes wide at the men who have come crashing into the room. His mouth clearly forms, as it did that night, two words:

"Oh shit."

CHAPTER 1

MY FIRST RIDE ON THE STEAM-POWERED STREETCAR;

OR, THE MOMENTUM OF CANADIAN EXCEPTIONALISM

THE DAILY GLOBE, October 30, 1890

Editorial of Valentine Vanstone, national correspondent

Citizens of the Dominion of Canada, I wish to impart to you a story of great national significance, and this story starts with a streetcar ride.

On this brisk autumn morning, I found myself standing on the corner of Adelaide and Brock among a mélange of labour party leaders, local politicians, suffragists, railway magnates, reporters and curious onlookers; we had gathered outside of the iconic Teston & Tinker workshop. If you have glanced at a watch or ridden a train, you will know the work of Teston & Tinker Co. After its incorporation in 1865, in a small workshop on the Toronto waterfront Ms. Mave Teston and Mr. Darius Tinker III began their work on the differential steam-powered engine, a cleaner, more compact and efficient source of steam power that has changed the shape of modern technology worldwide.

Since its inception, the T&T workshop has been comparable to a

Greek Symposium, inviting scientists and inventors from around the world, regardless of creed, colour or sex, to apprentice, applying various engineering sciences free from outside or nationalistic interferences. A series of commercial successes allowed the then young engineers to build the booming industrial building they currently occupy, and they continue to offer residency and apprenticeship programs to inventors from around the world.

Ms. Teston made a dramatic entrance on the Teston-model bicycle, her personal improvement on the Starley Rover, that features pneumatic tires alongside improved suspension, chain drive and steering systems. The attire of Ms. Teston, a spritely forty-two-year-old Irish immigrant, made quite a stir among the more traditional members of the crowd.

Known as an advocate of women's dress reform, Ms. Teston was, as usual, outfitted in the controversial women's bicycle suit, which consists of a long-fitted tailcoat and bloomers tucked into knee-high riding boots. Ms. Teston is a notorious head turner, especially since her costumes often complement her fiery red hair.

As per usual for public functions, Mr. Tinker was absent and Ms. Teston spoke in his stead.

After handing her bicycle off to a Teston & Tinker fully automated mechanical assistant (more on those strange machines later), Ms. Teston took a moment to greet invited dignitaries. This included Mayor Clarke, functionaries of the soon-defunct Toronto Street Railway, a representative from Canadian Pacific Railway and airship industrialist Hector Quigley Sr., there with his wife, the esteemed Dame Aveline Quigley (nee Jernigan) and their two sons.

Ms. Teston then addressed the crowd to considerable cheers, especially from a spirited group of members from the Dominion Women's Enfranchisement Association, a Toronto-based suffragist group.

"Greetings friends, sisters," she nodded then to the suffragists, garnering a degree of enthusiasm from the group of women that bordered on improper. "Today we embark on a new journey. When my good friend Mr. Tinker and I met, we shared a vision for Canada, one that I can say, with pride, that we are rapidly accomplishing. The power of steam gives us incredible momentum, and not just for our ships, airships, or trains, but as a country. Moving forward into the next century, Canada will demonstrate itself as a pioneer, both in the New World and in the unexplored realm of technologic potential."

With this, a chime came from the north. The crowd turned to see a blazing red, gold-gilded, completely horseless Teston & Tinker Co. streetcar rumbling southward on Brock St. An excited chatter arose; it was difficult not to feel electrified by the spectacle.

"The maiden voyage," Ms. Teston intoned, stepping down from the stage for an encore of handshaking and back patting with the honoured dignitaries, as thrilled as the rest of us.

"This new streetcar arrives, quite literally, at an exciting time for Toronto," she continued, bellowing from among the crowd. "Teston & Tinker, in partnership with Canadian Pacific Railway and the Toronto City Council, are excited to announce that our city has been officially selected as host of the 1892 World Exposition."

At this news, the excitement grew to a fever pitch, as it was clear that the new steam-powered streetcar was not to be the only development unveiled by Teston & Tinker that day. Although it is no secret that Toronto has been vying for candidacy in a close race with Chicago, New York City and Munich, the prodigious work of Teston & Tinker is, no doubt, what put us miles ahead of the Yankees, and leagues ahead of the Bavarians.

Ms. Teston invited forward those of us lucky enough to have received a special ticket (scarlet, gold scripted, matching the streetcar we were to board) each emblazoned with "Teston & Tinker Company: Ride into the future." Ms. Teston, with her signature impish grin, tore each ticket, with pride and received mumbles of appreciation and awe.

I stepped up, walking past a stationary mechanical man at the helm. The vehicle itself sat twenty-four in rows of seats and, if needed, could easily fit another twenty standing shoulder-to-shoulder.

Parents followed their chattering children rapidly filling most of the window seats, and Ms. Teston stepped aboard leaning against the driver's station. There was appreciative applause when the mechanical man exclaimed a stilted but resonant, "All aboard." The streetcar hummed to life and began to slide forward, as if a sled along a well-ridden winter path.

"How fantastic," a generously rouged society dame intoned. She nodded to the mechanical man engaged in avoiding collisions with confounded carriage drivers and their equally quizzical equine. "I've seen these queer things employed to rake leaves in Queen's Park. However do they work, Ms. Teston?"

"Ah, now this is Tinker's area of expertise," admitted Ms. Teston.

"A sort of pastiche of internal switches, clockwork and steam power. A wind-up toy on a grand scale, you could say. Don't understand a bleeding thing about it myself."

Darius Tinker, sometimes referred to as "The Toymaker," is famous for his oft-fantastical designs. The Clockwork Carollers stationed outside the construction site of the new City Hall building last Christmas season were his doing, as is his life-sized steam-powered riding-pony for children. The mechanical men, although crude in resemblance to their maker, are slightly more intricate than their automated animal companions, and are at the very least effective at the simple tasks they are designed for; say, sweeping the floor; shovelling the sidewalk; picking up and moving a box of railway parts too heavy for a single man.

"This," one union representative aboard voiced, "takes away jobs from the working class, already consigned to heavy and dangerous labour."

Ms. Teston was quick to assuage his concern. "Yes, one of Tinker's mechanical men may be able to pick up a dozen steel beams, but what will it do with them then? Think of them as a plough, or an industrial press. Fantastic inventions, indispensable, but useless, even dangerous without a human hand involved. They will not replace the jobs of the working class, but make them less labour intensive."

Ms. Teston rested a hand on the shoulder of the brass humanoid, who remained indifferent to the touch. "They're simple inventions at the core, no intuition, no empathy. No, the working class need not fear these clockwork creatures. Not until Tinker has another breakthrough, anyway," she said with a wink, espousing the laughter of most passengers. The union representative scowled but offered no further editorial.

Simple though they may be, the mechanical man is capable enough to drive the newest steam-powered streetcar, designed by Ms. Teston herself—her specialty being impressive feats of transportation engineering. She invited a few curious passengers, mostly excitable youth, to the front of the cabin.

I, a man of considerable age, though questionable maturity, accompanied them. The speed and technical marvels of the steam-powered streetcar notwithstanding, the children were most fascinated by the mechanical man. They tugged at its coat sleeves, which Ms. Teston assured us were wholly decorative. Adolescent Norwood Quigley, scion of the aforementioned airship entrepreneur, seemed especially keen on carrying out a conversation with the automaton. "What's your name?" he asked. "Do you like driving the streetcar?"

"Don't be stupid, Norwood," his older brother, Hector Quigley Jr., reprimanded his sibling. "It's just a machine."

"Please. Stand behind the white line. For your safety," the mechanical man responded, to the collective bemusement of the children, who dispersed, whispering and giggling to one another. I remained to observe this strange being, roughly human in form, despite being affixed to his driver's station as an extension of the grand machine. The friendly voice, although of a tinny, mechanical modulation, originated from a small electric speaker used in many of Tinker's creations, an improvement on the technology used in

Alexander Graham Bell's telephone machine.

Like the majority of its kind, the mechanical man was shaped from brass, that most resilient of materials. Our driver was exquisitely polished, and he sat almost regally at the front of the vehicle in his crimson jacket like an Oriental statue. I brought my head closer to study the way the thing was welded to the chair when I heard a slight whirring noise, drawing my attention to the eyes (if they can be called eyes—more apertures than anything approaching its human analog). They seemed to, in their own clockwork way, take in the world before them.

"You say there's no intelligence, Ms. Teston," I wondered aloud, "but the thing seemed to see that cat dash across the street, and slowed as not to squash it."

I turned to the world-famous inventor, a look of fiery delight matching her hair and bicycle costume. "The human body, the human mind, a clockwork man, it's all just machinery of differing complexity, Mr. Valentine."

"Next stop," came the dutiful, mechanical voice behind me, "the New World Exhibition."

As if a perfectly timed pantomime, the streetcar slowed, allowing two workers—human, not mechanical—to finish raising a banner that read "Future Home of the '92 World's Fair" between a pair of posts just beyond the Old Fort.

The Toronto Industrial Exhibition grounds are a wholly appropriate location to host the World's Fair. The waterfront has featured an annual exhibition for more than a decade now, drawing in visitors from across Ontario, Quebec and the United States. Many criticize that Toronto lacks an essential waterfront aesthetic beyond rail depots, shipyards and industrial edifices. As Ms. Teston presently demonstrated, the Toronto waterfront could meld the industrial and the cultural essence of our developing metropolis, while creating a proud piece of Canadian heritage.

Ms. Teston escorted her passengers a short distance onto the Exhibition grounds to a small open tent near the athletics Grandstand. Beneath was a small edifice housing boards with various plans and conceptual drawings of the World's Fair waterfront.

"The firm of our good friend, Mr. Lennox, will be employed to design and carry out the construction of the World's Fair buildings." Edward James Lennox, the famed Toronto architect, is renowned for his construction of the new City Hall on Queen Street, a commission received due, in part, to his efforts on the Teston & Tinker building erected in 1881. His work has come to epitomize the Herculean industrial atmosphere of Toronto, that meeting place of steamship, airship, and locomotive, and his success is closely related to that of Teston & Tinker.

The passengers marvelled at plans for the Gallery of Fine Arts, the Canadian Pacific Railway Exhibition Terminal (one that will no doubt rival Union Station), the Automata House, and the almost cathedral-like Electricity Pavilion.

"An American manufacturer, Westinghouse Electric Company, will be working with one of Teston & Tinker's young American engineers, Mr. Nikola Tesla, to make the exhibition fully electric," explained Ms. Teston. "We will also be rebuilding the Grandstand, and refurbishing the Dufferin Gate to the Exhibition ground as well, giving them our own small twists."

Of course, it was clear that the Teston & Tinker Machinery Building will, rightly so, be the centrepiece of the New World Exhibition. The artist's rendering was almost palatial, a massive, ornate workshop with a brass statue of Athena sitting in the courtyard.

Young Norwood Quigley pointed to the artwork of the proposed exhibition pier that will allow for arrivals by steamship, and also feature waterborne exhibits of various shipping companies. Young Quigley drew the crowd's attention to a fantastically large steamboat docked within the drawing, exclaiming, "Ms. Teston, I've never seen a bigger steamship!"

Ms. Teston smiled indulgently. "Something of a personal project of mine. The Hanlan family asked if I would design a luxury steamboat, a floating hotel, to be christened in time for the Exhibition. At ten-decks I believe *Hanlan's Pride* will certainly make waves when it first sails." She motioned to an adjacent picture, one featuring a number of airships of various sizes and functions. "We have no doubt that the Exhibition will have the most airships ever present in one place. Teston & Tinker will be launching the Royal Airship Fleet, among a number of my own commercial designs."

Airship transportation has boomed since Teston & Tinker revolutionized lighter-than-air travel, and the sky above Toronto is daily filled with oblong silhouettes.

"Ms. Teston, I must say that all of this inventing must not give one much time to find a husband," joshed the gentlewoman with the liberally applied blush.

"No, it won't allow time for such frivolity," retorted Ms. Teston, to the appreciative snickering of the present suffragists and others, and disapproving frowns of the rest.

No stranger to criticism, Ms. Teston, while a prodigal transportation engineer, has received the brunt of a certain amount of controversy regarding her involvement with foreign powers beyond the Crown, supplying domains such as the United States and Prussia with military grade airships, steamboats and weaponry. All the more grave in the public's eye are allegations of "ungainly dress," "unwomanly behaviour," and her self-appointed spinsterhood. Ms. Teston, while not formally affiliated with local suffrage groups, also does not distance herself from them, gaining her the ire of society men and women alike.

Indulge me, dear reader. My opinion on suffrage being widely known, I will not freshly harangue my readers. But I will say this: when I recently dined with a friend visiting from the Windy City, he explained to me that if Chicago won the World's Fair bid they planned to dub it the "World's Columbian Exposition". Naming it so would celebrate the 400th anniversary of Columbus's landing and pay homage to the female personification of our neighbours; Columbia, a poetic invention representing the mythic spirit of the United States.

Now I ask you, have our homes not been built on the sacrifice of both the men and women, both the Indigenous Peoples and those who traversed from one coast to the other, carving a country out of this oft cold and inhospitable, albeit eternally beautiful land? Have women not worked twice as hard, building this country from the foundation up while propagating generations of Canadian children?

If the United States has Columbia, I propose that we accept as the female personification of our great industrial nation the "New Woman".

If you are yet to be convinced, simply look at the accomplishments of our own ruling monarch, Victoria. Under her eye, the British Empire has expanded to the four corners of the Earth, and the Dominion of Canada, though in the rough, is the biggest and potentially most beautiful jewel of her crown. If Her Royal Majesty is to visit during the Exhibition, I should hope the earth she steps foot on is worthy of her power and dignity.

As we ambled our way back to the streetcar at a leisurely pace, I noticed a number of female passengers, from young girls to august society dames, excited, chatting to Ms. Teston about becoming involved in the planning and execution of the New World Exhibition.

A formation of airships hurtled above our heads as Ms. Teston shook each of our hands, accepting kind words and congratulations. "I wish I could accompany you back, but there's much to do here," she said in an assured voice. I could not help thinking about how this is a world on the verge of a great change and how exciting that is to be a part of.

I turned to one of my fellow passengers near me, the bright-eyed young Norwood Quigley as it happened. "What do you think of this new Canada, my young friend?" I asked, motioning at the intense activity surrounding us.

My adolescent companion grinned from ear to ear. "Well, it's quite exciting, isn't it? It's a chance to build something new, I think. Everyone working together for something better. It's something I want to be a part of!"

I chuckled and patted my utopian-minded young travelling companion on the back. Like young Mr. Quigley, it's clear that all forward-thinking individuals feel energized by the momentum of Canadian potential. Should you need a little invigoration, simply step aboard one of the new Teston & Tinker, horseless, steam-powered streetcars and ride into the future. Hopefully a better one.

CITY OF TORONTO, 1893

CHAPTER 2

IN WHICH NORWOOD ATTEMPTS TO ATTAIN A PHOTOGRAPH OF MR. TINKER AND HIS FANTASTICAL WORK THROUGH THE USE OF A SMALL EXPLOSION

I find it strange that something as simple as a picture, a portrait of a small, frail, cagey, scowling old man accompanied by a little less than five-hundred words can so drastically change the course of events. Had I not been assigned to photograph the great inventor, Mr. Darius Tinker, I wouldn't have been present for the events that unfolded over the next few days. I would have ascertained no knowledge of the grave injustices being committed, and the men who do so. I would have been unable to play my small part in sparing the lives of countless innocents... but I get ahead of myself.

It was a sunny, late April morning that I quit my lodgings on Duchess, on the eastern end of the city, and took to the warm Toronto streets. The city was in its usual throes of chaotic business, exacerbated by the impending opening ceremonies for the New World Exhibition. Kodak camera in hand, I was unperturbed by the busyness—indeed, I revelled in it; the soothing hum of people going about their lives, punctuated by screeches of machinery, whinnying of horses or curses of derelicts.

An enchanting, heady haze dappled the city's rooftops. I decided to forgo a trip on the horseless streetcar—still quite a novelty among city folk, even though Toronto had been fully outfitted with the technology the previous summer—to enjoy a walk in the vibrant, intoxicating spring weather.

I made my way down bustling Adelaide, taking in the sight of small repairs being completed on the Grand Opera House, no doubt in anticipation of thousands seeking entertainment during the World's Fair, occasionally bidding a hearty "good day" to familiar neighbours. A shopkeeper and I chatted a moment, remarking on the Opera House's advertisements for the world-famous Lady Song's appearance next week, sure to be a sold-out run of performances and a boon to local businesses.

With such a novel piece of equipment under my arm and, as it's been described to me, my signature dazed sense of wonder, many took passing notice of me. As a youth of eighteen, even in a tailored sack coat and trousers, I managed to appear in a constant state of slight dishevelment, through no conscious design. Unlike my father, brother and many of my peers who, even when in their shirtsleeves or athletic dress, appeared wholly proper and on the edge of fashion, my more liberal sensibilities shone through preparations made in the morning.

My father had often remarked affectionately on my "bohemian" appearance, untamed hair, clothing slightly askew, a camera case strapped to my shoulder or a sketchbook wedged beneath my arm, my fingers stained with charcoal or graphite dust. I looked wholly an artist, as many observed. I chose to take that as a compliment, though many, including my father and brother—secretly and not, respectively—would not consider it such.

My aim was to be a great journalist and writer, though I'd been warned by multiple published authors that the profession was undervalued—not to mention woefully underpaid—and seen as ignoble. Ironic, as there seemed to be no small public interest in the humble scribblings of word mercenaries. I planned to couple the skill of setting ink to paper with some small talent for photography and join the growing rank of "photographic journalists."

The problem: I was an idle, moneyed boy with nary a journalistic credit to my name. One of the worst sorts to boot. I was a well-heeled child desperate to make a name for himself independent of his family fortune and reputation—while relying on those very things to do so.

My father had purchased my camera for my eighteenth birthday. My comfortable apartment in the city, my well-tailored wardrobe and my exceptional education were all the products of my parents' success. My father had even offered to put me in touch with members of the press in hopes that I would make something of myself, but I had politely declined. The only thing that was all my own was my ambition, whatever good that was worth.

To Lionell Hackerman, the *Globe*'s editor, it was worth little enough.

"I've got no need of more writers, Quigley. The useless lot are thick on the ground here," Hackerman had put it bluntly when I had turned up at his office a day previous. He had barely glanced at my photographs and had completely ignored the few writing exercises I had prepared for the impromptu interview.

I'd been inquiring after a number of other publications, but had been politely and roundly rejected for lack of experience or reputation. The *Globe* was the only game left in town for me, and I had reluctantly included my pedigree when I called on the secretary of Mr. Hackerman. I had been unwilling to do so leading up to this interview, so with little choice, I figured the only thing that would get me into his office was my family name. I still hadn't counted on such an obstinate wall of a man hunched behind his desk.

"Perhaps I can offer my photographic expertise," I suggested, wincing. "I've made an extensive study of airship workers, and the working cla—"

He bristled at this. "What good are pictures of the downtrodden when all the world wants to see are photographs of this blasted carnival?" He punctuated the rhetoric with a dismissive wave of the hand. The editor returned to eviscerating a draft of writing on the desk before him, ignoring me as I gathered my samples off his desk. I was reaching for the doorknob when I heard an annoyed grunt behind me, and I turned for fresh rejection and abuse.

"I'll admit, having a Quigley could be useful, would drive the competitors mad," he admitted. I suppressed an urge to groan. Here I was trying to prove I could be more than just a name, yet that was all I was to the world. "I'll give you one chance and one chance only, and I don't expect you to succeed, no one else has."

He laid out my probationary assignment. Mave Teston, one of the founding inventors behind the Teston & Tinker workshop here in Toronto, had been documented widely in the lead-up to the World's

Fair. She gave interviews freely and was well liked enough by the public, despite her feminine sensibilities listing toward "sturdiness" and "ungainliness."

Teston was a celebrity, sure, but the real public obsession was her elusive compatriot, Darius Tinker III. While his work in the venture was prodigious, he was rarely seen and was remembered as an eccentric, but not the entertaining kind—more an anti-social recluse. The inventor had eluded the public eye, to the annoyance of investors and the confoundment of the public. With no small amount of sneering, Mr. Hackerman admitted that a photograph of Darius Tinker coupled with a few hundred words about him would capture the imagination of the public.

"We've sent a hundred reporters before you to speak with this mad old codger, and they have yet to catch a glimpse of him," he growled, aggressively organizing a pile of papers in front of him. "I'm starting to believe the only tinkering in the enterprise is with the patience of those of us with a serious job to do.

"I've got no faith in you, Quigley," he repeated a third time. I only nodded but was secretly thrilled at the assignment. Even if I was unsuccessful in the endeavour, I could simply add this failure to the long list of ways I didn't live up to my family name.

I assured Mr. Hackerman that, indeed, the endeavour was futile—I had heard from a few other writers that pessimism in the face of existence always seemed to calm editors—although I pointed out that there'd be no shame in allowing myself to become the hundred-and-first reporter to fail to meet Mr. Tinker.

Begging "more important things to do than speak with a writer," with a few expletives thrown in for good measure, Mr. Hackerman shooed me away. "And don't come back without a ruddy photo."

This is how I found myself cutting through the city to the corner of Adelaide and Brock the next day, my destination now in sight. My fate as a journalist rested on doing the impossible, getting a picture of a world-famous inventor who had not been seen in decades.

Down on the corner of Brock and Adelaide, I could see that edifice of industrialism, the Teston & Tinker Workshop, looming above the garment factories, synagogues and such on the west end of town. The three-storey stone building assumed a more palatial front than the warehouses and factories surrounding it. Large windows adorned the sides of the building framed by dramatic arches; whimsical, cylindrical towers broke up rusticated walls. Above the main entrance was an enormous, elegant clock held in place by exquisitely wrought iron fretwork. Below the dial, shaped into the fretwork, read: ET IPSA SCIENTIA POTESTAS EST

Once within, I expressed my business to a young Ojibwe man in the vestibule who I (to my mortification) took to be a clerk or attendant. He peevishly waved me down a hallway before returning his attention to a section of an enormous clock—I had failed to notice he was sitting within the carriage-sized machinery. Flushed with embarrassment, I proceeded onwards, peering when I could into the dozen or so workshops. Only two were occupied; one by a Negro woman immersed up to her elbows in a large steam engine; the other by a boy of a swarthy complexion, no older than myself, snoring lightly, propped up at a desk, surrounded by cogs and switchboards of varying sizes. The other rooms, only affording a soft light diffused through heavily glazed transom windows, were mostly steeped in shadows. Outlines of various grand technologies loomed in the dark. Within one workshop a half-finished brass automaton turned to watch me pass.

I found myself at the designated room. Crude signs, the result of some small trickery, adorned the door frame that read "TOYMAKER" and "Enter at your own risk". Clutching my camera in both hands, I ventured into the workshop of Darius Tinker.

Upon entry, I was convinced the room must be uninhabitable. In fact, it was in such a state of complete disorganization, I assumed I had been given incorrect directions and had walked into the building waste depository. The workshop was a dark, cavernous room that occupied two floors of space. Semi-completed constructions piled upwards to the ceiling and occupied every inch of the room; brass parts, gears and springs jutted outwards dangerously, in no obvious arrangement. Through the detritus and gloom, I could make out two large loading doors on what was certainly the farthest end of the building. I took a few tentative steps into the gloom, unable to determine any sign of life.

I prepared to turn about and head back to make a nuisance of myself to one of the other inventors when a sparkle of light from a nearby pile caught my eye. There were two enormous glowing emerald orbs starring from the darkness. For a moment I could make out a faint and rapid ticking. The strange apparition blinked once and sprung to the ground, giving metallic clicks and pops as it moved.

I leapt back as the shadow creature approached my feet. However, a little light spilling in through the doorway behind me illuminated the thing; a mechanized approximation of a small cat. The feline machine brushed against my leg and glanced up at me with two shimmering emerald spheres. The ticking noise emanated from what was, I'm sure, a very complex system within, and the clicks and pops came from its segmented parts and intricate joints that allowed it to move like its flesh and bone analog. Despite the surprise of the creature's sudden appearance, and its hairless, skeletal look, the mechanized animal seemed quite harmless, even friendly.

"Tickertape, who are you bothering?" a thin, mumbling voice came from among the rubbish. The cat's eyes blinked once with a click, and it sped off, dodging around piles of debris, showing me a path. Emboldened by this discovery of life, or at least life-likeness in the clockwork cat and the voice of its master, I followed, taking care to avoid the labyrinthine jags of various machine piles and half-constructed clockwork creations.

I rounded what seemed to be the largest mountain of junk. This, I had to assume, was based around some sort of workbench. The small patches of space still visible on the surface were scattered with various canisters of chemicals, tools and scraps of paper scrawled with schematics and designs.

Finally, I found a small clearing in the chaos where a strange little man, dressed in dirtied shirtsleeves and trousers, hunched over something. He was small, thin and had light brown skin; pallid, it seemed to absorb, rather than glow, with the dim lamplight in the room. His coiling moon-white hair fell about his head in no attempt at order. Tickertape, no doubt the name of the clockwork cat, sat haughtily beside its master on a cleared surface studying my approach, its tail flicking side to side in interest. I cleared my throat, to no response. I did so again, louder, and still nothing. I could feel my face turn red as I uttered, "Mr. Tinker, I presume?"

The man turned and, with little more than a glance at me, returned his focus to his machine. "One moment, please. This work—very delicate."

"Of course," I replied in a whisper, barely daring to breathe should I disturb something, though I was sure my answer did not register as his attention was already on his work again. For a moment I watched as his hands, wrapped in bandages, administered quick and efficient to the machinery. I glanced around the small space lit not by electricity, like the rest of the building, but by a small, simple oil lamp on a nearby table. The table was otherwise clear apart from a pile of schematics and almost empty plates of food. A small cot, the sheets cast aside, was the only other piece of furniture not covered with mechanical parts, with a small pile of books and technical manuals pile, haphazard, beside it. On top was a beautiful, ponderous tome, Whitman's *Leaves of Grass*. Curious.

Lost in my observations, I hardly heard the man mumbling. "I beg your pardon?" I stuttered, not entirely sure he spoke to me as his attention seemed to be completely on his work.

"Your camera, may I see it?" He held out a free hand, each finger grease-covered and mummified in yellowing bandages. Fumbling, I deposited the device in his palm and he finally turned away from his work.

"Hmm, an Eastman Kodak box camera. One of the first models of its kind. Kept in good enough condition." He carelessly held the camera out. I grasped my dear device before it could fall from his hand to the floor and decline in condition. "Who are you?"

I attempted a regal pose with my camera, although he had already turned away and was indifferent. "Quigley, sir. Norwood Quigley. I—"

He continued grumbling to himself, "Quigley... That name sounds familiar..."

I swore inwardly; I hadn't meant to reveal the familial connection, but I couldn't lie to so eminent a person. "No doubt my father, Sir Hector Quigley, of Quigley Airships, the family business. We fly exclusively Teston & Tinker models."

He turned from the machine on the ground, his face shrouded in shadows by the light behind him, again studying me with caution. "I don't handle transportation business. You'll have to go to the administrative offices on the... second floor and speak to... well someone else."

I realized my error before he'd finished his directions. "My apologies, Mr. Tinker! I'm not here on my father's behalf. I'm not involved in the business end of things, really, though I do know my way around your airships. No, I'm here on behalf of the *Globe*." He stared blankly at me. "The newspaper." I held up my camera, as if an explanation. "For coverage of the New World Exhibition." His brow furrowed in consternation. "That's the... international festival of technological and cultural marvels?" Nothing. "I telephoned ahead yesterday... I was told you might pose for a picture..."

I recalled the amused female voice on the other end of the phone. "Oh, he *might* pose for a picture." I realized how loaded her words had been.

Mr. Tinker's eyebrows knitted closer. "I'm afraid that is not my area of expertise. I'm a simple craftsman." He motioned awkwardly around, at the gatherings of such fantastic machines, including the clockwork cat that had leapt off the workbench and was brushing against his shin. "If you want to take a picture of someone, I would seek out Mave—Ms. Teston. She looks much better on film. I am... really far too busy."

He turned his attention to an intricate machine on a nearby table. It appeared to be the chest of a man in the dim light, although when Mr. Tinker removed a front plate, cogs and gears were revealed within. Our exchange seemed to be complete, but I remained where I was.

I crouched, reaching out my hand—as if to any household pet—and with a click of its eyes, the clockwork creature approached, causing soft metallic ticking with its paws on the stone floor. I allowed my fingers to find the crook between ear and skull, a favourite place to be scratched for most cats. "Interesting creature, this." I smiled down at the mechanical feline, pretending to speak to no one in particular. Mr. Tinker, I'm sure, feigned deafness, so I continued, "Beautiful, really. Nice kitty, Tape... Taper..."

"Tickertape," Mr. Tinker interjected gruffly. I apparently had his attention. I repeated the name, with some awe. "After the sound he makes, like a stock ticker," Tinker muttered as if explaining it to a simpleton.

"Of course," I replied. "Quite a complex machine, I'm sure. Much like the mechanical men around the city."

"Nothing like them," he grumbled. "Crude things, utilitarian."

I chuckled. "Teston & Tinker seem to be doing swift business with them. I hear there's to be a whole building devoted to them at the World's Fair, a fully automatic home."

Mr. Tinker scoffed. "Such mindless mechanical drudgery. I don't wish to denigrate the work of my peers, but the wonder these philistines have for automatons that sweep the sidewalk, and dust the fine china..."

I watched as Tickertape stretched, groans and pops coming from the metal he was fashioned with. "What would you propose in their place? Litters of mechanical kittens? Toronto is overrun by irritable toms as is."

At this Tickertape let out an annoyed, mechanical, "Miaow!" and Mr. Tinker turned away from his administrations again. "And why not? Oh, I know, people laugh at my work. 'Toymaker' isn't necessarily a respectful endearment," he continued in the same quiet grumble, though there was an edge to his voice. "Clockwork children's ponies, orchestrions, leisure flying machines for young people. Frivolity, they say. Little money to be made in a mechanical cat but for a novelty, a toy, they say. But where is the whimsy in the world? Where is the joy in our fantastic technologies? The artfulness? Will children grow up in a cold, automaton world?"

Tickertape and I watched as Mr. Tinker finished his quiet but impassioned speech, the cat's apparent clockwork stupor mirroring my own.

Mr. Tinker turned away from me, embarrassed. "My apologies. The ramblings of a daft old madman who wants nothing more than to build toy cats." He waved over his shoulder just as Tickertape dashed off into the shadows as if after something, perhaps a clockwork rat. "Mave's work, improving my designs, is beyond belief. She understands the necessities of the times. The industry, the military demands. The politics," he spat this word as if he'd ingested machine grease. "She's a genius, and deserves all the praise in our venture."

"Mr. Tinker," I said after a brief silence, "if I may, I feel the same way about my work."

He glanced over his shoulder and we made brief eye contact before he looked at the workbench beside me, pointing to a tool, which I promptly handed to him. "My father is one of the world's most successful businessmen. He was the son of a simple English sailor. Built Quigley Airships from the ground up, so to speak. Knighted for all of the work he's done in the New World, in the name of England. He's accomplished all these great things, travelled all over, and impressed his success on my older brother. He is the strongest, kindest, most generous and intelligent man I know.

"But," I continued, hoping I still had Mr. Tinker's attention, "he's a businessman. Like a lot of his peers, he finds those things beyond the scope of making money... frivolous, I suppose.

"He bought me one of the first Kodak cameras, thinking I could take some pictures of the airships, contribute something, anything, to the family business. He couldn't understand why I started taking portraits of the men who worked for him. The airmen, labourers, pilots. And beyond that; blackguards, thieves, immigrants, Catholics, homeless, the destitute, street urchins, sinners, all on the city streets."

I paused. Noticing Mr. Tinker had ceased working momentarily, I pressed on, "Don't misunderstand me. He is a compassionate, loving man, working for the good of the world, but we differ in our feelings for these people. They live their lives much as we do, although with considerable more hardships, I suppose. 'We Quigleys must shape the world,' he often says. But I know, while he loves me, I'm not included in that assessment. I'd like to live up to my name, but despite my best efforts, I find it a challenge. Even with his success and genius, Father can't understand my creating something solely for myself, which becomes a piece of my life I'm able to share with others."

I ceased haranguing Mr. Tinker, prepared to be banished from his property, either politely or by force, but the older man stood, propped against the table before him. "I would," he almost whispered, "very much like to see some of your pictures sometime."

I couldn't suppress a grin. "I'd like that very much."

He remained where he was, as if in deep thought. I interrupted his rumination with what I hoped was a polite question. "Mr. Tinker, I'm curious. The *Globe* has two or three photographers and a dozen writers—the others being far more experienced, and technically able than I. None of them have ever even seen you before..."

Although still masked in the gloom, I could swear I noticed Mr. Tinker smirking a little. "They would always stick their head in the door and shout like there was a fire," he explained, the tone of his quiet voice bordering on amusement. "One of them tripped on an engine and cut open some vital artery a few years back—none of the lot really tried after that.

"I figured someone would persist hard enough eventually. Someone who wasn't a complete cretin. And I hoped that person would be quiet, thoughtful... bright. And kind."

Again, in the darkness, I couldn't tell, but I believed Mr. Tinker flushed at the implied compliment to me. I beamed once again and was returned with a smile that seemed to take a pained effort on the inventor's part. "Mr. Tinker, I would like very much to photograph you, and I would like to share it with everyone with a little something written about your wonderful workshop."

He seemed to think about this for a moment. "Yes, well, I suppose... some small public concession... Go ahead."

"Oh." I had been preparing to engage in shameless begging and found myself unprepared for this simpler outcome. "Good then!"

However, I realized the darkened environment would not work for a photograph, and I shook my head—both at my small victory and the small challenge. "Might we step outside into the sunlight? I'm afraid the camera would yield only darkness if used in here, even in the presence of the lamplight. You see, the sensitivity of the film to light is—"

But Mr. Tinker cut me off with further grumblings, "Yes, yes, of course, I understand the concept of photographic sensitivity. But... but I can't step outside."

I cocked my head in question. "I can't abide it," he continued.

I repeated the gesture, and Mr. Tinker flushed deeper,

embarrassed. "That is to say I'm far too busy."

I inhaled for a breath, about to launch into shameless begging in my request of an outdoors portrait, but he held up a finger to silence me before rubbing his forehead with the other hand, deep in thought again.

Mr. Tinker began to move about the workshop in extreme agitation, from one pile to the next as a honey bee travels among a field of flowers. By this point, Tickertape had returned from the depths of the workshop to take stock of the sudden flurry of activity.

As the clockwork cat and I looked on, Mr. Tinker seemed to be cobbling together a crude device of some kind; a long cylinder topped with a shallow oval cup with some wire connected to a small switch. After disappearing from view for a moment, he returned to the bench beside me that was piled with chemicals. He took a generous helping of chalky white powder, placed it in the cup and offered the device to me. "This will provide some improvised light." After explaining how it worked, he took his place.

He patted the workbench, and lithe Tickertape leapt up beside his master. "When you are ready, Mr. Quigley."

I wish I could say I was, because when I pressed the button to release the shutter function, the small explosion that ensued in the cup of the device I held aloft inspired a less than masculine shriek from me. However, the resulting flash of light, simultaneous with the shutter's click, mimicked a window thrown open and closed again to temporarily let in light, as Mr. Tinker promised. When I had gained some composure, I couldn't help but wonder at the innovation. "A portable flash lighting device. Marvellous..."

"Perhaps a little liberal on magnesium, but the desired effect, no doubt," Mr. Tinker grumbled to himself, and I warranted that it was as I handed the device back to him, hoping my expression was more dignified and less abject surprise. He studied the device in his hands. "Quite a brilliant young man, George Eastman. I hope to meet him someday and discuss his innovations, maybe offer some consultation."

I laughed. "And I hope to someday take a photograph with a Teston & Tinker non-explosive flash-camera."

As I shook his hand, I realized I was no longer registering in Mr. Tinker's mind. Already I could see, as they say, the gears in his head turning. I scratched Tickertape's ear before a final wave goodbye, and let myself out of Tinker's wondrous workshop.

CHAPTER 3

IN WHICH THERE IS MUCH ADO ABOUT THE NEW WORLD
EXHIBITION AND A MURDER

Later that afternoon I walked into Mr. Hackerman's office, my completed story and developed photograph in hand. I approached his desk as if a departed soul coming to Saint Peter before the Pearly Gates. Mr. Hackerman accepted my submission with the utmost gravity, and I stood before his desk, paralyzed, awaiting judgment.

Mr. Hackerman glanced cursorily at the photograph, set it aside, and then skimmed the few hundred words I had written on the incredible things I had seen in Mr. Tinker's workshop.

He nodded, his mouth twitched a little. "Passable, Quigley, I'll give you that."

Only the deepest reserves of composure kept me from leaping up and down and hooting in a most improper manner. Instead, I shook his hand—perhaps over-enthusiastically, as he growled a warning at me. Mr. Hackerman admitted that it may be featured somewhere in tomorrow's edition if they could find a little space.

And they did just that; on the front page of the *Globe*. "INTERVIEW WITH ELUSIVE INVENTOR DARIUS TINKER: GLOBE EXCLUSIVE by Norwood Quigley"

The picture of Mr. Tinker in his workshop seemed to surprise the world. It had surprised me, as well, as I processed the film and churned out a story on my experience in his fantastical workshop.

There he was, despite the darkness, his lined and tired face lit up; though his eyes remained guarded, maybe even a little contemptuous, or perhaps I was reading too much into it. The picture was the first any beyond the walls of the Teston & Tinker workshop had seen of him since... well, since the building had gone up.

As the photograph and story passed through the staff, and then into public circulation the next morning, I found it strange that everyone was more interested in Mr. Tinker over the intricate clockwork cat perched beside him or the marvellous, incomprehensible contraptions that framed the picture. We were surrounded by the wonders of his imagination every day, but it was the man in the flesh that seemed the most impossible.

The picture was a success though, both professionally and personally, no doubt. When I reported to him the day my story entered circulation, Mr. Hackerman promised with great reluctance that he could find me some insignificant place at the *Globe* to make myself useful. As I arrived at my boarding house that evening, my porter was in an absolute panic. A flurry of notes had arrived for me all day, including a coveted press ticket to the opening ceremonies of the Exhibition care of the *Globe*, and an invitation to the opening ceremony gala hosted by my parents.

Sir Hector Daedalus Quigley Sr. created one of the most successful air shipping businesses while the technologies were still in their infancies. A shrewd, calculating, charismatic businessman, my father convinced several of the most prosperous English Colonial families to invest in the developing technology of lighter-than-air transportation which, after a number of uneasy years, benefited everyone greatly, my father most of all. Quigley Airships arose to the top of lighter-than-air mercantile transportation and is the only company in the world that offers passenger flights, although many "landlubbers" are dissuaded by consistent turbulence once aboard.

My father is also one of the bravest, noblest, most well-studied men I knew, all the more surprising given his rough birth. The Quigley name is renowned in the well-to-do parlours and ballrooms of the New World, and many in the United Kingdom as well. When not travelling to various company airship fields, expanding business, brokering deals and what have you, my parents are usually throwing parties for industry partners and visiting friends and dignitaries; my mother, Aveline, often fundraising for various charitable causes. My older brother, Hector Jr., had followed in the steps of my father, and despite an aptitude for sport and a friendly demeanour among his peers, has big shoes to fill, and is a clumsy businessman at best.

Mine is a family of philanthropists, well recompensed and knighted for it, and as I have previously described, a life I had no interest in. It was something my father, though genial and forgiving, always seemed vaguely disappointed about, though he seemed to recognize a little of my intelligence, resourcefulness and independent spirit. As was common among my wealthy peers, I claimed that most common of traits shared between a progenitor and his artistic offspring: an unfortunate difference of values—although Sir Hector did indulge my talents and made sure I led a comfortable life.

My parents knew I had little interest in society, so it came as some surprise when I received an invitation; *"Hanlan's Pride* Launch and Gala, hosted by Sir Hector Quigley and Dame Aveline Quigley." Although "invitation" is too mild of a word. Written in my mother's ornate cursive scrawl, the invitation was a request, or a contract to "grace the launch of our good friends the Hanlan's steamship gala with your photographic skill," a begrudging though welcomed compliment. My mother, ever the supportive parent, added an encouraging postscript at the end. "I know your father would love to see you there."

The launch was to be the most anticipated social event of the New World Exhibition's opening ceremonies. The steamship, a veritable floating hotel, would dock every night in front of the Hotel Hanlan, a grand building on the Toronto Islands that faced onto Lake Ontario, and a centre of leisure for those who wanted to escape exhausting urban life. The revolutionary steamship was booked solid through the first few months of the Exhibition opening. The Hanlan family being investors in my father's ventures meant only the most well-connected people would be there, of which I would normally not be included in. Businessmen, socialites, politicians, minor royalties. There was even a rumour that the Marquess of Lorne and Princess Louise would be rooming aboard at some point, perhaps during the opening ceremonies!

I had been charged by my parents to present myself at the party, "properly attired, please. We will have the tailor send over a new dinner jacket for the occasion," camera in hand, as a photographer of fine society. I had no doubt this would allow me to be presented as "the one who captured Tinker," surely a worthy accomplishment of their youngest son (finally).

Whatever the obligation, the invitation was a pleasant surprise, and I was looking forward to the opportunity to be aboard *Hanlan's Pride* when it launched, although I was hesitant to explain to my parents that unless the steamboat was illuminated like the sun, my camera, a simple machine, would capture vague, shadowy images for the most part.

This anxiety was relieved on my return home the day before the opening ceremonies. One of our maids had laid out my new jacket, which fit superbly, and beside that a long and cumbersome package. Though no name was included, I recognized the contents to be the device Mr. Tinker had cobbled together to produce the temporary flash of artificial light in his workshop, although a much more sophisticated and refined iteration. A short letter, barely legible, accompanied:

Jigged about with it a bit. Should be reliable if the need to photograph in the darkness arises.

The note went on to instruct me as to how to affix the flash stick to my camera, and how to apply a pinch of powder, enclosed in an accompanying pouch. Mr. Tinker's letter assured me it was all "relatively safe," however, he'd scribbled an afterthought: "If you or the device catches fire, best to cease using it."

I and, as it turned out, half of the world rose early that morning for the opening ceremony of the New World Exhibition. I joined the throngs of people who had taken to Toronto's streets, and it was clear that even those who would not be attending had got caught up in the festival mood of the Exhibition. People leaned out of their windows, watching the mass making their way to the grounds on the southwestern extremity of Toronto. The city's major buildings—the New City Hall building, still under construction, the courthouse, Union Station, a number of the larger manors in town—were decorated with streamers and flags of every nation participating.

In the streets, people waved their flags with pride—Irish, French, Scottish and, of course, the Union Jack being the more popular choices. I felt like I was part of a grand parade snaking its way through Toronto's gridded streets, making carriage passage almost impossible. My heart felt light to be at the centre of such an electric mass of people from every corner of the world. I documented the sights for the *Globe*, and for my own pleasure.

I was somewhat less enthusiastic about the crowds when I was forced to elbow my way to a number of sweating journalists in the press seats, a disappointing distance from the massive, wooden grandstand beside the main Exhibition entrance, where speeches would be made, hands shaken, etc. I could just make out, among the blob of people of status seated in rows on the stage, my father, and mother who, I assumed, was one of the more smartly dressed ladies in the crowd. From the enormous bandstand, an orchestra played a rousing rendition of "Rule Britannia!" that carried over the crowds, joined in by hundreds of patriotic voices among them. The journalists around me mostly swore at the heat and smoked with professional expertise. I suspected my neighbour was sneaking drinks from a flask, for he bent over into his bag to search for a pencil more times than necessary, and would return upright with a smell that stung the eyes. I waved at Mr. Valentine of the *Globe*, who I had been introduced to in passing after my story had been published. He'd received a much better seat than myself despite our ostensibly being colleagues. I would have to hunt him down at some point and get his take on it, though I supposed I could read it in tomorrow's paper as well.

At the conclusion of the hymn, a stocky, dour-faced gentleman took the stage. A number of people in the crowd questioned who he was, followed by embarrassed nods when he introduced himself as John Thompson, Prime Minister of Canada.

The prime minister, it turned out, was an exquisite orator but not very good with the newer technology; a fully electric *sonus* amplifier had been mounted on a podium. He had a tendency to pace during his speech and it was therefore lost somewhat to us further back due to the quiet roar of a thousand voices chattering away, giving their own commentary. I and every other fretting journalist caught one line on the "superiority of Canadian ingenuity, with a little bit of British Tory know-how" contributing to the success of the Exhibition. We duly noted the line in perfect unison.

Below us, the crowd was thrown into a fresh patriotic fervour when a woman, stout, elegantly dressed, despite her being clad in mourning-black, took to the stage, trailed by another man and woman attired in opulence visible even at a distance. This, it turned out, was our monarch, the Empress of India and Queen over the Dominion of Canada herself, with her daughter Princess Louise and the Marquess of Lorne, Louise's husband. The Queen approached the electric *sonus* amplifier, directed by a bowing prime minister. Attendants brought out a strange contraption, a short podium, the details of which escaped us from such a distance. The crowd clambered over one another to get a better view of the monarch. There were a number of cries of "Long live the Queen!" from below, although my neighbour, well into his flask, uttered an oath about our monarch that I will not reprint.

The Queen's voice came clear through the electric system—perhaps she was a more practiced hand with the new technology? She sounded tired. "It is with the greatest honour and pride that We pronounce the New World Exhibition open."

There was a moment of mass inhalation as she fumbled on the podium. She seemed to give an annoyed shrug, Prime Minister Thompson and the marquess rushed to her aid, although she figured the device out, and an audible hum filled the almost silence that had fallen over the crowd. Lights above the grandstand flickered to life—electric lights, for the Exhibition was to be an all-electric miracle—and a welcoming beacon held aloft by a robed statue above the main gate shone as the New World Exhibition twinkled to life. The Queen waved lamely to the audience as she hobbled, in as dignified a manner as possible, off the stage and out of public sight.

Thus were the gates to the Exhibition grounds thrown open to the thousands who awaited, myself among them.

Of the countless curiosities I saw on the opening day of the New World Exhibition, the most widely anticipated, and well attended, was the Automata House.

Although to describe the building as a "house" did the exhibit some injustice. The latest mechanical innovations of Teston & Tinker resided in what would be considered a modest mansion. The Automata House was designed like all of the towering edifices in the New World Exhibition—in the Royal Industrial style (as the architecturally savvy call it).

Intricate, dark-stoned masonry made up much of the outside, iron fretwork decorated the perimeter; the Automata House like the hundreds of other buildings in the style, appeared to take the most whimsical elements of Victorian architecture—themselves calling back to classical designs—and the most functional forms of industrial factories and marry the two. On the inside, much of the appliances and steam-powered technologies were a glimmering, almost gold-shining brass. The Royal Industrial style was becoming quite popular among the wealthy in the country's developing, affluent neighbourhoods.

Each room was roped off so visitors could regard demonstrations from the hallway. The rooms were occupied by T&T employees charged to maintain and guard the wares, utilizing amenities of the Automata House in a demonstration of clockwork precision. Among the many wonders, a few stood out. There was a closet that allowed the user to select full outfits at the touch of a button, based on mood or occasion. There was a mechanical woman that was programmed to tell fairy tales, children's stories and poetry (it recited some Walt Whitman to the crowd, in turns appreciative or scandalized by the agnostic verse) while also employed to dust, sweep and clean fine china with a delicate touch. There was also a clockwork contraption that spanned the entire kitchen and consisted of a number of mechanical appendages, which prepared a set number of meals depending on the time of day. For the late morning crowd I was a part of, the machine served toast with marmalade, some fresh slices of fruit. I accepted a cup of under-steeped tea from a mechanical arm, which delicately dropped two scoops of sugar in.

A uniformed man called through the house for a demonstration in the backyard, and many of us ambled through the hallways, overwhelmed by the house going about its clockwork life. The man ushered a few dozen of us onto a terrace wrapping around the back of the house, where we waited until the demonstration began. Flowers and trees on either side gave some privacy from the lanes and buildings beyond, which hemmed in the backyard complete with a beautiful glassed-in gazebo—which employed a novel self-cooling feature, we were told.

We watched three men milling about a great bulk beneath a draped canvas. With a final glance at his pocket watch, a tall, handsome, blond-haired Englishman with the grandiose voice of a ringleader stepped forth and addressed the chattering crowd. Right away he reminded me of an adult iteration of the jocular, athletic schoolboys that had terrorized me throughout my youth. This, perhaps unfairly, coloured my judgment of the man.

"Ladies and Gentlemen," he began, hands raised, "the rapid expansion of major urban areas presents new problems to the Empire's constabularies. These brave men dedicate their lives to protecting the honest citizen by rifling out bad eggs, but of course, the power of the just man can only reach so far. A hunter can only poke his head into so many foxholes in a morning. So, we offer an efficient addition to the lawman's ammunition. A bloodhound, if you will. I present Mr. Shackles."

The two assistants threw back the sheet to reveal the mechanical wonder beneath, although I'm sure I'm not the only that day who would describe the thing as a mechanical monster.

The creature was more than seven feet tall and seemed to be almost as broad. The dark brown greatcoat that swathed the so-called "Mr. Shackles" was circus tent-like in scale; the hat covering its domed, brassy skull seemed ludicrous. Dressing this colossus was like swaddling a monster out of a fairy tale in a baby's blanket. The hands, which peaked out from under the cuffs of the jacket, were two great claw-like hoops that seemed to twitch excitedly, opening and closing like the pincers of a crab—the shackles of the creature's namesake.

Most frightening was an iron grill over where a human's mouth would be. A terrible, choking exhaust emanated from within.

I shivered despite the warm spring day.

The handsome Englishman rocked forward and back on his heels, smirking. "He does cut an intimidating figure, does he not?"

A few in the crowd warranted it did. The man drew a small glass slide from his pocket, seemingly marred with some soot or dirt, though I recognized it as a photonegative with an image upon it. The man brought the slide forth so the crowd could observe the photographic portrait of the assistant, a tall, lanky, athletic man who had removed his coat and was rolling up his shirtsleeves.

"Mr. Shackles runs on an Advanced Analytical Engine, veritably the most intricate piece of machinery on the face of the Earth. Bend over, if you would, old chap."

The brass titan removed its hat and entered into a very deep bow. The presenter was able to open the thing's head, revealing minuscule machinery, unimaginable depths of gears and cogs, switches and lenses, springs and rubber belts.

The gentleman slid the photonegative into a slot ready made for it. "Light filters in through the frontal apertures, and Mr. Shackles can, nine times out of ten, seek out and capture the subject of the photograph. Man, woman or child, no matter how far away they are, within reason, he uses advanced switchboard calculations to sniff them out like a bloodhound. Ladies and gentlemen, this is the future of the constabulary!"

The top screwed back on, and with a mumbled command, the giant stood back up to its full, menacing height, placing the hat atop its head.

The presenter nodded at his taller assistant who, as if in sincere fright, began running away from the crowd, the Automata House, and Mr. Shackles. The handsome man smirked and faced the crowd. "Find him and bring him back... alive, would you, old chap?"

A growl rumbled from Mr. Shackles' chest, like a train passing nearby. It took a threatening step toward the crowd on the terrace, many of whom gasped and shrunk backwards.

"No need to fear, ladies and gentlemen, unless it is your picture within!"

It swivelled about, no doubt taking in the faces of the crowd, but ignored them as it surveyed the area. Mr. Shackles caught sight of the man, who peered back over his shoulder either in a pantomime of what a fleeing criminal may do, or in genuine terror. Upon sighting him, the machine took off in a leaping, thunderous stride. Within seconds it had already caught up to the scrambling assistant, who had only made it halfway to the gazebo down the lawn. Mr. Shackles swept one great arm across the assistant's shoulders and easily tumbled the man to the ground, stunned but otherwise unharmed. Without hesitation, it leaned over and scooped both of the man's wrists in one claw, locked the shackle in place, and lifted him onto his feet to be dragged back in front of the smirking demonstrator.

There was a smattering of cowed applause from the crowd. The demonstration was impressive and frightening. I couldn't bring myself to imagine one of these great brutes stalking through the bustling streets of Toronto, knocking down hungry pickpockets, downtrodden prostitutes, troubled vagrants and destitute labourers.

The presenter seemed smug with the success of the demonstration and muttered a command. Mr. Shackles dumped the assistant at his feet, who seemed genial enough with his capture, although he rubbed his bruised wrists. "Imagine," the gentleman cried out, "a Mr. Shackles installed within every stationhouse! Sociological surveys have been done, ladies and gentlemen, that find the mere visible presence of a Mr. Shackles in the neighbourhood reduces crime by fifteen percent!"

As he spoke, the assistant had lifted himself from the ground and took a few steps behind the portly gentleman to retrieve his coat. The crowd looked on with interest as Mr. Shackles' eyes (or the mechanical equivalent) followed the other man and, without hesitation, sprang into action, sweeping about and almost knocking the presenter over.

The assistant, realizing what was happening, attempted to dive out of the way of his aggressor, but the thing's claw swept about and awkwardly caught hold of his arm. There was an audible crack, a cry of pain and a number of gasps in the audience. The blond Englishman was crying out, "Enough! Enough! Cease and desist! Enough! Stop, would you, old chap?!"

The creature gave a shudder, as if in resistance, but gave up its assault and released its captive. The assistant fell to the ground, crying out in pain, his arm twisted oddly. "The bleedin' thing broke me bleedin' arm!" he cried out.

A woman in the crowd fainted dead away, and I must admit I felt a bit queasy myself. One man volunteered himself as a doctor, and some staff from inside the house came forth as well to assist and clear the crowd away. I raised my camera and snapped a picture of the handsome Englishman, who no longer seemed so friendly, standing beside the hulking machine. He scowled at me before leading the machine away

In turning to follow the crowd, I caught a glimpse of winking, emerald orbs and a glint of brass. Perhaps it was just my imagination, but I thought I could hear the sound of a fading ticking. The mechanical cat, Tickertape? Or simply another strange invention haunting the grounds of the World's Fair?

The fairground itself was laid out like a massive bicycle wheel, with spokes running in every direction leading to the various attractions along each road, as I learned from my official *New World Exhibition Guide for the Easily Lost*. The main thoroughfare led south from the Dufferin Gate entrance to the waterfront's main pier that stretched out into the green-blue span of Lake Ontario. The path was a long, broad, almost uninterrupted stretch of lush gardens called the "Industrial Esplanade."

Every main artery of the Exhibition met at the centre of the main grounds, a wide-open plaza, Victoria Circle, with a towering, gilded, larger-than-life statue of the Queen, crowned and clutching a sceptre. Here, too, was the cage-like, domed Administration building and the British National Society for Aid to the Sick and Wounded in War

Hospital. The sizeable brigade of nurses and doctors within treated the immediate onslaught of injuries and maladies—mainly dehydration and the fainting of overexerted ladies, I was told upon investigation—with military precision.

Each wedge of the grounds was dominated by one towering main structure complimented by concentric arcs of grounds housing smaller exhibits, gardens, restaurants, courtyards and attractions. The palatial Steam Engine and Liberal Arts Building towered above all, a great hall, the largest building ever constructed, housing hundreds of displays within. Around it, a visitor could find the extravagant Ontario Provincial Building (which matched the recently completed New Parliament Building down to the last stone), the cavernous Teston & Tinker New Waterworks Building, the Paris House, the Dominion Post Office Exhibition Pavilion to name a few. And that was simply in one of sixteen wedges.

I spent the rest of the afternoon wandering the sprawling exhibition grounds, from the airship fields and the Lighter-Than-Air Pavilion on the southwesternmost extremity of the grounds, to the Gallery of Fine Arts. Within, I found a photography exhibit and spoke to an excitable young man at an Eastman's Kodak booth that instantly recognized my camera. Cameras, I was pleased to see, were to be a significant craze at the fair. They were to be rented out to curious fairgoers, the pictures processed professionally. Though some called amateur photography a fad, I welcomed the new generation of photographers.

I ambled along the Global Boulevard, a series of storefronts, kiosks, edifices and "villages" dedicated to the various nations of the world, and their entertainments. The volume of attractions on this midway alone could occupy the better part of a week, so I only took the time to indulge in a stein full of "Weizenbier" in the German Village's beer garden.

Along the Global Boulevard, there was a great deal of excitement at the prospect of a cowboy show being set up in the fields outside of the Dufferin Gate. This, I learned, was an unofficial attraction. *Buffalo Bill's Wild West and Congress of Rough Riders of the World* led by the titular gunslinger had been rejected from a spot in the fair, but had shown up anyways to great acclaim.

Among the many celebrity cowboys, like Sitting Bull and his braves, Annie Oakley, her husband Frank Butler, were claims of a legendary, immortal gunslinger from New Mexico. The Obsidian Devil was a negro man who had been present at the revolution in Haiti and the slave uprising in the south back when it was French-owned land, in what had become in the Free People's Republic of Louverture, before he'd disappeared into the desert for decades. This would make this "Obsidian Devil" well over a hundred years old, a bold claim for one who could still ride a horse, but Buffalo Bill had certainly captured the imagination of the crowds, and it sounded like his show would be the main attraction, however unsanctioned.

For lunch I poked my head into an almost empty storefront in the Japanese Bazaar—exotic in design, with flamboyant paper lanterns, sliding doors and strange archways. The small staff, who seemed militant in their friendliness, all turned as I peered through the door, and cried, "Irasshaimase!"

Not being fluent in the Japanese language, I simply grinned as they escorted me to the counter with bows and indistinguishable but what I believed were gracious welcomes. A cup of green tea was plunked before me, and they began to parade samples of what they called "Edomae zushi" out for me to try. I was only slightly horrified when I realized that among slices of various vegetables were raw fish and seafood, wrapped in seaweed and rice, or placed neatly on top of it, but I was resolved to continue my day of adventure. The colours and presentation were gorgeous, the texture terrifying, the taste... not terrible, actually!

I pointed to a couple of the samples that I enjoyed, and the "chef" behind the counter began to prepare the meal before my eyes with machine-like precision and speed. Meanwhile, one of the waiters, his English a little more functional than my Japanese, did his best to teach me how to use the chopsticks. The cutlery was beyond me, and as I fumbled with the pieces of food, I began to giggle and dropped a piece of "zushi" into my tea. The staff found this uproariously funny, and the volume of laughter was so much that other Exhibition goers began to glance into the restaurant, and every time the waiters cried, "Irasshaimase," the curious pairs and groups felt compelled to enter the strange little place.

After I had paid for my meal and stood to leave, I held up my camera and the staff gathered, amused by the novelty of the picture taking process. By the time I left, followed by a chorus of what I guessed was Japanese "thank-you's," there were an additional four tables occupied and other wary patrons were presented with the bizarre though delectable food.

I realized as I was making my way through the crowds how many people were there with families, or friends, or with their sweethearts. As the day wore on and I visited different pavilions by myself, I wished very much that I had someone there alongside me. The sights, sounds, and tastes of the Exhibition were so magnificent they were an adventure to be shared with another.

I recalled with fondness the days my family would vacation together, although even then this was usually to suit my father's business schedule, and my mother was concerned with her parties and fundraisers, and making sure her children were educated and cultured, more than letting us have real fun.

I was a sensitive, shy child, and my brother only tolerated me as far as making sure I wasn't picked on by other boys at the different schools we ended up in—it wouldn't do to have a Quigley humiliated, even if he was a lesser branch on the family tree. I had a few chums as a child, but never anything lasting. Boys my age were either brutish or boorish, or a combination of both. The few I had associated with similarly interested in the life of an aesthete were therefore unpopular, like myself.

As far as the fairer sex went, I enjoyed talking to them enough when we could find something to relate to, and when they didn't inspire crippling social anxiety within me. My mother had introduced me to many eligible young women, but I had little interest in those dull, flighty things, and they probably felt the same about me. I was, of course, familiar with a breed of New Women, those concerned with securing the right to vote, and advocates of dress reform, and they had my sympathies, but their type would probably think of me as a privileged, ineffectual man of leisure... to which they would, unfortunately, be correct!

I guess my one consolation was that I had my camera, and it never stopped snapping pictures the entire day.

As the day pressed on toward the evening's festivities, I ambled toward the docks, though stopped to take in the occasional sight or amusement.

One in particular caught my attention outside of the grand Sciences Lecture Hall: a demonstration by a young Oxonian professor, Dr. Merlin Hawking, presented by Watts Applied Mechanical Sciences. I recognized Hawking as a contentious figure in Britannia's academic circles, and I soon learned why. A pamphlet handed out to us by Exhibition staff explained how his work concerned hypothetical "cosmic energies" and "metaphysical sciences," and he purported to have invented a machine that could gaze into "other worlds that are not our own." Even to my rather liberal, open mind, this idea seemed fantastical though preposterous. That he was considered a charlatan outside of Oxford did not surprise me, but the festival attendants promised a spectacle, so a line duly formed.

The small crowd was ushered into an ornate lecture hall in the elegant Royal Industrial style where, at the front, a mousy, dirty blond-haired man frantically moved about an enormous machine of unimaginable design. Combustion chambers and gaskets, cylinders and modules, pinions and spindles, wires and widgets going every which way, and atop of it all sat a great glass lens as tall as an adult, and just as wide, held aloft by thick metal casing about the rim of the lens. Wires snaked all over the casing and seemed to connect to the machine every which way, although the lens was otherwise clear and refracted light like any other, despite its size and connection to such a bizarre machine.

Who I first mistook as some dishevelled assistant was introduced as Dr. Hawking, young Oxford professor of theoretical cosmic studies. He stuttered a greeting to the crowd, motioned to his machine, but then seemed to reconsider and instead approached the lectern, knocking a stack of notes onto the floor, which he scrambled to pick up. There was some uncomfortable shifting in the audience as we looked on this pitiable display before such a grand machine.

"The cosmos!" he announced, a little too loud and overexcited, and then adjusted his volume at the quizzical looks and snickers from the audience. "Uh... vast... unknowable... and yet I posit. Well, my theory is... many worlds, yes. Ours isn't alone!"

Someone in the audience coughed.

Dr. Hawking seemed to be sweating, some of his notes tumbled off the dais, which he ignored, though he had lost his place—if indeed he'd ever had one.

"Think of it... like blankets... Or, rather... paper!" he held up his notes; more pages escaped him and fluttered to the ground, "stacked one on top of the other! Pages that repeat infinitely, but each with a slight difference. A different word here, a different spelling there, a different number, a different language, over and over again, endless."

The man in front of me scratched his head, and a woman leaned over and muttered something to her husband, and they stood and began to edge out of their row.

"Uh... On their own, each page appears mundane... completely normal... but gestalt... endless combinations... and I believe I have found a way to peer into these other worlds!"

The husband and wife stopped. There was an emotional shift in the room to curiosity rather than pity.

Dr. Hawking stepped down from the lectern, relieved, and began to flick switches and turn wheels on his cosmic machine, which hummed to life. Each pulsing vibration could be felt from the ground up; a disturbing sensation, as if experiencing the heartbeat of the very world we found ourselves upon.

Hawking moved to the far side of the machine, and threw his entire body weight onto an enormous lever. Something deep within the machine gave a mighty clunk. He winced as a high whining came from the lens; a frightening, otherworldly sound, as if it was singing some ethereal, unknowable melody.

Sparks shot from the wires connecting the lens to the thick metal casing, and the audience gasped, some ducked for cover, but I watched on, mesmerized. The lights in the room, especially around the machine, seemed to dim in comparison as the lens charged, glowing a colour I could not name—something between a luminescent sea green and the darkest purple of the night sky.

Those who looked on saw faint, flickering images as if ghosts danced across the lens. In rapid succession I saw a lighthouse of foreign design, a woman singing on stage, a city glowing with lights unlike anything I could imagine, a hoard of fur-robed barbarians. Strange music or noises filtered through the lens, but inconstant, distorted, distant, as if heard from underwater. Nothing I saw or heard made sense as one image flickered into the next with increasing rapidity, but Dr. Hawking seemed elated, surprised that his own machine was working, and he watched like the rest of us, wide-eyed in wonder.

Then the machine whined into an even higher pitch, followed by a series of pops as every light in the room exploded, showering the audience with glass. There were terrified screams from all, myself included, as the room was thrown into darkness, although after a moment, quiet descended and Exhibition attendants rushed forth to throw open the lecture hall's blinds, filling the room with natural light.

We all gazed up at Dr. Hawking, who looked on his now lifeless machine with horror. The humongous lens had cracked down the centre; wires connecting it to the rest of the machine were frayed and smoking.

Exhibition staff instructed the audience to evacuate the room in a calm manner, but immediately, if we please. I followed, dusting glass shards off my clothes and out of my hair.

"A fraud," one man opined, "but a bloody good show."

Others seemed to agree and debated how he had achieved the effects. Another man who worked in a theatre explained to his wife how, as soon as we were out of the room, the staff would go to work replacing the dummy light bulbs for the next so-called demonstration, and the charlatan professor would replace the lens of the so-called cosmic machine with a new one and prepare his rehearsed idiocy for the next group of dupes.

I wasn't so sure I agreed with the disbelievers as I glanced back over my shoulder at Dr. Hawking, who stood stock still, staring at his machine in abject misery.

I decided a picture would be inappropriate, and filed out with the rest.

Another display of note was the Krupp Building, a German pavilion displaying artillery machines by the weapons company, at great cost, said the Exhibition staff on hand.

Within the building, which resembled a German manor, was a gargantuan artillery gun almost fifty feet in length—a coastal gun, it was explained by a heavily accented German employee of Krupp.

"Tested in ze field, it can penetrate a wrought iron plate zree feet zick," he said, proud as a parent, patting the base of the enormous cannon. He called it a "peacemaker," but the gun, like the great and intimidating Mr. Shackles, gave me chills. I pitied any enemy on the receiving end of the "Thunderer," as the German named it. Ever the hypocrite, I took some notes and snapped a picture for the *Globe*. Guns and war ever seemed to fascinate the mind of man, and I had no doubt Mr. Hackerman would be thrilled to run a story about a device that so thoroughly matched the personality of an editor.

My job satisfied, I vacated the Krupp building even quicker than from the accident of Dr. Hawking's demonstration, hoping to distract my mind from thoughts of war with less frightening exhibits at hand.

As the sun began to dip toward the horizon, I made my way to the Steamship Pier, where the *Hanlan's Pride* was docked. An enormous crowd had gathered at the waterfront, and the steamship towered above them, in fact, it towered above most of the other steamboats, passenger vessels, warships and buildings along the edge of the lake.

At ten decks, *Hanlan's Pride* was the world's biggest steamship and did the image of a floating hotel perfect justice. From bow to stern, the ship stretched the length of the main pier, and on each side were two enormous paddle wheels, three or four storeys in diameter each. A trinity of smokestacks jutted upwards from the aft.

Those who had already boarded or made their lodgings on the *Pride* were leaning off the promenade deck and above, in front of their rooms on each level, dressed in exquisite finery. The men were in austere dinner jackets and tuxedos of blacks, whites and greys. The women were in evening gowns so voluminous and colourful they complimented the multi-tiered cake-like appearance of the *Pride*, their plumed and elaborately adorned hats only adding to the confectionary effect.

I was late in arriving at the *Hanlan's Pride*, so I was further down the pier from the stage than I would have liked. The pier was so packed, not even my press pass would get me closer until some of the non-passengers dispersed. I could see familiar blobs in the distance that vaguely resembled my parents, and I could hear my father's voice, electrically amplified, echoing across the water, though I could only make out the occasional word or two in his deep, reverberating voice. "Proud day for the Empire," "Canadian ingenuity" and "unwavering loyalty and power" were just a few in what was surely a very inspirational speech to those close enough. Perhaps I could later beg a copy of the speech from Father for inclusion in my writings for the *Globe*.

There was a great deal of applause as Sir Hector and Dame Aveline descended from the stage and cut a ribbon before boarding. A regiment of steamship crew in spotless uniforms descended the gangplanks and began to sort through the crush of a crowd for attendees with bookings or invitations. The pier was chaos as the porters and roustabouts of latecomers with stacks of luggage struggled through the crowd; guests of the gala were sorted from enthusiastic though non-invited fairgoers.

As the sun began to descend over the western lakeshore, I presented my ticket and boarded without incident, though found myself jostled and lost in the excited crowd on the lower level. I greeted a few familiar faces, searching for my family aboard, Hector Jr., Mother or Father...

Hanlan's Pride completed boarding just as the sun dipped into the lake, and the youthful and energetic aboard leaned over the railings, waving their handkerchiefs to the landlocked, jealous onlookers. As the darkness of the summer night swelled above us, the electric lighting system aboard the *Pride* began to sparkle off the water, reflecting back the span of lights from the fairgrounds. A pretty, novel sight as the steamship paddled its way out onto the lake. I could start to believe the claims of industrialists and engineers that someday the city reflected off the lake's water would be fully electric.

The evening was fair, with a cool but pleasant breeze off the lake. On every deck guests and party goers were conversing, laughing, dancing. On the top level, on one of the larger leisure decks, a string quartet had set up and was playing a lively tango. Immaculately dressed, white-jacketed servers moved about the decks with drinks and hors-d'oeuvres that seemed to replenish themselves out of nowhere.

My, or should I say, Mr. Tinker's flash stick turned out to be a lightning rod for conversation that evening. I circulated on the public decks of the *Pride*, requesting groups of people to pose for pictures and duly taking down their names to appear in a society section of the *Globe*. After each initial shock following the minor lighting explosion, which, admittedly, I had yet to become accustomed to, a polite conversation would reveal me as Norwood Quigley, of the Quigley airship empire, the photographer of Mr. Tinker. When it was further deduced that the flash stick was an invention of his, I would be bombarded with questions about the poor old man and, despite my brief encounter, it appeared I was now the chief authority on his character.

I believe the only thing that kept me alive among the number of T&T investors aboard that evening was my family name. Many of them had put so much money into the company and felt it was their right to meet the man, though they never had, and they seemed personally slighted that I was able to meet Mr. Tinker in their place. "We've all met Mave, though," said one of the men with a knowing smirk to another.

"Ms. Teston," interjected another investor, an edge of warning to his voice.

"Is Ms. Teston aboard this evening?" I asked, hoping to divert the conversation away from my interactions with Mr. Tinker. "I'd very much like to meet her."

The investors gauged that would be a possibility, although commented on her absence from the festivities thus far. I pledged to make it my mission to locate her before the night was out and bid them a hasty adieu, untangling myself from the awkward conversation and accusatory looks of these men, each one wealthier and more affluent than the last.

Who I was most keen to seek out, however, was my father for, despite his appearance among the dignitaries at the opening ceremony and his speech before the launch of *Hanlan's Pride*, I had yet to speak with him, to thank him for the invitation. On the uppermost deck, the leisure deck and promenade around the great steam stacks of the *Pride*, I found a Hector Daedalus Quigley. Junior, however, my older brother.

I was distressed to discover him leaning against the railing in a state of significant intoxication, bent close in consort with a shifty-eyed young lady. Although by no regards teetotalers, my brother and I were taught by our parents to respect a certain amount of social decorum and moderation in life's pleasures, and I know my mother and father would have been mortified and disappointed to see Hector in such a state.

"Ah!" he cried out as I approached him, a little over-loud. "Ze artiste, Monsieur Quigley! Come, we will have our portraits done and on the cover of the *Globe* in the morning!" He made an obscene gesture in posing with the giggling young woman on his arm.

"I'd sooner save the film," I said in what I tried to be a good-humoured tone, although I was a little off put. I knew Hector had a reputation as a drinker, but I hadn't ever seen my brother so red-faced and staggering. I nodded toward his ardent companion, to whom he bid a salacious good night. I repressed the urge to comment on this fraternization. He had often mocked me as a prude for doing so.

We exchanged some formal brotherly pleasantries, Hector slurring as he spoke. We chatted about the opening ceremonies and some of the amazing sights of the day. He boasted about the important men he and Father had been working with in preparation for the Exhibition, and all the job offers he'd been extended—I nodded, indulging my older brother's sense of vanity as I'd done many times.

Begrudging the compliment, he impressed on me that Father was rather pleased with my getting so close to Mr. Tinker as none outside of the workshop ever had, which made me flush with pride.

"I haven't seen Father yet today," I said, a little surprised. "Is he with Mother now?"

Hector took a long drink from his glass and seemed unable to find the words he needed. "I believe he wasn't feeling well, went to his room, didn't want to be disturbed." I expressed my desire to speak with him and asked which room he and Mother were staying in, but my brother ignored me and seemed distracted. "He didn't want to be bothered, Norwood. So I really don't feel..." His statement trailed off as he glanced behind me and blanched. "I have to go."

My brother shoved past me with a great urgency, and I turned to watch as he pushed his way through the crowd, garnering cries of upset and disdain at the impropriety. My eyes followed him, and I saw someone disappear around the corner, away from the deck. I heard Hector cry, "Ms. Teston!" before being swallowed up in the mob of revelry. What business Hector had with Ms. Teston, I couldn't say— perhaps something regarding Quigley Airships or the Exhibition—so I saw no reason to further interrupt his evening. My brother thus proved useless, I sought out my mother, Dame Aveline.

As I mentioned before, my family are all entrepreneurs in their different spheres, my father among the growing class of industry magnates, my brother being a sort of protege of his and quite popular among his peers. While there was genuine affection between my parents, theirs was a marriage arranged to maximize assets, familial, financial and political. I always admired how Mother and Father functioned, even better than marriage partners, as business partners.

Where my father has made his fortune in boardrooms and building projects, my mother made a battleground of dance floors and dining rooms. There is no single person more capable among the parlours of society. Aveline Quigley, nee Jernigan, was a woman destined for the stage before she met my father. A flair for the dramatic, on the cutting edge of fashion, ability to charm and warm up to even the coldest of hearts and a predisposition for European erudition, I admired my mother a great deal. I also found her exhausting.

As I began to make my way through the crowds, I caught sight of my mother seated with a scowling Chinese man, parked at a bistro table on the far side of the leisure deck. From his severe expression and his thin beard, I believed him to be the Chinese ambassador who had attended the opening ceremonies, though I'd only seen the dignitaries from afar. He was flanked on either side by hulking Chinese men I could only assume were his protectors. Mother, of course, looked heavenly in the golden glow of electric light, her dark, curly hair piled smartly atop her head, a cream evening gown adding to the beatific effect.

The orchestra finished their song, and the dancers lapsed into a breathy stillness, applauding politely before the band struck up the next number, a quick, spinning waltz.

The song started and I watched my mother, a beguiling, mischievous look on her face, invited by one of my father's business partners onto the dance floor. I cursed to myself as the deck crowded with dancers, it would be impossible to talk with her for the duration of the song, and beyond that, if she stayed on the dance floor. Unless...

I turned to the closest figure in a voluminous dress, a young English maiden close in age to myself; smaller in stature, her hair in long, elegant ringlets—pretty enough, though sporting a look of irritated boredom on her face.

"Miss...?"

She grinned, eyeing me up and down, "Ms. Cassie Watts." She

emphasized the honorific in a lewd manner. The name sounded vaguely familiar, but then again, they all did to me at these sorts of functions.

"Ms. Watts, may I trouble you for a dance?" I asked stiffly.

She nodded with enthusiasm, giving me a bawdy appraisal. "Trouble me all night!"

We swished rather clumsily—I've never been much of a dancer, despite my mother's best efforts—onto the floor, and taking advantage of the dance, I began to make my way across the deck to my mother, taking pains not to brain any of my fellow dancers with the photographic equipment strapped to my back. The waltz called for the occasional switching of partners, one after another, and though my original partner seemed dejected as I switched my way across the dance floor, from one pair of arms to the next, I closed in on my prize.

With a flourish, I soon found myself bowing to Aveline, and she laughed as her gloved hand met mine, her face flushed with the fun of the evening.

"Norwood, my darling!" she cried as I pulled her away from her dance partner, although she would not be led off the dance floor, so I was made to continue the waltz with her, panting and sweating copiously with the effort, a dancing disaster. "You're looking well," she lied. "We were all surprised to see your picture of Mr. Tinker, your father the most. I think he's very interested in the piece you wrote!"

I narrowly dodged a rather intoxicated pair of Dutch dancers before regaining some composure. "I was hoping to speak with him," I replied.

We swirled about again. "Yes, darling, though he's been in our room all evening, a spot of fatigue. It was a tiring day for him, you can imagine. As a director-general of the Exhibition he's been scheming away over everything at this bloody fair for months—years even, you can imagine." She seemed to be glancing over my shoulder. I could tell another partner switch was coming. "I'm not sure you should bother him."

"Please Mother, I was hoping to thank him for the invitation."

She smiled. "But of course, we wouldn't have you miss this party for the world," her reply unconvincing. My disdain for these sorts of evenings was well known to her.

The moment in the dance came and Mother spun away from me, bowing to another partner. At that moment, the comely lass from before found her way back into my arms. I heard Mother laugh as she twirled around behind me. "902, darling. Send him my love," she called before she was swallowed up in the dance.

I managed to work my way to the edge and abandon the dance, to my relief and my partner's sincere disappointment. "Trouble me again, if you will, sir! I have a brother too, if that sweetens the pot!" she called after me, to my intense mortification.

As I made my way from the top deck down to the ninth, I could hear the waltz finish, followed by applause from the crowd. To my relief, there were few people on the lower deck as it was mostly occupied by private lodgings. As I made my way along the broad walkway of deck nine there was a flash of light and an explosive pop from the sky above the city, followed in quick succession by others; fireworks in celebration of the opening night. There was laughter and "oohs" from the upper deck, and I paused momentarily to take in the lights reflected on the water. I hoped the sound might rouse Father from his rest so I wouldn't be the one waking him.

I found Room 902 easy enough on the starboard side of *Hanlan's Pride*. The ten-deck steamship chopped across the placid summer waters of Lake Ontario, the electric jewel of the New World Exhibition glittering off our starboard, easily outshining the modest gas-lit Toronto streets. Explosions of celebratory fireworks lit up the waterfront every few seconds, an effect I wished I could stop to admire more. The deck was empty other than a couple of sailors interrogating a slight, dark-skinned, suited man in a bowler hat at the end of the walkway. Stopping outside the appointed room, I rapped on the door and heard a frantic shuffling from inside. The door opened a little, but not onto my father, as I had expected.

Inside the quarters was a squat, scowling little man, his hair so blond it was practically white, with a complimenting, exaggerated walrus moustache, a tad askew. He was dressed in a plush, exquisite robe, though his posture was military, his demeanour severe. Behind him I saw a slight, nude figure duck into the room's water closet. My face flushed. I had interrupted something.

"Ver is der champagne?" he growled, eyeing me up and down. His accent was thick, most certainly German, or maybe Austrian.

"My apologies... I was looking for Hector Quigley. 902?" The moustached man seemed startled by the sudden explosion of fireworks over my shoulder. He glared at me nervously. "Clearly he is not here." The door almost took my nose off as he slammed it shut. I stood a moment, bewildered, studying the number on the door: 902B. I took a couple of steps backwards, looking up and down the walkway, before realizing my mistake. Another dozen feet down the deck was another door with the same style of brass numbers, though they read, "902A". I would have to chastise my mother for her making me disturb the ill-humoured foreign gentleman and his companion.

The fireworks popped overhead as I walked the short distance to the next door, and just as I raised my hand to knock, I heard a muffled scream from behind me from within the quarters I'd just disturbed. Without thinking, I turned from my father's room and rushed back to 902B and threw myself against the door. The commotion got the attention of the nearby crew members but, afraid someone's life was in immediate peril, I continued to batter the door until I felt a strong hand grasp my shoulder. I spun around and faced the imposing figure of the famous adventurer, airship pioneer and my father, Sir Hector Daedalus Quigley, Sr.

Sir Hector, in my mind, always had the sombre, handsome gravitas of a stone bust; the same permanent, unwavering calm. In recent years, his hair had thinned slightly around the temples and gone grey, his tanned face now lined with age, but he was still the hero of my childhood, my father, the strongest, most dignified, gentlest man I knew; a world traveller, a fierce intellect, captain of the *Halcyon*, one of the fastest airships in the skies.

"Allow me, Norwood," he said calmly, as if offering to help me tie off a difficult line on an airship. I nodded and backed away from the door. With a mighty, calculated kick, he sent the door crashing open, and he, two sailors and myself pushed our way into the cabin to a horrific sight.

He stood over the body, a boy no older than I, though of significantly different demeanour. He was of Asiatic stock, no doubt, clear in his golden-brown skin and dark eyes. He had a strange beauty, augmented by the loose-worn, red and gold-stitched robe of an Eastern cut he wore. The robe terminated shortly and disconcertingly below his hips, revealing slender, shapely legs.

Though his admitted comeliness was not the most distracting sight in the room, for the body of the foreign gentleman I had bothered moments ago lay in a pool of blood at the boy's feet, the dagger in his hand still dripping blood. He held it delicately, the handle between two fingers out away from his body as if it disgusted him. Upon our forced entry, he gazed up at us, a look of shock and terror on his face. He glanced at the dagger in his hand, then back at us, strands of long, dark hair falling in his eyes, which widened as he uttered, almost inaudibly, "Oh shit."

CHAPTER 4

IN WHICH THERE IS AN INQUIRY, AN ESCAPE AND A
BLOODHOUND ON THE TRAIL

I did not sleep well that night and awoke early the next morning, images of the murdered man—his head lolled against the ground, his milky-white skin set off against the ruby-red blood still flowing from his chest—were more than enough to inspire a restless sleep. I ate and dressed quickly, then departed without waiting to be summoned. As I made my way to the station house where they had taken the suspect, I went over the events of the previous evening, my brow furrowed, my mind troubled despite what was certain to be another beautiful day.

A murder had been committed, there was no doubt. It was a mercy that my father was present, for I fear that the two sailors and myself would have stood gazing incredulously at the scene, overwhelmed by the sight of the corpse and the young murderer.

My father, a much more hardened man, had experienced his fair share of death in the course of foreign battles and airship piracy and was able to process the situation with stronger wit.

Sir Hector addressed us, though did not at any point take his eye off the other boy, who seemed in a similar state of shock. "One of you fetch the second officer," to which one sailor stumbled out of the cabin. "Norwood, close the door, and let no one but the second mate in," he commanded, his voice strong but sympathetic to my horrified state.

I complied as he motioned the remaining sailor over with him, murmuring another command. I looked on as the second sailor and my father approached the boy with caution who, snapping out of his shock, dropped the blade and held up his hands.

"Please!" he cried out in a strange, stilted accent, "I no kill him. I no hurt anybody!" The sailor restrained the boy with little struggle, though he squirmed and continued to protest. My father removed some of the linen from the rumpled bed and moved to cover the body with a sheet, of which I was especially grateful for. He then lifted the blade with a handkerchief, careful to disturb the bloody weapon as little as possible.

Other than the foreign boy's quiet pleas and the occasional firework exploding beyond the walls, there were a few moments of tense silence, which gave me an opportunity to gaze about, take in what I could.

The room wasn't large, though there was space for the four of us to move around the now concealed body in the centre of the floor. It was elegantly furnished, a broad, tall, sturdy armoire against the wall to the right of the door, a writing desk to the left, and a plush bed with the water closet through a door beyond on the opposite wall. I was so engrossed in my studies, trying to keep my mind off the dead man before me, that I flinched when there came a rap on the door.

My father bade me to open it and in came who I assumed was the second mate, another grave looking Canadian sailor, followed by, to my surprise, the tall, handsome, bombastic English man from the Automata House, now dressed in a more formal black suit and matching bowler hat. "Willard." My father nodded gravely before turning to me. "A military consultant to the crown."

The man, Mr. Willard, returned the greeting, looking excited. "Quigley. Who's that then?"

"This," my father bent over and pulled back the sheet, "is Herr Rudolf von Conrad, the Prussian ambassador."

"Good lord," interjected the second mate. A final firework exploded and there was enthusiastic applause from above. I did not know this Herr Conrad or the immediate significance of his death, but I was nonetheless part of the shared, shocked silence, interrupted only when the orchestra on the deck above resumed playing a lively, maddening waltz.

The men began to discuss immediate plans to dock at Hanlan's early and get in touch with the local constabulary. Mr. Willard kept punctuating sentences with phrases like "international security" and "diplomatic crisis" and "Chinese assassin," while the second mate just stood there, pulling at his beard and shaking his head. My father bade the second mate to go relay instructions to the captain, and after he left, Sir Quigley began discussing the situation with Mr. Willard who spoke with the same animation and, I dare say, excitement used in his demonstration earlier in the day.

I continued my watch at the door, listening as best I could to their hushed voices, but my eyes were drawn back to the boy who, released from the sailor's grasp and allowed to sit on the edge of the bed, still under guard, had lapsed into silence. He was scowling at his feet, however, feeling my gaze, he glanced up and our eyes met. There was pleading in them I could not ignore and I had to look away from the pitiable site.

My father and his companion finished grumbling to one another and Willard turned as my father consulted with the remaining sailor.

"Young Mr. Quigley, a pleasure. Your father says you are handy with that camera." He nodded at the device clutched beneath my arm. I admitted as much, and Willard requested (or ordered, rather) my services in documenting the crime scene. I stuttered I would, though he had to lead me by the arm over to the body of von Conrad. I raised the camera and flash stick as he pulled back the sheet. Up to that point, I had been surprised how little feeling the body inspired within me, though I could now see that the camera shook within my own trembling hands.

"This is the future of police procedure," said Willard glowingly, gazing on. "These cameras will transform the way we categorize evidence. No more basing things on the verbal, he-said-she-said nonsense. Nothing will escape the eye of the law!" He directed me to the other boy. "Best get a picture of the perp, old boy. For identification, police files and all that."

There was a slight shuffling in getting the Chinese boy against the wall, and to give me enough room to take a picture of his person without stepping on the body of von Conrad. This set off a fresh set of pleas in his strange accent. "Please! Please! I no kill him!"

"The boy is obviously a foreign dimwit," Mr. Willard growled angrily. "Some lowly pawn in the Chinamen's game, whatever it is."

My father seemed slightly more suspicious of the boy, especially when he caught the look of scorn on the boy's face at Mr. Willard's observation, pointing out, "Or perhaps he simply doesn't have a grasp of the language."

We were finally set up in the corner of the cabin, with the boy's back against the wall and I stood by the water closet door. As I raised my camera, there was a great ado from the outside corridor, just beyond the door to the cabin. It was thrown open and a woman with fiery red hair and bicycle suit of autumn tones elbowed her way past a pair of sailors flanking the door.

Of course, I recognized her as the inventor Ms. Teston. Behind her, curiously enough, she was followed by my brother, a sober, grim look on his face. The man I had noticed earlier being interrogated by the sailors stood just outside, looking in with a neutral expression on his face. From a few interactions with his people, I hazarded a guess that he may be Ojibwe from his appearance. As soon as I gazed on him, he disappeared into the small crowd that had gathered.

Ms. Teston stood a moment, studying the scene, an impassioned scowl on her face. My father approached her as if she was a riled animal and cautiously, almost whispering, said, "Mave..."

"Goddamn it," she growled, her eyes fixed on the body. "Goddamn it all."

Mr. Willard was crying, "Get her out, dammit, and close the bloody door!" Although he needn't have bothered as Ms. Teston turned and brushed past everyone surrounding the door, her face contorted in anger and as red as her hair. The few onlookers outside gasped, either at the small drama unfolding, or catching sight of the body on the floor.

During this distraction, the Asiatic boy and myself were momentarily ignored, in fact, I had forgotten he was nearby until he grabbed me by the collar and pulled me close to him. "Listen," he growled quietly, his teeth bared, "I didn't kill this dirty old pervert."

I was speechless. I realized his accent had evaporated and he spoke in a comprehensible, even eloquent English. Strangely enough to notice, given the circumstances, I could smell a subtle floral scent and felt his warm skin against mine. "I may be a criminal and a lot of other not so nice things, but I'm not a murderer. He told me to go into the water closet and stay there, and when I heard the scream, I unlocked the door and came back into the room. And he was dead. You have to believe me, no one else will listen, I know it! I'll hang! You have to believe me!"

"That's enough of that," came a voice from behind me. My brother, Hector Jr., had noticed the boy grasping at my collar and pried him off me, throwing him violently against the wall. I was stunned but observed Ms. Teston was now gone, along with the sailors and the second mate. All that remained behind were the body, the boy, Mr. Willard, my brother, my father, and myself.

"You must watch out for these Chinee, young Mr. Quigley," Willard stated, patting my back with aggressive friendliness. "I served in Her Majesty's Royal Navy in Shanghai. Slippery bastards. They may be good at cobbling together a railroad, but we should've shipped 'em all back to Peking the second they finished. A picture of the perp, would you, old chap?"

"Up, you," my brother snarled, pulling the other boy up by his arm.

He glared at Hector, then Mr. Willard and said, as if challenging them, "I no kill him."

Although I had no reason to believe him, I wished, as I lifted the camera, that I could apologize for my part in the arrest.

About then we could feel the boat shudder, meaning that we were docking at the Island, the party cut short. The sailors returned and took the boy by his arms, leading him to shore. As I watched after them, he threw one final pleading, accusing glance over his shoulder before disappearing down the walkway to his imprisonment.

"Very good. A coroner will be called for, and we can put this awful business behind us," Mr. Willard decried jovially. "You and your sons have been a wonderful help, Hector, I wonder if..." he raised his hand at me.

"Oh... Norwood," I answered, my voice warbling.

"Yes, Norwood. I wonder if you would give me your camera, old chap." I realized it wasn't a request.

"My camera?" I stuttered, clutching it to my breast as though it were all I had to hold on to.

"Yes, unfortunately it now contains evidence," he replied, unconvincing apology in his voice.

"Give him the camera, Norwood," my father commanded, placing a hand on my shoulder, his voice sympathetic but firm. Everyone could see the camera trembling in my hand as I handed it to Mr. Willard. He grabbed it and stuck it beneath his arm before, turning on his heel, marching out the cabin with a tip of his hat to my father.

We followed soon after, the three Quigleys. My father kept his hand on my shoulder and smiled sadly down at me. "I'm sorry I didn't get to say this until now, given the circumstances, but I was very impressed with your picture of Mr. Tinker. And your help..." he motioned backwards at the ugly business in Herr Conrad's cabin, now guarded by two other sailors. "Why did I not notice my son has grown into a skilful young man?"

"Father," I stuttered, my face flushed from the unexpected compliment. "Why did Ms. Teston seem so..."

At my side, my brother scoffed, as if such disdain for the woman explained all. My father nodded. "I understand Herr Conrad was a patron of hers, maybe a friend."

"Not to mention a bloody degenerate, apparently," my brother remarked snidely at my side. My father ignored him.

"I'm not surprised she was upset. Mave is an... impassioned woman. Any other woman would become hysterical with a friend dead at their feet. From what I hear about Mave we're lucky she didn't pull a weapon on us," he said, attempting to lighten the conversation while patting my shoulder gently.

My brother threw his arm around me and said, "Come on, chum, let's go get a drink before they lock up the bar."

Father grumbled his thanks to Hector as my brother led me from the deck. I turned back as we walked away and saw my father gazing down at the blade, still glistening with ruby blood and half-wrapped in the cloth, clutched tightly in his hand. My heart felt a pang of pity, for I could see how much the murder of this prominent man had shaken him.

I had drifted through the rest of the evening in a state of shock and had somehow been ferried to the mainland and wandered home, a sense of emptiness where my camera should have been, or at least that's what I convinced myself the feeling was. With a constricting anxiety I retired to bed that night; emotions that persisted in my dreams and remained as I departed for the station house the next morning. Even greater was a sense of dread and the feeling that something was terribly wrong with what had happened.

My dark humours were juxtaposed by the already warm, almost cloudless day; what was sure to be a beautiful summer day for the city's fairgoers. It was a short walk from my lodgings to the station house, a squat stone building just off of Church Street on Court. The street was bathed in shadows of the dramatic, Gothic spires of St. James Cathedral cast by a hazy morning sun, giving me a chill despite the warmth of the day.

I am, by no means, a detective or agent of the law, but a murder had been committed, I could ascertain that much, though the details of the event nagged in my brain. When I had spoken to the victim, Herr Conrad, who I learned was the Prussia-German ambassador, a dignitary on a goodwill mission to the ceremonies, the Chinese boy had not been in the cozy but small compartment, having just disappeared into the water closet where—he alleged—he had remained secluded.

The only other entrances into the room were the main door and an adjacent window that looked onto the deck. I heard the scream mere seconds after, myself a few steps down to the neighbouring door. A swift assassin, that, to evacuate the bathroom, make his way to the opposite side of the cabin and stab a man the moment the door closed behind me. The murderer would have had to be in the room, almost directly beside the victim when he was stabbed.

Furthermore, if the Chinese boy had been the murderer, why stand over the body, awaiting an inevitable arrest instead of making his escape by whatever means necessary. And the boy himself: his switch in language from a strange broken accent to functional English. He was clearly not what he seemed. What of his attire, a barely covering, exotic robe. Strange clothing for a criminal act. And then Ms. Teston's interruption on the scene, Mr. Willard, the Ojibwe man dressed in a dark suit, watching. My father, my brother...

The boy's assurances of his innocence would not let me be. Perhaps, I reasoned as I approached my destination, if I explained my concerns in the matter to a member of the constabulary, I could persuade these details to be investigated further.

As I entered the station house, I was greeted with an explosion of activity. The Chinese man I had seen talking to my mother the night previous, the ambassador, flanked by his two hulking countrymen, was storming by the front desk.

"This is outrageous!" he cried, his face a mask of fury. "Never have

I been treated like this, such accusations!" His bodyguards loped after him, scowling at one another, though they didn't seem particularly attentive and he did not wait for them.

Following behind him came a constable and Mr. Willard, looking grim and exhilarated respectively. The officer chased after them as they threw open the doors, shouting, "Ambassador Chen, you're required by law to remain in the city for further questioning," before the diplomat disappeared beyond the doors of the station house. Mr. Willard stared after them a minute, a dark smirk on his face, before recognizing me and hailing me warmly.

Now dressed in a plum-coloured suit with a matching bowler hat atop his head, he beckoned me to follow him, a hand clamped on my shoulder as if expecting me to turn tail and run.

"We were just about to send for you. Yes, old chap, of course, your camera's safe and sound. Had officers working on developing the film through the night. You'll get it back in good time. Right in here, young Quigley."

The Englishman led me into a comfortable office, no doubt vacated by the station's inspector. I was surprised to find my father seated behind the office desk perusing the morning paper, a cup of tea on a saucer before him, and my brother leaning against a cabinet behind him. "Morning Norwood, good to see you again," Father greeted me curtly. "Nasty business, this." He laid the paper out and there was a photograph (not my own) of the German ambassador, alive, accompanied by a picture of the *Hanlan's Pride*. The sensational headline "MURDER AT THE EXHIBITION" took up a portion of the front page in large, bold letters.

"Please, young Mr. Quigley," Mr. Willard motioned to a chair, "make yourself comfortable. Much to discuss. Yes, of course, your camera and negatives will be fetched, but in the meantime, we need your help."

"The situation is more serious than we could have anticipated," my father said, his deep, rumbling voice adding further gravity. "We have reason to believe the boy found at the scene of the crime is a Chinese nationalist, an agent."

"Assassin would be my word, although some would believe it a tad dramatic," Mr. Willard commented, excited, grabbing a pot from the table. "Tea?"

"No, thank you," I answered, bewildered.

"The Chinese-Prussian relationship has been tenuous for a time now," my father continued.

"Ambitious empires," Mr. Willard added. "Competing military powers. Nothing compared to Old Britannia, however."

"And it would seem that beyond the political situation, the relationship between von Conrad and Ambassador Chen has been… strained."

"To say the least," Willard grinned. "I think the word the Chinaman used was 'nemesis.' Something about the Prussian ambassador poaching a Chinese explosives expert from the Imperial Military some time ago. Rather amusing stuff."

My father continued, paying the other man's amused commentary no mind. "A sort of peace talk was to take place during the opening ceremonies, but we fear this is a blatant message that could escalate into something rather unpleasant. The Prussians blame the Chinese. The Chinese blame the English. We're not sure whom to believe, but it's clear there was a plot put into action. Both power hungry nations. It could lead to hostilities."

"A war, no doubt." Mr. Willard seemed to be boyishly delighted at the idea.

"I... don't understand, Father," I said, trying to work this out. "The boy is no older than I am. I don't believe that he's an..."

"Assassin," Mr. Willard finished my thought.

Hector gave another of his signature scoffs, leaning against a cabinet behind my father, his arms crossed. "Don't be naive, Norwood," my father replied, not unkindly. Hector nodded in agreement as if to show how he was right. "You've led a sheltered existence. You don't understand the darkness that drives men's hearts."

"War is an inevitability with these types," Mr. Willard continued his commentary as he eviscerated a biscuit. "Can even be a good thing sometimes. Cull out weak blood, make men of boys, stir up patriotic hearts, get the rabble-rousers under control."

My father seemed disturbed at Willard's suggestion and apparent bloodlust, and he frowned at the grinning man. "We don't know what motivates them, and we will try to sort this mess out before it comes to any further violence, but as civilized, lawful hosts, it's up to us to make sure justice is served," my father said with a measure of gravitas.

"With extreme prejudice," Mr. Willard concluded, taking a punctuating bite of his biscuit.

Father was correct in describing my sheltered existence. I knew nothing of war, and had never come in contact with death before the previous evening.

"Ah, here we are. What do you have for us, Constable Sherratt?" Mr. Willard called at the door, and in entered a ruddy-faced, bearded constable holding a file.

"Not his first run-in with the law, as is usual with these types, it seems." Constable Sherratt began reading the papers. "John St. Andrew, Chinese in origin, estimated to be about eighteen years of age. Abandoned as a babe at the Sacred Heart Orphanage, placed in the Toronto Boys' Home, ran away a few years ago. Two previous arrests, the first for petty theft at fourteen, although he was not charged on account of his age and the vouching of his guardians, the charitable brothers."

"And the second charge?" my father asked with a raised eyebrow.

Sherratt shuffled the papers and cleared his throat, his face reddening further beneath his beard. "Herm... He was found on the docks... soliciting, Sir Quigley."

The room fell silent, except for a stifled chuckle from my brother, ceased by a glance from my father.

"Solicitation?" Mr. Willard asked, incredulously.

"Yes sir," Sherratt replied, his face becoming a shade shy of purple. "Brought into this very stationhouse. He was soliciting for acts of an indecent nature. Acts so abominable, I dare not utter them as a good Christian soul."

Mr. Willard coughed and my father studied his empty teacup in mild embarrassment. It seemed I was the only one present who did

79

not understand the implication. From what I gleaned, he was selling something on the docks that deeply disturbed these men. My brother, of course, noticed and was amused by my lack of comprehension, and ever tactless in delicate situations, elaborated, "He's a prostitute, Norwood. The boy is paid to lay with men as a woman. He's a sodomite."

My stomach twisted uncomfortably, and I felt my face flush red to match Sherratt's. I made a study of my hands clenched in my lap and managed to utter, "Oh."

"Is that all, Sherratt?" my father asked, hoping to move the inquiries along.

"Well sir, as a..." he cleared his throat, "prostitute... St. Andrew poses as a Japanese boy with his given name as Katashi, I believe. He... managed to escape before he could be jailed, the last time."

"So!" Willard said, slamming his fist to the desk. "A seduction of unnatural means so this criminal could attack the ambassador at his most vulnerable."

"It would appear that way, sir." Sherratt dropped the papers on the desk, clearly anxious to be free of the matter.

"I tell you, these damn Chinee. Bringing their decadent practices into our God-fearing Empire! They should be shot, every bloody one of them!"

"Norwood," my father's voice cut through Willard's curses. I looked up to meet his eye, my stomach in knots.

"Yes, Father?"

"He asks for you, specifically," he said as if this is the most damning thing the criminal could do for himself, which it likely was.

"Not by name," Mr. Willard assured me. "Whenever we try any... lighter methods of interrogation, he just keeps saying 'Camera Man' in that Chinee-speak of his. We know he somehow got his hands on an invitation to board, as we've spoken to the sailor who remembered taking it from the scoundrel, but beyond that, we've been able to get little out of him, his English being so poor." I did not think it wise to contradict the military adviser of Britain, so I merely listened. "We hesitate from using our usual methods. Rough him up too much and he won't be able to confess, much less refuse to."

My father nodded. "I don't like it, but perhaps he'll be willing to talk to you. We'd like for you to go in, talk to him, get as much out of him as you can. Who he's working for, why he killed von Conrad. I have a feeling he has quite a bit more to say than he lets on."

Mr. Willard frowned. "I doubt it, Sir Quigley. These immigrant criminal vagrants are mostly illiterate, stupid things. Probably couldn't tell the difference between a queen and a quince."

If anything, I now felt more unsettled about what was happening. It was clear Mr. Willard had already decided this boy was a murderer without even speaking to him, and this St. Andrew called for me for whatever reason. My help? What could I do? But I couldn't refuse just as much as I couldn't ignore the nagging feeling I had of the boy's premature judgment. Mr. Willard assured me that there would be officers outside the interrogation room at all times, along with himself and my father, so it was all perfectly safe.

"We'll at least listen to what he has to say, right son?" my father said, sensing my unease. "Help us bring justice where it's due, Norwood." I nodded, feeling as though my involvement could only make the situation worse.

I followed Sherratt and Willard through the station house with my brother and father following behind us. I felt more a prisoner than someone assisting in an investigation.

We came to the holding room, a small, windowless cubicle furnished by a table and a couple of simple wood chairs, just around a corner from the cells, the only entrance a single door. Through a screen, we could see John St. Andrew, his back to us, seeming to meticulously rearrange the chairs with great agitation. When Willard wordlessly opened the door and motioned me through, the other boy jumped and turned around.

He had at least been afforded the mercy of some modest clothing, for his strange robe had been exchanged for a dirty looking shirt, a pair of threadbare trousers and a pair of scuffed, mismatched work boots. This seemed the end of mercy. Since the previous evening, he had been given a split lip and matching bruises on each cheek. We made eye contact for a brief but affecting moment wherein I felt a renewed sense of shame for my part in his treatment. Even if he was a criminal on any number of charges, he was a boy my age, and none deserve that kind of abuse.

St. Andrew broke the gaze and moved to a chair on the far side of the table and sat, then motioned me to sit on the one he had been fiddling with. I did so, feeling a little flustered by the gesture.

"John St. Andrew?" I asked cautiously once seated.

"Yes," he said, his voice cracking. "Please, water, thirsty." He touched his throat. There came excited whispers through the screen at his first words. I nodded, realizing he probably hadn't been given any luxury such as water since his arrival. With a little more authority than I thought myself capable of, I requested a glass of water to be brought forth immediately before the interview—interrogation, rather—continued. It was produced immediately, and the other boy sipped it, looking relieved.

"You came to the station for your camera," he stated.

I stuttered. He wasn't speaking in the accent he'd affected the night before, which seemed to confuse everyone beyond the wall. "Well, also to talk to someone about... what happened." He waited for me to continue, so I explained, "I don't think it's what it looks like."

He nodded, and I sensed from his expression that he was a bit impressed. "You believe me, that I didn't kill that man?"

"I don't know," I admitted. "I don't know what I think, but I'll say nothing seems right. Really though, I'm a bit out of my league. I'm just a writer... a photographer, and not even a very good one at that."

St. Andrew smirked at my self-deprecation, though this was followed by a wince. I noticed the cut on his lip had reopened. I quickly grabbed a kerchief from my pocket and held it out to him. He reached out for it, but in doing so, our hands touched briefly. I retracted mine, feeling the same knots in my stomach from before. St. Andrew, on the other hand, seemed unaffected and dabbed the blood from his lip.

I rallied my courage to speak. "Would you, uh, tell me a little about the whole affair."

Holding his lip, he grimaced. "Poor choice of words." When I realized what he was implying, I'm sure I turned a fresh shade of scarlet. "I guess it's appropriate enough, though. I don't expect to change their minds." He nodded over my shoulder at the screen behind me. "They've already set my hanging date for tomorrow, I've heard." He sighed as if annoyed by the inconvenience of his immediate demise. "I was asked to... take my business to that man. The ambassador, though I didn't know who he was at the time."

"By who?"

He shook his head. "I don't know, I never actually saw him, the man who hired me. I got a letter through certain... channels, inviting me to an address in the Chinese quarter a few days ago. To a smoking den in a basement down an alley. It was empty, other than two men, two Chinese men. The one giving me the job sat behind a curtain and spoke to me through another one of the men."

"Why through another man?" I asked, genuinely curious at the mysterious circumstances.

The other boy's eyes fell to the floor. "He... tried to speak to me in Mandarin Chinese but I... speak very little, so the other man, a servant I guess, a large, bald, tattooed Chinese man acted as a translator. Not a very good one either." St. Andrew scowled. "He seemed like a sailor, maybe. Didn't speak a lot of English. The servant handed me an envelope. Special entrance to the Exhibition, and aboard the steamship. With the room number."

"To von Conrad's room?" I offered.

"Yes, he let me in, like he was expecting me, and we spent the next couple of hours... well, I worked," he smirked as my face flushed once again. "They offered me money to entertain the... von Conrad. That was all. They gave me more money than I'd ever make in one night, saying there was more coming to me if I was successful. I should have known something was wrong about that, but money's money. So that's what I did, and when the fireworks started, von Conrad told me he was expecting someone, and to go into the bathroom and not come out until he said so. I heard a knock, so I rushed to do as he said. Nothing more."

There was some excitement outside the room. I could hear Mr. Willard bellowing, "He's lying, of course!" There were some further commentaries from those attending my interrogation... but...

Suddenly there was another voice in my ear. A voice that was almost whispering. As Mr. Willard continued his protestations, I heard St. Andrew. "Don't panic," it said. "I'm throwing my voice. Just move your mouth, they'll think you're talking to me. Stop looking around like an idiot and just listen to me. I need to escape, and you can help me if you really believe me." I was frozen in place, my eyes wide in disbelief. I noticed how the other boy's mouth was twitching very slightly as the ghost voice continued. I did not stop him, and I realized I would help him any way I could, though I could not say why. "I'm going to threaten you, or pretend to. I won't hurt you. Go along with me, and I think I can get myself out of here. Blink twice if you'll do this for me."

I did.

It happened in a flash. St. Andrew lifted the glass, downed the water and then brought the top of the glass smashing against the edge of the table. He leapt across and pulled me out of my seat, one arm around my shoulders and the other with the broken glass pressed against my neck. "Here we go," he breathed into my ear, which, added to our sudden proximity and the shard against my neck, sent shivers up my spine.

There were shouts from the corridor, but St. Andrew pulled me close to the door and bellowed, "You do everything I say or I'll stick him, I swear! Now someone open the door, and then everybody back away into the main room. Do it!"

The door swung open and Constable Sherratt, his hand resting on his pistol, scowled at his prisoner. I could hear my father's voice growl, "Do as he says, damnit!" The officer hesitated before he backed away into the station. St. Andrew and I followed, cautious. Despite the ruse on his part, St. Andrew still had to be careful and not allow himself to be snuck up on from behind. Satisfied there was no one of danger to us in the jail area, we quickly edged our way after the rest.

Further into the station, every person present had congregated a distance away from the holding room hallway, no doubt at my father's command, all dead still, each officer with their hands ready on their pistols.

"No sudden movements, or he dies," St. Andrews called as we inched our way into the room. I, for my part, was making a convincing act of struggle, for I was doing my best to keep from slipping and slicing my neck on the glass. Trying to stay upright and match the other boy's desperate gait was a challenge, and the jagged glass at my throat was by no means pretend.

There was a look of intense concern on most faces present in the room. My brother looked more scared than I had ever seen him, and my father glared at St. Andrew venomously. Mr. Willard, on the other hand, had turned purple in rage, no doubt at his prisoner's attempted escape. When we hesitated, St. Andrew strategizing his next steps, Mr. Willard cried out, "What are you idiots waiting for? Shoot the little bugger!"

My father turned about the room. "You'll do no such thing. I'll have the head of the man who risks my child's life."

Despite the situation, I was touched by the sentiment, though resented being referred to as a child.

"No sudden moves or I swear," and with St. Andrew's voice in my ear, I felt a stinging warm sensation against my neck as the glass made the slightest contact, drawing blood.

"Let him by," commanded my father, and as we worked our way across the room, our backs always to the wall, the officers moved out of the way for us.

I realized we were making our way toward a door that would lead out through an alley, which led to the city morgue. We were a few feet away from our escape, clearing the last of the officers, when I saw on the corner of the last desk in our way, sticking out of a canvas bag, my camera.

"C-c-camera," I rasped quietly as I could as we neared it.

"What?" he looked, and let out a sharp sigh when he realized what I meant. "I'm taking the camera with me to... destroy whatever evidence you have against me! Grab it!" A ridiculous excuse, but no one protested when he allowed me to snatch the camera bag.

We cleared the couple of feet between the two of us and freedom, and without another word, St. Andrew released me and launched himself through the door into the alley.

And damnit, I followed him.

We burst onto the alley only to be accosted by two constables. Of course, in the time it took us to get out of the holding room into the station, they had preempted our escape and had sent officers to trap us.

The first lunged for St. Andrew but he was small and fast enough to duck, and the officer tumbled toward me. I maintain that I brought my foot out into a kick to his face completely by accident.

The second officer, a few feet behind the first, was reaching for his pistol, although St. Andrew leapt, flying through the air, and brought the jagged glass into the man's hand. As the officer cried out, the other boy brought his knee into the unlucky officer's groin, and the man crumpled.

I was almost tempted to stammer an apology to the men, but St. Andrew was already running full tilt down the alley and I could only follow or lose him. Behind us, police bellowed orders and blew whistles as they gave chase, but we had enough of a start that we were able to duck a corner and get lost in the crowd.

We had taken two corners and crossed the street into another alley when St. Andrew afforded a moment to glance back over his shoulder, and I saw his eyes widen in surprise. "What are you doing?" he cried out in between panting breaths.

"Coming with you!" I managed. "I must!" And as we were currently in flight, he took this as a sufficient response and continued onwards with me tailing him.

We began to sporadically weave our way through the alleys bordering the bustling thoroughfare of King Street, dodging piles of rubbish and leaping over the occasional vagrant. We dodged our way through crowds, past busy storefronts, around carriages and wagons across Bay Street, before cutting north and slipping into an alley off the big mail office building. St. Andrew skidded to a halt behind some mail crates and motioned for me to join him. We had ducked out of sight just in time because we heard a clatter of hooves pass in the street and some shouts of a coordinated search effort.

"Police, but we should be clear now. Keep low," he muttered and I, a novice to evading the law, nodded my agreement. We ambled nonchalantly past a mail cart being unloaded into the sorting room and made a couple of turns behind other buildings before circling around to the corner of Bay and Adelaide. With a final glance around the corner, I followed St. Andrew out into the street. Luckily for us, with the continuing opening ceremonies, the streets were thronged with people. Tourists, vendors, entertainers, hucksters, pickpockets, a crush of vehicles and animals added to the usual chaos of downtown city life. We were able to lose ourselves in the crowds, hiding in plain sight, though the other boy snatched a cap out of the pocket of an unlucky elderly man and pushed briskly through the crowds, glancing back down Bay from the direction we'd come from before starting to head southwards as he pulled the cap down over his face.

"Excuse me... uh, St. Andrew... John?" I said, getting as close as I could to the boy as we cut through a group around the front of a grocers.

He snorted. "Please, St. Andrew is just a name the brothers gave me. John isn't my real name—if I even have one. Call me Jing."

John St. Andrew. Katashi. Jing... I supposed my companion had admitted readily enough that—while not a murderer—he was part of the criminal element. And I supposed that one needed to employ professional handles and multiple identities in that industry, but that did little to ease my mind. I had helped him escape without hesitation, but the gravity of the situation weighed on my conscience. I knew little about this young man standing before me. Who was he, really? Was Jing merely another pseudonym?

"Okay. Jing, where are we going?"

He stopped so suddenly I crashed into him. This gave him the chance to grab me and force me into the mouth of the closest alley. Jing studied me a moment as if taking stock of me for the first time. "We? Who said we are going anywhere together? I am going to Union Station to sneak on the first train out of the city." He paused and slapped his forehead. "I don't even know why I'm telling you this! Who are you, anyway? Wait, you're..."

"Norwood. Norwood Quig—"

"Christ's crutches, that's right," he interrupted. "In the eyes of the law... literally, I've kidnapped the son of the richest man in the country. I have to get out of here."

He shoved past me down the crowded street, and I continued to pursue him. "You won't be able to get a train," I called after him, and he turned around, glaring at me, so I dropped my voice. "Security is tight enough already with the Exhibition in town. Mounted police, soldiers, the Exhibition Guard. You know they will already be all over Union Station. They're probably on their way now. They'll search every train, airship dock and carriage in town. They'll probably arrest every Chinese man until they have you. And anyway, why run if you're innocent?"

Jing stopped and turned on me again, practically snarling. "What would you have me do, Mister Quigley? If you didn't notice, your friends back at the station, not to mention your close family, want my blood. I'm just a foreigner whore-boy turned murderer to them. Even if I had your money, I couldn't talk my way out of that."

This stung, more so because he pointed out my blatant naivety. "Can't we prove you're innocent?" I protested. Jing's laughter was callous but then, seeing my face fall, he threw his hands up in exasperation.

"Look, Quigley, I appreciate all you've done for me. Probably more than anyone has ever done for me, but kindness won't build an airship to fly me away into the sunset." I was about to further protest when I noticed a poster for the opening ceremonies hung in a storefront window over his shoulder:

WITNESS A DEMONSTRATION OF
THE NEW ROYAL AIRSHIP FLEET!

GREAT FEMALE INVENTOR MAVE TESTON UNVEILS THE ROYAL FLEET,
ALL NEW MODELS, AT THE QUIGLEY AIRSHIPS FIELD!

The date was the second day of the Exhibition, early in the afternoon.

"Mave Teston!" I cried. Jing jumped and turned, as if expecting to find the inventor herself directly behind him, but found the poster and cocked his head in confusion. "She was the woman who stormed into the room last night," I elucidated. "She seemed to know von Conrad and was distressed by his murder. Maybe she'll know something, or at least be able to offer some insight into what transpired."

Jing pondered this a moment. "Or she'll turn me in for killing her friend," he added, although he seemed softened somewhat to the idea.

"And think about it! What better place to hide than among the Exhibition crowds? Sure, security will be tightened, but it'll be even busier today than yesterday! That's the last place they'll look for us! We can even sneak onto the Queen Streetcar to get us to the Exhibition grounds. It'll be so packed no police could ever see us."

He thought on this. "*The* Mave Teston? And she'd listen to you? Well, of course she would, you're a white-as-white-can-be Quigley." I shrugged, there was no arguing with that assessment. "I guess it's as good a plan as any. But Quigley..."

I stopped him. "Norwood, please."

He let out a sharp, quick sigh. "Fine, Norwood. Any sign of trouble, if you fall a little behind or get caught, I disappear and hide, then catch the first ride out of town I can, and don't think for a second I'll look back to help you." I supposed that was fair. "Fine then, before we go to the fairground, I have to check something. Then we'll catch the streetcar in front of the New Town Hall. Keep fast and low."

With Jing in the lead, keeping his head down, we continued dodging our way through the crowd, cutting down another alley that led us behind some shops, and then we were working our way toward the towering New Town Hall construction site just beyond, a short distance away on Queen. Despite the urgency of our situation, I still couldn't help but marvel at the grand stonework of the half-constructed building, the dramatic design which inspired the Teston & Tinker workshop. Just as we rounded a final corner and saw Queen Street mobbed with people, a church tower chimed noon in the distance. We had a little less than two hours to make our way to the Exhibition grounds.

Jing turned left on the crowded street and pushed his way across Queen with me in tow. The crowds started to thin out as we cut into St. John's Ward, a less than savoury neighbourhood.

As a prosperous, dynamic city had grown around it, St. John's Ward had become the depository of the unfortunate and destitute. Freed slaves from Canada and America, and their descendants; Jews fleeing massacre in Europe; Chinese immigrants, mostly men, imported to complete the railroad and then cast aside; Irish families escaping famine only to find it here. Children huddled in doorways, either forgotten or lost to their parents. Cramped, ramshackle homes, mostly no more than one or two storeys, were subdivided by greedy landlords who wanted to cram as much human misery as possible and feed off their meagre earnings.

At a dinner party hosted by my mother last year, a wealthy Jewish doctor and philanthropist, an earlier import to Canada than his impoverished kinsman, had described how he had visited a family of nine living in a single room in St. John's Ward, and that was typically the norm.

Jing seemed to know where he was going, skirting the southern extremity of the Ward until he came to a decrepit Chinese herbalist shop, paint-chipped and shabby. Passerbys gazed on at the exotic script in wonder, none brave enough to enter, but were arrested by a nearby vendor, an elderly Chinese woman who was stooped over a wheeled cart decorated in fanciful gold and crimson red paint, not unlike the new streetcars. She was dressed in an outrageous, equally flamboyant robe of blue and silver, her hair done up in curls and knots, her face powered white with exaggerated eyebrows drawn on.

"Authentic Exhibition Chinese dumpling!" she cried in a stilted accent similar to that which Jing had employed the previous night. "Same dumplings sold at Fair! Ten cent each for authentic Chinese dumpling! Just like in Peking!"

We approached, though held back as she made a sale to a wide-eyed, middle age European couple in modest farmer dress. The Chinese woman reached into a boiling pot within her cart and ladled two bread blobs into cheap paper cups. The woman's face turned green upon seeing the "dumpling," but the man seemed thrilled. "Is China close to Winkler, Manitoba?" he asked.

"Oh yeah," the Chinese woman said, grinning from ear to ear. "Just a couple mile west'a there."

The man departed, satisfied with the answer, his wife looking queasy as he began to slop the food into his mouth. Jing and I approached, my companion sneaking behind her and lifting the lid of "dumpling" container and peeking in.

"Looks like... bad bread rolls?" he said, a snide, accusatory tone in his voice.

The woman jumped, but then smirked when she saw Jing beside her. She pinched his cheek and muttered, just loud enough for me to hear, her accent vanished, "Quan's sells me yesterday's burnt rolls a dozen for a nickel. You boil anything long enough and white people will believe they're dumplings." She turned, noticing me standing there and grinned, her accent rallying. "Nice man want authentic dumpling?"

"Drop it, Yaling. He's with me." She raised one of her arched eyebrows at me before snorting and turning back to Jing.

"Heard you murdered someone," she scoffed, pulling the cart into the shop, with Jing and I following. She shoved it haphazardly into a storage closet filled with jars and sacks of herbs. Yaling pulled off the robe, more humble, loose, simple men's clothing underneath. She used the robe to wipe off the thick layer of makeup on her face, then tossed it into the pot of "dumplings" to wash. Finally, she removed the thick twists of hair atop her head, a ratty wig that followed the robe into the water. Beneath was a tight bun of silver-grey hair. The change was immediate and incredible; I would have taken her for Jing's kindly grandmother if she hadn't sworn about the heat of the wig.

She waved at us to follow and we continued into the herbalist's store, past shelves full of tinctures and balms, roots and baskets of fragrant herbs. Yaling nodded at a bored looking elderly Chinese man behind the counter. He nodded in return and immediately went back to snoozing in his seat. I glanced over and noticed his hand resting lazily on a rifle under the desk.

The room behind the herbalist's store was an office of sorts. While the premises were run down, this room was opulently decorated, a solid, elegant oak desk and plush chairs not unlike a Quigley Airships boardroom. Art decorated the walls, Chinese and Western, beautiful landscapes mostly. Yaling waved absentmindedly at the seats before she plopped into her own behind the desk. She and Jing held a long, tense glance before she smirked again. "You want information, you have to pay."

Jing's scowl intensified. "After your job put me in this situation?"

Her smirk widened further, she looked like a friendly, grinning cat waiting to claw out our throats. "Not my job, my dearest. You know I'm just the messenger, and you've been all too happy to accept 'my jobs' in the past."

Jing swore and then turned to me expectantly. They both stared at me until I got the hint and produced a dollar from my pocket and placed it on the table before Yaling. She raised an eyebrow as if insulted. I produced another dollar, then another. Soon ten were stacked on the desk in front of her, a small fortune, and I was afraid she'd keep going until all my pocket money was gone, but she snorted again and snatched up the bills, counting them.

"I never saw the man who arranged this, just got his note in Mandarin. Asked for a young Chinese man who would 'entertain' an official. Gave a generous finder's fee."

I sighed inwardly, relieved. A charlatan this woman may be, and a criminal sort to boot, but if she could be believed, as I was wont to do, this proved Jing was simply a pawn in a larger scheme.

"Where's the note now?" I asked. Her head whipped around to face me and fixed me with a glare that would curdle milk.

"Oh, I just left it on my desk for anyone to read, of course!" she purred, a dangerous tone in her voice. Her finger stabbed at an ancient coal stove behind us. Destroyed, of course. I was about to protest, suggest she come forth to the police with this information, but Jing kicked my leg. I lapsed into silence.

"There's more?" Jing pressed.

Yaling turned away from me, opened the desk and reached in. She drew a cigar and a box of matches, taking her time to light it and take stock of Jing. She exhaled a plume of smoke from her nose, shrouding her face in a nauseating cloud.

"This wasn't the first note," she offered, finally. "The first one came last month. Just like yours, except requesting the services of a couple of strong Chinese men looking to be paid well who weren't too picky about the work." She let that hang in the air for a moment.

"How do you know it was the same employer?" Jing asked. I nodded, curious myself.

She blew another plume of smoke; I assumed she was considering if this information was worth another few dollars, but she relented. "Not often I get anonymous notes in Mandarin. The writing was elegant, literate, not the usual scrawl I'm used to. Someone studied and cultured, I'd say."

My stomach turned at the possibilities. Perhaps Willard was right, was this a plot of the Chinese ambassador? Jing an innocent pawn in a grudge between feuding empires? If that was the case, claims that war would escalate did indeed seem inevitable.

"I passed along the message to a couple of brutes who were fresh out of the Penitentiary and looking for work. Jiao-Long and Qiang Li the Ox. I'd avoid them if I were you, my dearest. Get out of town. Go to Vancouver, or further. At the very least get out of my sight."

Jing stood. "We're going."

Yaling didn't move to stop him, so I stood and followed. When we reached the door she called after us, "I could probably turn you in and make some good money if I wanted, so consider that my apology before you storm out of here like a child. It's just, as they say, business." I glanced back as she stubbed the cigar out on the back of her hand. "And don't come around here again while you're a wanted criminal, or I'll do worse than turn you in."

Jing's face was contorted with anger as we breezed through the herbalist's. He clearly felt betrayed at having been passed along into this plot and, although I was no criminal mastermind or even a person of particular skill or resource, I resolved that I'd do whatever I could to help him out of it.

We dashed back through St. John's Ward. The warmth of the afternoon had drawn out more souls into Toronto's streets than I had imagined possible. The streets were a riot of gaudy fashions and gaudier sights, entertainers and dubious salesmen plagued us every step of the way, looking to rake in what they could from fairgoers out on the town.

"I knew this job was rotten the moment I stepped into that smoking den," Jing grumbled as we dodged our way through the throngs.

I, taller and broader than my companion, had trouble keeping up. "Do you think it's true, then? Do you think the Chinese were retaliating against some slight?" There seemed to be no other explanation.

"I don't give a damn about politics," he snapped back at me over his shoulder. "I just want to find out who pinned it on me."

Jing stopped a short walk away from Yaling's shop, at the corner of the New Town Hall construction site and I joined him. We both glanced up and down the street and, fortune on our side; a streetcar was cutting through the foot and bicycle traffic and neared the New Town Hall stop.

"Let's go," Jing said, and we began shoving our way through the crowd as quickly as we could. We received some fairly irritated reproaches for our rudeness, which Jing answered with passing curses, and I could only hope our urgency would make up for our impropriety in the grand scheme.

We were some of the first to board as the streetcar doors chimed open, joining a rush of passengers disembarking in front of the construction site. We brushed past the automaton driver, ignoring its tinny greeting and into the already rather full cabin, though we were able to steal two remaining seats at the back of the vehicle. The streetcar reached its capacity of laughing, excited riders, the door chimed shut and we began to trundle west along Queen Street.

Jing and I sat low in our seats so we could not be spotted from the street, but we both sighed at the momentary rest. He turned to flash a lopsided, relieved grin at me, which sent my stomach into the same nervous knots as before, and I'm sure I blushed once again. However, the grin quickly switched to a look of concern. "Your neck!"

I lifted my chin and brought my finger to the spot where the glass had grazed into the skin. In doing so, I was awarded with a stinging sensation as I had opened the cut anew. I let out a hiss. "I'm sure it looks worse than it is."

"Here, let me." He produced the handkerchief I had given him earlier and dabbed at the wound with a clean corner. His touch was so light the sensation on my neck caused me to shiver. Noticing this, he smiled slyly and opened his mouth to say something, but at that moment there came shouts of terror from outside.

In our escape, I had completely forgotten about my camera in the cloth bag, now slung over my shoulder. Jangling about within, in a small case accompanying the negatives were a series of glass slide copies of the pictures I had taken during my first day at the Exhibition, which the police had prepared. If I had looked through the slides, I would have noticed, logically so, all the pictures from von Conrad's room had been removed. However, if I had considered the implications of the missing slides, I have no doubt Jing and I would have proceeded more cautiously. The moment we had escaped from the station, a bloodhound had been loosed on our trail.

We learned this presently because with a massive, groaning shudder, the entire streetcar pitched to the side and we were falling, drowning in a sea of limbs, metal and broken glass.

CHAPTER 5

IN WHICH TWO FUGITIVES FIND A PRESSING
NEED TO CONSULT WITH A GREAT INVENTOR
AND PROPONENT OF WOMEN'S LIB

A heavy pounding noise assaulting my ears, coupled with frantic squirming and wailing all around, brought me back from brief unconsciousness. Reorienting myself in the mess of panicking bodies was a challenge. Even more alarming was reorienting myself with the streetcar lying on its side, having been knocked over into the opposite lane. Glass crunched beneath my feet as I braced myself upright.

Once I had righted myself and determined my body was whole and mostly uninjured, my mind was concerned with two things. The first being to help people closest to me and directing them through the hole where the windows at the back of the streetcar had been, allowing for people to climb through and out of the wrecked vehicle. The second was to locate my missing companion, lost in the madness of the wreckage.

And still those terrible, rending slams from outside the vehicle, as if God's fist was beating down upon us. It was maddening and did nothing to quell the general panic. In between each resounding blow,

I could hear the mechanical driver at the front repeating, "Please. Stand behind the white line. For your safety."

Luckily there seemed to be no major injuries that I could detect as I directed the passengers out. A little blood here and there from scrapes and cuts, maybe a broken limb or two, but most of the poor frightened men, women and children were able to leave on their own steam. I imagined Jing had already escaped and had probably put a block between himself and the accident until the streetcar cleared and I saw a heap cradled between a couple of chairs a few rows ahead.

I clambered over broken glass, debris and abandoned personal effects through the overturned streetcar to him and shook his shoulders. He stirred slightly, so he was at least alive, but the blood trickling over his face from a gash on his forehead communicated that he had smashed his head in the tumbling. Despite the situation, my heart melted a little when I noticed he still clutched my handkerchief in his fist.

I scooped the smaller boy up from under his arms and pulled him as gently as I could out onto the street, and two waiting men aided me when I reached the smashed windows at the back. We laid Jing out as comfortably as possible and turned our attention to reviving him, when someone in the crowd surrounding us cried out, "It's... It's—"

I followed the onlooker's finger to the creature that had been tearing at the underside of the streetcar, what had been making the horrible pounding noise. As I looked up, it turned its massive body to face us, and my blood ran cold.

The crowd had given it a wide berth, but hundreds of people stood and gazed on the hulking brass brute, the one Mr. Willard had demonstrated the previous day...

Mr. Shackles.

At once, everything in my mind clicked. They had used the picture of Jing from my camera, the one I'd taken in von Conrad's room an evening previous, and developed it into a glass slide. The thing, Mr. Shackles, must have been within walking distance of the station. In fact, Mr. Willard may have even anticipated an escape and merely needed to relay orders to the creature to hunt down actual prey. What better product demonstration to the Canadian constabulary than the Mr. Shackles prototype capturing the von Conrad murderer on the streets of Toronto?

As it gazed over the crowd and its attention fell on Jing and I. I could see that apertures within the frames of its eyes spun, analyzing the scene, before a low roar emanated from inside of it, like a huge engine surging with power, and acrid smoke and steam filtered out of the grate where, given human anatomy, its mouth would be.

I knew once it had Jing, there'd be little I could do to help him, and in spite of my best judgment, I stepped between my companion and the machine. The beast took two thunderous steps, and then suddenly there was a heavy, metallic thud and it stumbled and fell. Behind Mr. Shackles stood a small group of large people who had stepped out of the crowd, three men and a woman. They were dressed in rough garments of the working class and held tools and pipes, workers from the construction site of New City Hall, no doubt. One had stepped forward and broken a wooden plank over Mr. Shackles' back.

"Feck off ye great broot," bellowed the first attacker, and the other three flanked him, brandishing improvised weapons.

"Terrorizin' these good people," screeched the woman indignantly. "Ye shood be ashaymed!"

As if sensing their hostility, Mr. Shackles stood with a mighty roar and turned its attention away from us, onto its assailants. Not wasting any time, I gave Jing a shake. "Wake up," I cried over and over. After a moment his eyes fluttered open, and he squinted at the light.

"I think I'm dead," he said in a matter-of-fact voice, his speech noticeably slurred.

"Not so fortunate," I replied, attempting to hurry him to his feet. "We have to go, we have to run!"

As Jing managed to stand on shaky legs, I turned to witness Mr. Shackles lift and toss one of the burly Scotsmen into the crowd, easier than a sack of laundry. The woman managed to duck the first swing, but the second that followed caught her in the side of the head and she went sprawling.

Whether he was able to or not, we had to get away. I threw his arm around my shoulder and, grabbing his waist, began to shove through the crowd with Jing wobbling along, bracing himself against me.

Luckily we were just another pair of injured, scared, fleeing passengers to the crowd, so they parted easy enough, distracted by the battle between man and machine before them. We dodged between halted carriages in the street who were cursing the blockage or calling after us, wondering what had happened.

Jing, after a few minutes of slow, steady movement southward, was a little more coherent and able to pick up the pace, though he continued to need my support to walk. I explained to him our renewed peril. How, from the little I knew about the gargantuan that now stalked us, it would stop at nothing until it had captured him. "In fact," I added, "it may not even be ordered to take you alive."

He scoffed. "That's such a relief, Norwood. Thank you for pointing that out."

As we rounded a corner and we passed Adelaide Street, the Opera House nearby, he at last noticed I had a general direction, and he asked where we were going. "South, to the ferry docks. We'll find a boat for hire. I have a bit more money on me. Or we can take the ferry to the Island and find some way to the Exhibition from there."

He was silent a moment, thinking very hard in his slightly addled state. "Why a boat? Why not walk, or take a cab?"

I hastened him along, across the street, glancing over my shoulder. The thing hadn't caught up, not yet. "Unless that thing can buy a ferry ticket, it'll have no way to follow us. That might throw it off our trail."

He laughed deliriously, as if the situation were a child's game of tag. "Norwood, you're a genius!"

We hobbled together down Bay Street, where things were quieter than the scene of the accident we'd left behind. Busy with tourists and businessmen in dark suits, but no sign of our pursuer or police. I saw the grand construction of Union Station. Jing, in response to an engine sounding off, exclaimed, to my intense worry, "Choo choo... I would love to take a train, but I never have before, Norwood."

The childish way he spoke was alarming, perhaps from the blow to his head. I could only hope it was not permanent as I responded, "Of course. After we take care of things here, we'll take a vacation. We'll have a grand train adventure. How does that sound?"

"How romantic!" he said, an edge of sarcasm returning to his voice. All was not lost.

At the ferry docks I located a toothless old man normally in the hire of the rich desiring a private ride to the Island Hotel. Given our condition he seemed suspicious, eyeing us up and down.

"I promised my friend I would show him the Exhibition grounds from the water." He cocked an eyebrow dubiously as Jing, blood still streaming down his face, laughed and interjected, "Choo choo!"

I, however, remained assertive. "We're on our way to see Mave Teston unveil the Royal Airship Fleet!"

The man looked skeptical. "Tha' so?"

"Yes, so we'd prefer not to be delayed further... And..." I dropped triple his usual fare into his hand, which happened to be all the money I had in my pocket, "we are in a tremendous hurry."

This convinced him. "Right y'are sir. T'only be moment. This way."

He led us to an old steam dory, a dingy, rusty little boat barely polished up for its passengers, but the man assured me she was seaworthy.

As he coaxed the clanking engine to life, I almost didn't hear the distant roar, but I followed the sound and caught a glimpse of something in the distance.

The thing had lost its hat in the scuffle, so the shiny dome of its skull caught the sun. It was striding parallel to the water line, glancing back and forth. I prayed it would miss us, though this prayer went unanswered. Mr. Shackles stopped a dock's length away from us and let out an awful roar. "Now!" I cried. "We cast off now!"

I unceremoniously dropped Jing into the boat with my camera bag, and despite the sailor's terrified protests, I went about untying the mooring lines. He continued his protests until he saw the mechanical beast charge straight for us, at which point he started shouting instructions and curses.

"Push off!" the man screeched, and I did with the resounding steps of Mr. Shackles on the rickety wooden planking. I leapt for the boat just as he lunged toward me and, as I soared over the water, I heard a terrible crash of splitting, snapping wood.

When I was finally able to open my eyes, I found Jing lying next to me on the bottom of the boat. He grinned stupidly and whispered, "Choo." It took every ounce of strength to force my trembling legs to stand. The boatman was alternating between a steady stream of prayers and curses, working at steering while glancing over his shoulder at the shrinking shoreline. Steadying myself on the railing, I looked at the dock we had just departed from, or what was left of it.

The end of the old wooden dock had been shorn off, and jagged planks hung, dangling into the water. Much of what I had just been standing on now floated in the brine below, bobbing in the wake of the small dory. Something below the water bubbled, although I was thankful to see it moving back toward the shore.

As the boatman and I looked on, the terrible figure of our pursuer walked, step by ponderous step, out of the grimy water, clambering over rocks and pieces of debris. Water poured out of the joints and inner workings of the mechanical beast, a plume of superheated steam trailing out behind it, yet still it moved. Once ashore, the thing turned, raised its arms as if in enraged and gave such a mighty, gurgling, resounding roar that it scattered the dozens of dock hands and sailors who had witnessed the scene unfold.

"What in the name of Solomon's flopping left teat was that?" the boatman cried as the clockwork beast stalked back into the city. I ignored him, instead attending to Jing, who seemed to be having trouble sitting up on his own.

"It looks like I'm bleeding," he said, rubbing his head, his words still slurred. "Was I in an accident?"

I located the handkerchief, still clutched tightly in his hand, and after recovering it, began to administer to the blood on his face. "You were in a bit of a wreck, and you look like one, too."

He smirked. "You don't look so great yourself." He attempted, again, to sit up, although this seemed to dizzy him. "My head hurts, Norwood. I wanna sleep…"

"I don't think that's a good idea." I was able to prop him up against the side of the boat, though he still seemed disoriented. "We have to go see Ms. Teston, remember?"

"Maybe I should be putting you two back on land," the boatman called to us gruffly. "I don't much care for trouble being brought on my humble vessel."

I tried to keep my voice as kind as possible, but I may have sworn at the man. "We're in no shape to get to the Exhibition on foot. Plus,"

I added, "you start into land and that thing will likely get a hold of your humble vessel."

He swore right back at me. "I'm just sayin'... you coulda taken a streetcar if you was in such a hurry."

The boatman made what was undoubtedly record time to the Exhibition docks, and left us there even faster.

I had managed to clean Jing up enough, and he was made a sight more presentable when I gave him my jacket. By the time we returned to land, however, he had at least recovered his capacity to walk on his own, though he complained of a headache.

The fairgrounds were busier than the day before despite—maybe even because of—news of the murder, and we moved as fast as possible through the crowds. We passed the Machinery Hall and came onto Victoria Circle where the paths diverged from the statue of the Empress. Both Jing and I tensed as we heard people in the crowd gasp, though when we turned, we could see it was no immediate danger, and why they were so awestruck.

Like a storm rolling in from the horizon came more airships than I had ever seen all at once in my life. As they approached, I could see they were flying in military formations, the smaller single-seater fighter models soaring in concentric circles around the colossal warship models. Each warship had a gondola the size of a small mansion suspended beneath the massive frame. Imposing enough on its own, five warships surrounded by their fleets were inbound from the East, and they blotted out the sun as they flew overhead.

"This is real... right?" Jing murmured, barely audible above the shouts of delight and shock all around us. "I'm not just tetched in the head?"

"Come on," I replied, pulling him along. For some reason, I was shaken by the sight of the Queen's Royal Airship Navy. "The airship fields are a ways down here. The demonstration will be starting soon."

We passed the Electricity and Farming pavilions and walked through the Canadian Pacific Plaza before Exhibition Station. The crowds swelled, to our relief. Everyone seemed to be headed toward the airship fields on the western extremity of the grounds. Finally, we rounded the Lighter-Than-Air Pavilion and could see a number of the airships touching down in the fields.

"What now, Captain?" Jing muttered, and I was about to ask for suggestions when I heard my name being called from behind us. I froze, horrified at what would come next.

"Norwood! Thank goodness!" I willed myself to turn calmly in the direction of the voice.

The man calling my name was a Quigley Airships administrative employee. He was approaching from the pavilion in a hurry, but he was smiling, relieved. Jing, a more visible minority in the crowd, did his best to make himself inconspicuous, keeping his back to the man I recognized as my father's Toronto secretary, Mr. Lightly.

"Oh Norwood, thank the heavens! Have you seen Sir Quigley this morning? He was to be here to preside over the demonstration an hour ago. It's to start any minute now, and Ms. Teston is waiting for him and she's... well... she's temperamental at the best of times."

An idea of deception seized my mind, though I normally would not be so devious. "Of course, my father was detained at the constabulary. Something to do with the awful business last night."

Lightly's eyes nearly bulged out of his skull at the distressing, somewhat fabricated news. "Yes... Of course... how terrible..." Though his tone implied the bad news was interference in the itinerary, not the murder.

"He sent me in his place," I added, as much bravado infused into my voice as I could muster.

Mr. Lightly seemed to battle apoplexy. "You?!" he squeaked, which was commentary on a number of things, though most presently my appearance.

"Yes... well, I had a bit of a rough commute this morning," I said, and Jing snorted in response behind me. "Please, take my lowly assistant and I to Ms. Teston at once, for I must speak with her..." I hesitated, then quickly added, "about the demonstration."

We were led through the atrium of the Lighter-Than-Air Pavilion, which featured to scale replicas of almost every airship ever flown held up by thin wires, in flight against the glass-domed roof, a cloudless blue sky visible through it, a pretty sight.

To my discomfort, the halls of the pavilion were thronged with armed Exhibition Guards, their red, white-crossed and gold-laureled uniforms spotless. However, they paid Jing and I little enough attention, though why they were present in such number I could not say. We continued down a hallway and Mr. Lightly opened a door into the Quigley Airships Room. Within, and sporting a look of extreme irritation on her face, we found the great inventor, Ms. Mave Teston.

She opened her mouth to make a reasonably incensed remark, but it fell agape when she recognized Jing and I. Mr. Lightly began to give Ms. Teston the excuses I had made, but she told him to shut up and leave us alone a moment and he blathered off back into the hallway.

Ms. Teston glowered at us in silence until the door had closed behind Mr. Lightly. She was dressed in a sky-blue bicycle suit, her hair a fiery nimbus lit from behind by the afternoon sun. She motioned us closer, and at the table in front of a window, we found a modest meal of fruits, sandwiches, tea and a pitcher of water. She quickly realized the two of us were eyeing the spread voraciously and motioned to the chairs. "Please, help yourselves," she said, a sardonic edge in her voice. We pounced on the meal without hesitation, hungry and parched from our exertions, especially Jing, who had not eaten since the previous evening.

"You're Quigley's other son, aren't you?" she asked, gravely, though a smile in her eyes in regards to our atrocious dining manners.

"Yes ma'am," I managed to say between bites. "Norwood."

"Of course," she said. "And I expect you aren't actually here on your father's behalf?"

I winced. "No, ma'am."

"And you," she turned to Jing, a neutral look on her face. "You're the murderer of Rudolf von Conrad."

Jing shot her a resentful look. "Accused murderer..." he paused, then added, "ma'am. Truthfully, I prefer to be called Jing." The statement was polite enough, though there was an edge of defiance in his voice. "I didn't kill him, Ms. Teston."

She nodded, as if this settled the matter. "I believe you."

Jing and I were wide-eyed in surprise at the ease she accepted this fact, and simultaneously cried, "You do?"

She took a seat with us, looking out at the airships in the field before the windows, the crowds milling about the stands, a sad look in her eyes. "Yes, and if I could tell you why..." I opened my mouth but anticipating the question, she held out a finger. She peered about the room, then moved to a table in the corner. Ms. Teston fiddled for a moment with a strange machine, removing and replacing something; some part, or accessory. The inventor flipped a switch and then when she lowered a strange needle onto a spinning discus, the room filled with a blaring orchestral piece that caused Jing and I to jump in our seats.

"What is that thing?" Jing shouted to be heard over the crashing of cymbals.

"A phonograph musical machine, one of our prototypes, reproduces sound transposed onto a disc," she replied in an equally vociferous reply as she strode across the room to our table. She motioned for us to reseat ourselves and she leaned in to talk, and we to hear. "Listen closely, and carefully. I can only say this once, and cannot chance being overheard outside this room." She spoke rapidly, so it was barely audible over the din.

"I fear I'm being spied on, watched, listened to. The guards are keeping me. They haven't said so, they claim it's for my safety, but I know I'm their prisoner. The people at fault are very powerful, eyes and ears everywhere. You must understand I am not afraid for the danger that would befall me, but they have made a threat against the life of someone I hold dear if I speak of what I know, and I am not willing to take a chance. All I will say is that you may be able to help me. There is a place, and someone who may be able to help you uncover the truth."

She scribbled something on a card and then slid it across the table. Jing's hand flashed out and it disappeared in a pocket. Ms. Teston glanced around, wary, before continuing. "You may be the only two people in the world who can help me. You," she nodded at Jing, "have been used as a pawn. Quigley, I can't imagine why you've involved yourself, but you need to proceed with the utmost caution. I believe your family is in danger, and I fear Willard—"

Ms. Teston gazed beyond my shoulder and rose, as if in greeting. "I was just showing young Quigley the machine of my dear friend, Mr. Tinker. The marvellous phonograph!" she called over the music.

I turned to find Mr. Lightly had returned, and stood wringing his hands, flanked by two hulking Exhibition Guards. I felt Jing shrink behind Ms. Teston and myself.

Mr. Lightly seemed on the verge of hysteria. "Yes, Ms. Teston, an impressive and, obviously, loud machine." He skittered over to the phonograph and removed the needle which danced across the disc with a blaring, scratchy noise. "I wonder if now may not be the best time. The airship demonstration is to begin any moment now."

Ms. Teston smiled politely. "Of course, Lightly, lead the way. Mr. Quigley, if you and your assistant would accompany me."

And so we followed Ms. Teston out a pair of doors onto the terrace, with Mr. Lightly in the lead and followed close by the two guards, who kept close to Ms. Teston. As she'd mentioned, it wasn't clear if they were serving in the capacity of bodyguards or captors.

The airship field lay before us, a stretch of grassy flat land sprawling westwards along the lakeshore with different areas marked and roped off for different companies and landing zones. In the spectator area the stands were overflowing, and many were content to sit on the grass. In fact, groups of families or friends had brought along picnic baskets and were feasting, anticipating the festivities of the afternoon.

There was a great deal of applause as we made our way across the field. There was no doubt, with her fiery red hair and signature bicycle outfit, that it was Ms. Teston being celebrated, for I was probably recognizable to few, and Jing even less so. The six of us mounted a stage, which had been temporarily erected in the middle of the field, in the shadow of a warship, which had landed and tied off just beyond. Just behind the stage stood the crew, a group of twenty men and their officers, all immaculately dressed and at attention. In the nearby stand, a series of dignitaries sat, overdressed for the heat of the day, roasting in the afternoon sun.

I suppose my desire to hide in plain sight had been fulfilled; Jing and I now stood in front of thousands. I could sense my companion's anxiety, which I shared, and as Mr. Lightly stepped up to the microphone, his voice amplified up into the bandstands. He welcomed everyone to the Exhibition on behalf of Quigley Airships and launched into a somewhat long-winded speech about the history of the lighter-than-air transportation, accentuating the narrative with sweeping hand gestures.

Speaking with Ms. Teston had produced the opposite of what I had hoped. Instead of answering questions, she had simply left me with more, and I only felt confounded, even fearful. She said my family may be in danger, and there was no doubt that they had been tangled up in this mess of murder and talk of war.

And what of the note she had slipped to Jing? I glanced over at where he stood, slightly behind me, attempting, without success, to stay out of sight. His hands were in his pockets, or rather, the pockets of my coat, and I imagined his fingers tracing the outline of the card. I had the sudden desire to wiggle my fingers in after his—if only to feel I had another person to hold onto—but at that moment he caught my gaze and jerked his head in the direction of the nearby stand.

"The Chinese ambassador..." he muttered, his whisper fearful. I followed his gaze slowly and recognized the man in a special box reserved for politicians. Behind him stood the two men he had exited the station house on Court Street with.

Jing leaned in close, his eyes wide with fear. "They're the ones from the smoking den... with the Chinese man..." he whispered, pulling his cap further down over his brow.

I noticed now that they were eyeing us and consulting one another behind the back of the ambassador. The politician, for his part, seemed to glower on in a cold-burning fury. "Jiao-Long and Qiang Li the Ox, the men Yaling hired for the mysterious Chinese man..." I muttered, clear that we'd made the same conclusion. I watched as the men left their patron and began to push through the crowded stands at a rush. They'd be on the stage in moments.

Mr. Lightly finished his speech to polite, though somewhat lacklustre applause from the crowds. As I panicked and looked about for an escape, I took notice of the carriage, flanked by mounted Exhibition guards, that had pushed through the crowd onto the field by the building we'd come from, out from which stepped Mr. Willard, my brother and my father.

Strangely, close behind them, I noticed a familiar face; the slim Ojibwe man in the same dark suit and bowler hat from the previous evening who was looking directly at me. That he caught my attention at all was a miracle, for as soon as we made eye contact, he glanced at the trio of men alighting from the carriage and seemed to disappear into the crowd.

Willard and my brother shared a scowl at the sight of Jing and myself on stage next to Ms. Teston, though my father's eyes went wide, a look of intense concern on his face. As any child may, I felt an urge to throw myself at his feet and beg for his help, to spare Jing, to call off the murderous automaton, to do something!

I thought it was the choked noise in my throat that had alerted Jing, however, at the same moment he clutched my arm with a painful intensity and pointed over the crest at the waterfront. Striding toward the stage at an alarming pace was our mechanical assailant, Mr. Shackles. The thing must have followed along the water at a delayed pace. Now we stood on a stage in full view, with nowhere to run. It pushed through the wrought iron fence as if pushing aside some light shrubbery.

In my mind time stood still in a tableau of violence and destruction during the actions that followed. The only thing that saved us was the interference of all the men and machinery that suddenly converged upon us at once, and the quick thinking of Mave Teston.

The Chinese men leapt onto the stage and advanced toward Jing and I, cries of surprise from Mr. Lightly. Jing, ever quick to action, ducked as the first lunged for him. I, on the other hand, was not as swift and the other, the larger of the two, an ox-like man, clasped me in his great, thick, scarred, tattooed arms. I shouted out for help as he squeezed the air from my lungs. Though everything was blurring, I could hear Ms. Teston scream, and just as my vision began to blacken, the man's arms went limp and we collapsed to the ground.

Jing had somehow temporarily felled the man, and my companion came to help me stand as the attackers rallied and were coming at us. Ms. Teston grabbed the two of us by our collars and hauled us backwards.

Then the stage exploded into a rain of splinters and metal parts.

Mr. Shackles, which had charged the structure at full speed, had been unable to slow itself and consequently ploughed right through the rickety construction. The Chinese men disappeared into the collapsing stage, though we managed to leap off in time. Ms. Teston had saved our lives, or at least our limbs.

There was a great ado all around us, and I was struggling to return from the brink of unconsciousness. I could barely distinguish what was being shouted, although I could see we were moving closer to a gargantuan structure that loomed above us, and Ms. Teston barked two unmistakable orders: "On! Up!"

We were pulled onto a lowered walkway by two rather confused uniformed men. Even as our feet left the ground, it was pulling away from us. I watched as the earth below quickly grew smaller and smaller. We were now cocooned in the great machinery around us.

"An airship," Jing said, breathless, dropped to all fours on the deck beside me. "I'm on an airship."

I listened as the steam-powered thrusters accelerated and the wind beat against the rigid structure. We were not only aboard an airship but a massive one in rapid flight.

Airmen swarmed around us, tending to their duties or making sure we were unharmed as Ms. Teston sat on the deck beside us both, catching her breath. As I met her eyes she laughed in mad delight. "I dare say that was the most fun I've had in ages." I wished I shared her sentiments, but I had already had more excitement in one day than I could manage. "What's the matter, boy?"

Ms. Teston addressed Jing, who lay as still as possible, his eyes squeezed shut. "I—I've never been on an airship before," he stuttered. "Nor did I ever want to be. I... I have a terrible fear of heights."

I could have laughed had he not been close to frightful tears. The other boy had been confronted by murder, almost gazed through the hangman's noose and was hunted by an unnatural machine of destruction, and what turned him to pitiable whimpering was an airship ride.

I helped Jing to his shaking legs and turned to Ms. Teston, who had also stood and was consulting a grave-looking uniformed man bearing an admiral's insignia. "I'm going to take Jing into the bridge. I think he'll fair a bit better out of the wind."

She nodded. "Admiral Montgomery and I will join you presently. I must first clarify to him why we have commandeered one of the Queen's finest warships," to which I was all but willing to leave her to explain.

Jing clutched to my arm, keeping his eyes shut, allowing me to lead him from the loading bay into the bridge. I had been on countless commercial and luxury airships throughout my life, but I had never been on an airship bridge with so many technical features and explained as much to Jing, both out of my own excitement and a desire to calm him down.

"You really must see, especially if you've never been on an airship!" He opened his eyes cautiously and raised them from the floor. Unfortunately, at that moment we ran through some completely routine turbulence. He gave a sickly groan in response and clenched his eyes shut once again, never letting go of my arm.

"Oh really, you mustn't be so dramatic!" I said, which garnered a rather colourful curse from him. "We are on probably one of the safest airships in the skies. I've never seen such equipment. Look at the navigation system over there." The navigator sat at a console adjacent to the helm, which was occupied by the second mate. The navigator was rapidly flipping a series of switches.

Jing, to my delight, followed my finger to the console, but snarled, "Just looks like a bunch of stupid nobs to me."

"Well," I said, leading him over to the occupied panel. The navigator glanced at us, curious, but didn't seem bothered by our intrusion. "Since it's so difficult to see above and around an airship, we do all our navigation by the landscape. Towns, terrain and landmarks during the day, or the Airship Navigation Point-to-Point System at night. Those are bright skyward beacons all over the countryside... at least countries that have them. Anyways, it's usually that you would have a point man or two, crewmembers with maps or who know the land well enough to gaze over the side and relay directions."

"What if there's fog and you can't see the ground?" Jing asked, his voice still anxious though now showing genuine interest.

"Those who have the choice wouldn't fly, although otherwise you fly low, or plot a course with a map and compass as usual and proceed carefully," I replied. "You have as many point men as the ship's size warrants. On a ship this size, I would say...three or four. But that's three extra bodies weighing the ship down, so what they've done is set up..." I turned to the navigator, "and please, correct me if I'm wrong, refracting lenses where the point men would be placed."

"Aye," the navigator, a toothy, freckled young Englishman, nodded. "That's right."

"At this console, he's able to alternate through each lens. It's a fantastically elegant system. I'm sure it will be quite common in newer models."

"You know your way around an airship," the navigator said, his eyes never leaving the console.

I grinned, and replied, as humbly as I could, "Well I am, after all, a Quigley," to which the men present seemed mildly impressed.

"That is very interesting, Norwood," Jing conceded, still gripping my arm, though no longer as pale.

"And this," I pointed to the helm, where the second mate presided, "controls the propellers, which provide momentum, and each of these throttles controls the steam thrusters. Most medium-sized vessels only have a rudder and four thrusters: up, down, port and starboard, but this one has double that. Affords for improved maneuverability."

"I expect you could pilot this," the second in command commented in amusement.

I grinned. "I expect you'll do better keeping us up in the air."

I turned to Jing, who had eased up on my arm slightly. The look in his eyes was strange, and it sent my stomach into fresh knots of nerves, though not necessarily unpleasant this time—more of the feeling when an airship dips due to turbulence, equally frightening and thrilling. I was about to comment that his fear had subsided when the navigator's back straightened and he barked, "Visual, directly behind and below us, coming up."

The second mate pushed a button, and throughout the ship there was a series of urgent chimes. Soon the admiral, followed by Ms. Teston, walked briskly into the bridge and approached the control. Admiral Montgomery was a tall, lean, dignified gentleman in a crisp, spotless uniform, a silvered beard framing his frowning mouth, though his eyes were sharp, scanning the horizon as he attended to his crew and the ship around him. The very picture of an airship navy commander. "Who is it?" he asked.

The navigator appeared somewhat distressed as he flipped a switch. "One of ours, Admiral. Right from the Exhibition. Looks like the *Princess Louise*."

The second mate made way for the admiral, who sat at the control panel. He flipped another switch and a fresh peel of chiming was heard throughout the ship. "I'm taking evasive manoeuvres. I hope you know, Ms. Teston, I will not fire on our own fleet, nor endanger my men. Not for these whelps, whoever they are or whatever their mission for you." Ms. Teston seemed offended at the suggestion, but gritted her teeth and answered in the affirmative. "We're matched in speed by the *Louise*. Best we can do is keep above them for a while yet." The admiral consulted with the navigator before attending to the helm with a dexterity I did not think such an older man capable of.

This time Jing was justified to clutch my arm as the ship dipped into an upward thrust. I could feel the steady climb upward beneath my feet as we made for the clouds. For a moment, this seemed to put us out of the *Louise*'s sights and I almost wondered aloud if we'd lost them so easily. Just then a nearby explosion caused the ship to shudder.

"Bloody hell," the admiral muttered.

"That was a warning shot," Ms. Teston added, her voice grave.

Admiral Montgomery turned, his face crestfallen. "We have to slow, we must let them board or they'll knock us out of the sky for treason. I'm sorry, Ms. Teston." He turned to us. "I'm sorry lads."

Ms. Teston turned away slightly with a hand on her forehead, as if she needed to concentrate to solve a puzzle before her. After a moment she turned back. "Admiral, might I ask... have you prepared the Skyjump Apparatus?"

CHAPTER 6

IN WHICH NORWOOD AND JING
ENJOY QUIET STROLLS AND HARROWING GETAWAYS

That is how Jing and I found ourselves dangling off the side of a vessel in the Royal Airship Navy.

Perhaps a few details for those who have only seen an airship from the ground: most lighter-than-air vessels contain only the bottom control cabin, with some compartments, or a cargo hold depending on the vessel's function. Other than the thrusters, propellers and engine, the rest is all a series of lightweight steel cables, or heavy-duty roping holding together the air compartment, large ballonets enveloped by a fabric covering of some kind.

On larger airships like the *Princess Louise*, which was pursuing the crew, Jing and I aboard the comparable *Victoria*, there is a bit more structure to the envelope. Like the warship we were travelling on, some airships even have a small compartment above the envelope called the stargazer, which can be reached by climbing rungs up the side of the structure.

Obviously no sane, life-valuing person would make a climb like this without the necessary gear, but that is where Ms. Teston led Jing and myself, so I suppose we were all completely mad.

Convincing myself to reach out and take hold of the first rung took almost as much courage as it did to lift my foot off the solid deck, which took almost as much effort to convince Jing to do the same who, for his part, was in mild hysterics. Off the cover of the deck, the air tugged violently. I assumed every inch upwards was my last before a short and, ultimately, fatal plummet.

Ms. Teston, who had slung herself indelicately onto the ladder as if it were routine, was already a ways up the envelope ahead of us. She called on Jing and me to make speed unless we'd prefer death. Frankly, this seemed the outcome regardless of whatever we did that day, but against all rationality, we followed.

Moments before, in the cabin, Ms. Teston had explained her plan. "I fear for your life and... well, the life of my dear friend," she said. "The crew are loyal to me out of honour, but I don't expect them to go to war against their own fleet." The *Victoria* had to allow the *Princess Louise* to board, although Jing and I could not be found aboard lest we be captured and the crew charged with treason.

Jing groaned, prophesying some inevitable skyward horror, of which he was not to be disappointed.

"This way," Ms. Teston motioned us toward a door that would lead to the vertical climb. "I need only say to them that in the attack on the ground I fled fearing my life and that you must have escaped in the chaos." A flimsy enough untruth, but one we would not inconvenience with our presence. "Admiral, are we nearing our destination?"

Admiral Montgomery consulted the navigator, and replied with a great deal of gravity in his voice, "Yes, Ms. Teston, but I ask you to consider an alternative. The Skyjump is untested, and the boys haven't the necessary training."

She waved off his alarming concerns, though seeing the terror in our faces she smiled apologetically. "I built the damn things, and used them myself in testing. They're great fun." She handed us each a pair of goggles, and would not entertain any further protests.

So there we were, minutes later, clinging to the side of a massive warship, once again for fear of our lives. Jing inched along as best he could a few rungs above me, with myself shouting encouragement and reassurances of his safety, despite my beliefs to the contrary.

A second explosion grazed the *Victoria*, rocking the entire structure. Jing's feet slipped and he flailed wildly for purchase, almost taking my nose off with a boot in the process. In one swift burst of motion I didn't believe myself capable of, I hauled myself up two more rungs, clamped my hand on one foot and guided it back. One found purchase beside the other and I could hear him gasping in terror or relief above.

"Faster, you fools! I can assure you that was the last warning shot before they riddle the *Victoria* with holes!" Ms. Teston bellowed from above us. "If they get above us, your escape is lost!"

"Norwood," Jing screeched. "Promise me, if I fall to my death... promise me you'll get to the top and push Ms. Teston off!"

This was a promise I ended up not having to keep—fortunately, for Ms. Teston was a sturdy woman and could no doubt dispatch me off the side much easier than I could her. I made the promise anyway to calm him as little I could, and I swear I heard Ms. Teston somewhere above cackling in delight.

We crested over the curve of the structure and neared the stargazer, scrabbling along the side of the *Victoria*, now crawling as much as climbing. Gazing past Jing, I could see Ms. Teston had reached the compartment and was moving about the stargazer. She helped Jing inside who, upon reaching its questionable safety, was half laughing, half sobbing, a condition I shared with him as Ms. Teston hauled me into the compartment.

The small enclosure was barely shielded from the wind and hardly afforded enough room for the two of us. Almost like the cockpit of a single-seater class airship, with a glass windshield, and one seat to sit in, however, at the tail of the enclosure was another seat, less shielded, and with some strange, mechanical rigging to it.

"Don't get too cozy, boys," Ms. Teston called over the roaring wind. "I need to strap you both into this, Norwood first." I crouched beside her so she could sling a canvas pack with a number of different cords and straps attached over my back, and proceeded to tie everything into place.

"Now Jing, squeeze yourself as tightly in front of Norwood as you can." She pulled Jing into place in front of me, sitting him in my lap to my intense... Well, it was a novel sensation being so intimately close to another. Ms. Teston wrapped some of the straps around him. When she was certain we were secured to one another, she pointed to one particular cord on the pack. "Once you've cleared yourself of both airships pull this. That should give you some time in the air to get your bearings. These handles control direction. You still have the card I gave you?"

Jing sobbed out a: "Yes..."

"Good, the rest is up to you two," she eased us backwards into the mechanical seat at the back of the stargazer, which I had assumed was the Skyjump Apparatus, and I had some inkling as to what might happen given the name. Jing and I, now an uncoordinated creature of four legs, plopped ourselves awkwardly onto the seat, so he was held tightly in my lap.

I still had so many questions, least of all about her Skyjump Apparatus, but more about the general intrigue and danger surrounding us, which Ms. Teston seemed to have some idea of. "Ms. Teston, if I may, I—"

I didn't have a chance to finish my question, for I saw the woman's hand reach for a lever. There was a loud whirring as the enormous spring-loaded mechanism slid into motion, snapped backwards so we were facing the sky, and shot us pitching wildly upwards through the air.

In hindsight, it was a genius contraption. Parachuting out of an airship, for that was our mode of travel now, is extremely dangerous. You risk being caught in the propellers or burned by the thrusters because the machinery is so close to the cabin and engine room.

Jing and I, using the Teston Skyjump Apparatus, were thrown so high above the ship we cleared it and at our apex, I watched as the *Princess Louise* soared beneath us, climbing steadily after the *Victoria*. Unless they had someone in their own stargazer on the lookout for bodies soaring through the air, there was no way they'd be able to spot a little speck in the sky, nor would they have been able to hear us screaming our heads off over the roar of wind, despite our considerable volume.

As I mentioned, this is all in hindsight. I was ill prepared to be literally thrown overboard and was applying every curse in my vocabulary directed at the great inventor, Ms. Mave Teston.

As our launch trajectory became a rapid descent, and despite the wind whistling past us in a near deafening roar, I could hear Jing's persistent and shrill pleas to "pull the cord," although including a number of his usual brand of colourful curses. I managed to gain some small control of my fear, and as I fumbled for the proper cord, which danced disdainfully in the wind, eluding my grasp, I glanced up to see the *Victoria* slowing.

As the *Princess Louise* pulled up alongside, I imagined the dastardly Mr. Willard crossing the extended gangway, searching every inch of the airship to no avail. This gave me some small sense of pleasure, for I couldn't empathize with the fierce resolve by which he pursued us, utilizing monstrous mechanical beasts and even the Queen's airship navy to hunt us down. What was his investment in the intrigue? Jing had done nothing but be discovered, albeit in a rather incriminating manner, at a murder scene. And what of the Chinese ambassador and his thugs?

I felt worse when I thought my father might be beside him, worried about my fate, captured by someone he suspected a murderous criminal. The disaster at the airship field would do little to convince him of my immediate safety.

These thoughts flew through my mind, fast as our plunge toward Earth, which was eager to reacquaint itself with us. A freezing mist covered our bodies in a momentary drop through some low clouds, and thus losing sight of the two warships amidst them, I finally grasped what I prayed was the correct cord. With a snap of my wrist, I felt the canvas parachute erupt from the back, and our fall was thankfully slowed.

Jing panted in the thin air, "I am going... to kill you... Then I'm going to find Teston... and kill her."

I laughed, for the danger was over and the view, the sensation of being suspended with the world a green, blue, yellow and brown pastiche below our feet was breathtaking. The farmland of York sprawled in every direction, dissected by roads, bisected by rivers, enormous swaths of forests and great stitches of train tracks, dots of towns and villages, with the city merely a distant dark smudge on the lakeshore. Sunlight streamed through the clouds above, and we could see it dance across the landscape below. Even Jing allowed an appreciative moment of silence instead of the steady stream of curses he'd been employing.

We touched down next to a small pond in the middle of a fenced in grazing field with little incident, though we both ended up in a tangle of parachute, rope and limbs, disturbing some nearby cows who had never experienced such an unmannerly arrival. Lost in a sea of cloth, I fumbled around for the clasps, which would release us from the mess. Jing, his sense of humour restored with solid ground beneath him, began to make perverse jokes about my groping hands at my expense, and we both fell into a relieved fit of mad giggles.

Once we were able to untangle ourselves from the mess, Jing leapt to his feet that, although continuing to shake from the excitement, allowed him to dance around the field expressing his joy of returning Earthward. I simply lay in the grass and let the sunlight warm my wind-chilled face. I smiled at the moment of peace, at least relative to our day thus far.

Jing found a small blackberry bramble. We scrounged a handful of berries each and drank heartily from the nearby pond. If any had looked upon us and was blind to our bruised and battered exteriors, they may have thought us two chums on a frolicsome excursion to the country, the unfurled parachute our picnic blanket. As it was the only witnesses were cows who remained indifferent to our moment of serenity.

"I think," I said after I had given our bodies time to cease their fear-induced tremors, "we should stash the parachute and be on our way. If Willard figures out what happened he may bring the *Louise* low enough to search for us."

Jing raised an eyebrow. "Which one of the prejudiced white people who's out for my blood today is that?" He cleared his throat, and then, in a shockingly accurate impersonation of Willard intoned: "You mean the bloody bastard who sounds like this, old chap? Damn the Chinee and all that claptrap!"

I was delighted and couldn't help but applaud. "You have a talent for mimicry as well as accents! That is the villain himself to the tee!"

"Oh, is it really, Norwood?" He now aped my voice and inflections, though a tad on the exaggerated side, and in wide-eyed enthusiasm.

"Incredible," I replied, a little miffed. "Where did you pick up such a talent?"

He shrugged as if his perfect mimicry was nothing. "I get by on being able to change my appearances and behaviour depending on whoever I'm dealing with. Being able to pretend I'm little more than some simple Chinese immigrant, or an oafish sailor, or an Indian beggar. Once I spent three months living as a young maid until... well, I guess that's a bit of a long story."

"Disguise as well?" I was amazed, but I believed his claim. I had seen the way he had fooled others, thrown his voice, and the talent for mimicry. "You were destined for a life on the stage, it sounds like."

He gave the same apathetic shrug. "Not much theatre work for a Chinese orphan. Criminals such as myself still need to be someone different from moment to moment."

There was a moment of strained silence, and I suppose the question that I wanted to ask might have been hurtful, but from what he had said, about changing himself depending on whom he dealt with, I couldn't stop myself. "So, who are you right now?"

He said nothing and I turned to look at him. He was glaring at me, that same, stony glare I'd gotten so accustomed to over the course of a day that seemed to stretch out forever behind us.

No... that's wrong, we locked eyes and I could see he was hurt by what I had asked, what I had taken for unfeeling indifference was him covering up how I had made him feel. I felt ashamed.

He shook his head, ending the moment. "We should pack this thing up." He moved to begin folding the parachute, and I stood to help him. We wrestled the great folds back into the pack, with enough room to tuck the camera bag which was, like us, a little worse for wear from the day's exertions. I checked to find my dear camera and the slides the police had provided all intact before tucking it at the bottom of the sack, beneath the parachute.

Despite the momentary discomfort between us, we still needed to figure out our destination, so once we'd packed the parachute into the cloth sack alongside my poor, now dented camera and the casing of slides, Jing retrieved Ms. Teston's card from the jacket pocket of my coat he still wore.

On one side was a cheaply printed photograph, one of those cards made for mass distribution, of a beautiful young woman with dramatic, smoky eyes, dark skin and a nimbus of carefully coiffed jet-black hair. The slip the woman wore seemed to provide very little in the way of modesty, though the Greek influence of the photograph's composition afforded a nymph-like naivete in her lack of clothing.

Jing seemed to recognize the woman, and took a moment of consideration, before exclaiming, "Of course! Cordelia Hart!" He looked to me as if I should recognize the name, though admittedly I did not. "Kissin' Cordelia? The American burlesque performer? Named the modern day negro Helen of Troy?" I shrugged, and he gave me a sly smile. "Really, Norwood, you'd think a virile, well-to-do young man such as yourself would be well acquainted with the burlesque halls."

"Yes... well..." I stammered, for I had never set foot in a burlesque hall in my life due to a lack of interest. "I much prefer the opera, or a good piece of classic theatre." Jing's smile grew bigger so, irritated by his veiled, arcane implications, I grabbed the photograph to read Ms. Teston's scrawled note on the back:

Newton Brook, big brown barn, Cordelia's dear neighbour, find Two Rivers, too

Jing cocked his head to the side in question, and so I re-read the note. "Well," I thought aloud, trying to compare airship maps of the area I could remember to what we had seen on our way down, "Newton Brook shouldn't be terribly far from here, maybe an hour or two east if we can find the right road. Do you think this Kissin' Cordelia lives in a big brown barn there? Perhaps it's near these two rivers?"

"She's from Manhattan, Norwood," Jing answered acerbically, and I hoped Ms. Teston didn't expect us to make our way from the Canadian countryside to that far away metropolis. "She's travelled through Toronto a handful of times, but I don't see her living in a big brown barn in some cow town for any period of time." Despite our confusion at the note, Ms. Teston clearly intended us to locate the big brown barn at Newton Brook, regardless of its residents there.

We mucked through a couple of cow fields bordered by woods before finally finding a wagon-rutted road that led to Newton Brook. At one point we were walking through a fairly wooded area, though the canopy afforded enough space above that we could observe the sun making its ponderous flight westward to our backs. The light suddenly winked out around us, as if a particularly opaque cloud had tumbled into place, although a noise caught my attention and I pulled Jing into the thicket off road.

I could hear the distant though unmistakable hum as it grew steadily louder above. The massive shadow spread across our entire view of the sky like a blot of ink spilt on paper. By its size and silhouette, I discerned it was one of the Royal Fleet warships, and I had no doubt in my mind it was the *Princess Louise* flying so low to the ground the lens system could scan the forest floor with relative ease.

Jing whispered, unnecessarily, "I realize they believe I... murdered some ambassador, but they seem to be sending the whole Navy after me." We paused as the passing airship's noise faded back into that of a peaceful forest. "Why all the bother?"

A reasonable question and I could offer no insight, so we continued along down the wooded road in apprehensive silence.

A short distance from where we'd seen the warship above, Jing and I came upon a clearing in the forest by a stream, a lumberyard. In front of a small cabin we found two smoking foresters who, after their initial surprise at our appearance, informed us we were a short distance away from Newton Brook, which was just around the bend.

The village was a small but industrious lumber depot and community centre for local farmers, with a couple of mills, a church, a sundries store, an inn and some taverns along with a small assortment of dwellings and other places of business. Our presence in the sleepy streets garnered little attention from the locals, and most glances were due to our dishevelled appearance—they likely assumed us vagrant youth, common enough wandering the roads.

Unsure of where to begin looking for the big brown barn, we poked our heads into the tavern and were greeted, and forcibly bade to enter, by an elderly matron who introduced herself in a heavy French accent as Madeleine. She plunked down glasses of ale in front of us without hesitation.

"I'm sorry, ma'am," I said sheepishly, "but we have no money."

She gave a theatrical shrug and threw in a guttural French curse. "You two look like you could use it." We thanked her for it, and the bread and cheese she quickly brought forward despite our continued, though feeble, protests.

"Funny thing, these airships flying about all afternoon," she commented as we downed the meal with voracious speed. "Must be something to do with the Exhibition, no?" We conceded as much, but receiving no further opinion she pressed us, eyeing our tattered and bloodstained clothing. "So what brings you boys to Newton Brook?"

Jing glanced to me warily, so I proffered, "We were given directions by a friend to... find someone."

I realized that likely sounded miles more conspicuous then I intended as Jing delivered a kick to my shin, but Madeleine didn't seem phased. "Your friend, he is a local?"

This time I looked to Jing for an answer. Since entering the establishment, he had been employing his feigned Chinese accent.

"She," he offered. "We told to find big brown barn. We given name... Cordelia."

Madeleine scratched her head. "Cordelia? This name is not familiar, but do you mean the barn of the bicycle woman? Of course, you'll just be 'eading down to the end of the road, past the bridge and mill, then take a left. A stable and 'ayloft is where the bicycle woman stops every few weeks and gets 'ammering away on great big machines, loud as the devil. Strange woman, comes flying into town 'alf-dressed like a man, she out drinks the boys on Saturday night."

Jing gave me an eye roll at this that said, *that all sounds about right.* "A couple of times she's visited with another woman. Maybe her sister? Though this woman is beautiful, and a...'ow you say... dark-skinned? Bicycle woman is more what you would say... strong? Perhaps they work on machinery together?" She shrugged, then went to refill our mugs, though we pushed away from the bar, sure she would keep us drinking all afternoon out of her generous and gossiping spirit. We thanked her for her kindness and she bid us adieu, looking a little disappointed to lose the company.

Sated and our stomachs a little fuller, we continued down the road and over a small wooden bridge, past the wood mill. "My, what an adventure we are 'aving today," Jing exclaimed, in a perfect imitation of Madeleine. "Inadvertent streetcar accidents, being thrown out of airships, and meals with French Canadians!" I was at least happy to see he was in a better mood after my insensitivity in the field, likely due to the restorative powers of a decent meal and a little ale.

We found the old barn as easily as Madeleine had predicted, no doubt one of the first built in the area from the looks of it, with an ancient looking pump and trough covered in weeds to one side. No neighbours, to speak of. The closest buildings were back in Newton Brook. The next challenge was to get inside. The large double door was shut and fitted with a heavy modern lock, the lower windows boarded up. The only entrance we could see was a shuttered window that at some point had led to the barn's hayloft, although the forest had been allowed to grow in around the structure considerably.

With a bit of effort, I managed to convince Jing to follow me up a tree, which would just barely put us through the hayloft opening; my reasoning of the difference between an airship's altitude and that of a tree branch finally irked him into action, though he explained it made no difference. "I stand on a chair and I get dizzy, so quit your sniggering Norwood Quigley."

A precarious but well-placed kick and a difficult jump put us inside the shuttered loft of the barn. After our eyes adjusted, we were able to distinguish the bare furnishings of a bedroom: an ancient frame of a large bed with a simple mat, a bedside table with a couple of empty bottles of wine decorating, along with some dried flowers pinned prettily against the wall.

"No one's been here in a while," Jing said, moving one of the bottles and revealing a layer of dust on the table, "At least a month or two." We glanced over the edge of the loft to observe a recreation, on a smaller scale, of Mr. Tinker's workshop. Piled about the room were engines, tools, machine parts, layers upon layers of schematics. We clambered down a ladder onto the dirt floor of the old barn turned inventor's workshop.

After a bit of stumbling around in the darkness Jing located an oil lamp and matches on a shelf by the main door, so we were able to begin to sift about the mess. The papers strewn about the first floor were largely airship plans, Ms. Teston's specialty, illegible in their complexity. I pointed at one table that was once a well-organized file of Exhibition plans, now distributed about a worktable, peppered with oil spots.

"Nothing to do with Cordelia..." Jing said, poking at a table of steam engine parts, then his eyes widened and he pointed at the back wall. "Norwood, look!"

I held the lantern up and followed Jing around the table. At the back of the barn, beneath the loft, was a sort of rough kitchen, or study. The area had been outfitted with a newer wood stove and some dry goods set on a shelf. There was a small writing desk, bare other than a small kerosene lantern and a few writing implements, though what had caught Jing's attention were the two pictures hanging above the desk.

Both professionally framed, the first was a more recent photographic nude of a beautiful woman reclining classically on a studio couch. "Kissin' Cordelia," Jing explained, and he was correct. The difference in the photograph in front of us and the small card Ms. Teston had written her message on was the sense of vulnerability and the innocent artfulness of the pose. For some reason, the picture made me think of a maiden roused gently from her afternoon nap.

"Why would Ms. Teston have a picture like this of Cordelia Hart?" I asked, but Jing simply gave me an incredulous glare.

In the other frame was a very old, though skilful, painting of a young noble. The portrait captured his shy, startled expression.

Despite the beginnings of a beard, he was more boy than man. The subject was so familiar, someone I knew… I just couldn't place it…

There was a rustling and a popping noise, just audible over the melody of summer outside, within. We both practically leapt out of our skin, so startled we were. I shone the lantern into the gloom and we both held our breaths. Something was, or had been, moving about. I strained my ears and I heard a sound that, like the painting, I could remember from somewhere. A quiet mechanical ticking.

"Hold this," I whispered to Jing who, with a look of anxiety, took the lantern from me. I stepped forward and crouched down, and held out my hand.

There was the sound of a shutter clicking somewhere in the dark, though I caught an emerald glint beneath one of the worktables, which was followed by a gentle whirr. Tinker's clockwork cat padded into the lamplight, making its way to my hand where my fingers found the crook of its ear, and the creature hummed in mechanical appreciation. "Hello, Tickertape."

Jing, astonished, stepped forward. "I've never seen anything like it." As he approached, Tickertape blinked and skittered away, studying Jing from beneath the table with cat-like wary. "I'm surprised we didn't notice the plans for this."

I shook my head, smiling, "This is one of Mr. Tinker's inventions, though I wonder what it's doing all the way out here, and how it followed us here… wait!"

I took the lantern from Jing and returned my attention to the portrait. The eyes, the slumped shoulders. "It's a portrait of Mr.

Tinker!" Though certainly one made decades ago, when he was little older than Jing and I. Tickertape, as if in recognition beyond the abilities of a cat, meowed to agree. We pondered this a moment before I muttered, "Cordelia... dear neighbour..."

As if in answer, Jing reached up and pulled the portrait of young Tinker off the wall. He bounced the portrait on his fingertips for a moment, as if appraising it, then wrenched a piece of the wooden frame off. I cringed, but he turned the painting upside down and a pile of papers, handwritten notes and letters slid out from between the canvas and its backing. "Cordelia's neighbour! Of course! Portraits side by side!" We began pouring over what was before us; Tickertape leapt onto the table, seeming interested as well.

From what we could glean from the letters, Ms. Teston was a polyglot, because within was a number of letters to Ms. Teston in different languages. Spanish, French, German, and scripts we could only guess were Chinese, Japanese and Korean.

"Look." Jing held up a note in Ms. Teston's hand, perhaps a rough draft of a letter in English. "She was writing to von Conrad about a... Teston and Tinker workshop in... Munich? I didn't know there was a T&T workshop in Munich."

"There's not... and how about this?" I held up a rough sketch of a building, and a draft of some floor plans with notes. "Ming Workshop. And here are some notes about a proposed site in Tsingtao. That's one of the largest airship ports in China. There's apparently some negotiation toward an end of German occupation in this section of the country." I pointed to an English section of a Chinese ambassador's letter, signed "CC," asking Ms. Teston to act as an intermediary to

"RVC"... von Conrad?

"They were going to build workshops in Munich, Tsingtao, Paris, Madrid... and look!" Jing held up a letter from an American industrialist, "Pittsburgh and New York City!"

I pointed to another. "And London, they were going to build them all over... Share ideas. Ms. Teston was acting as an intermediary between von Conrad and Ambassador Chen."

"I don't think the Empire enjoyed that idea very much," Jing added acidly. "Or that damned Mr. Willard, he's named chiefly. Here," he handed me the letter by Ms. Teston, unsent, that seemed to believe the mail was being intercepted. On the other side of that letter, dated about a month ago, was a scribbled note that read, "Fireworks 902A VC and BTR."

"Ms. Teston and von Conrad set up a time to meet... last night, with someone else... Something's not right..."

"No kidding," Jing replied, but I was trying to work something out, retrace my steps from the night before. I had danced my way to Mother, gotten the room number, knocked on von Conrad's room, gotten turned away. The scream, the murder, my father helping me. Jing... Willard...

No, before that. Just as the fireworks started, I had been speaking to my brother, he had shoved me aside to chase after Ms. Teston... just as the fireworks started, when she was about to meet von Conrad.

"Hector!" I exclaimed, to which Jing and Tickertape both cocked their heads to the side. "Junior, my brother. He was chasing after Ms. Teston just as the fireworks started. There's something strange, the timing is too..."

"Suspicious," Jing offered, his voice full of bitterness. My brother had not made a great impression on him thus far.

"He's not a bad man, but he's... ambitious, and suggestible. And greedy, I suppose," though I was a little ashamed to admit it out loud. "Perhaps he's caught up in some plot. He seemed familiar with Mr. Willard."

Jing could tell I was uncomfortable speaking ill of a family member. "He may not be involved. It could just be a coincidence." Though he didn't sound convinced, and from what was laid in front of us, this suggestion seemed implausible. On more than one occasion, Hector Jr. had relied on me to get him out of trouble acquired through drinking, gambling, women and sometimes a combination of all three. I could only imagine how some career gambit could see him swept up in a murderous plot. He hadn't seemed particularly surprised or disturbed by von Conrad's murder, after all...

"I have to talk to him," I decided. "I have to find out if he knows anything. If I can get him and Father away from Mr. Willard... He'll talk to me. Admit if he's involved in something, or gotten into some sort of trouble. He'll talk to me."

Jing thought it would be prudent to collect the documents we had found before we departed, so we located a solid, metallic tube used to transport blueprints and slid a majority of the papers in, although we didn't discriminate between letters and schematics, which he strapped across his back.

"You know," he said as we began to make our way through the clutter of Ms. Teston's barn, "it's very late in the afternoon and it'll be night soon. I realize we are all about packing as much action as we can into a single day, but at some point we're going to have to find a place to rest. To sleep, if convenient." I realized the truth in this. Whatever had been keeping us going was taking its toll on both of us; especially Jing who'd had little rest the night before. Last evening... which seemed like an eon ago.

"My mother," I replied, "Aveline. She will give us rest, and a proper meal."

"Let me get this straight," Jing said, dubious, as I placed the lantern on the shelf next to the barn's main door. "You're suggesting we go to your family's home? I don't mean to be critical of your logic, but I'm quite sure your brother wants me dead, and he and your father haven't exactly gone out of their way to provide you safety today."

I shook my head. "Mother keeps our old family home as a retreat on the lake east of the city proper, just outside of Scarborough Village. It's a rarity if Father or Hector visit when there's business to be done in the city. And if by some chance she's there... You don't know Mother. She can be a bit frivolous, but she believes in protecting those in need. You're like her, in a way," I added. "She has a wicked tongue at times, and she pretends she's a mean old thing."

Jing laughed at the comparison. "Oh, believe me, I don't pretend." He gave me an affectionate smile, which I returned, the first we'd shared since my awkward question in the cow field. In the lamplight, his skin glowed golden. I felt my face flush and had to look away, feigning interest in a collection of contraptions in the corner. I could feel Jing roll his eyes.

I cleared my throat. "In the unlikely event that Father is there, even better! If we had him alone to explain things to him without the meddling of warmongering politicians, I know he would listen to reason. He's an intelligent, just man." Then my eyes caught something and I moved into the darkness to grab something.

Jing shrugged his acceptance of the plan. "So I guess we'll be walking then? I'm certainly getting my exercise today..."

Having made a discovery, I wheeled my answer out from the dark corner: a prototype Teston Model Three-Speed Motorized Bicycle; a promising, convenient mode of transportation that silenced his complaints.

With some tools at hand, we managed to dislodge one of the boarded up lower windows of the old barn and get the bike out. I hoped Ms. Teston could forgive such abuses to her private space given the perilous nature of our mission. It took a bit of tinkering on my part with Jing looking on curiously, sometimes offering suggestions, before we had all of the tubing hooked up. I wound up the engine and the bicycle machine, a red Rover model outfitted with a rumbling motor about the pedals seemed, at least to the ears, to work. However, I couldn't find the switch or lever to engage the motor for the driving power.

I mounted the solid frame and wheeled into the front yard, attempting to get the machine going. Tickertape, who had been skittering about nervously, swished away into the underbrush at the sudden appearance of a figure in the woods.

I had to shield my eyes from the late afternoon sun glancing through the canopy and saw the figure standing just beyond the yard. It gave off a golden glint in descending sun.

It was Mr. Shackles, a little worse for wear but if anything more frightening in appearance because of it. In addition to losing its hat long before, much of the thing's greatcoat had torn away, and what remained hung ragged and stained. Underneath the missing cloth was a system of pistons and joints, great metal parts that made the thing's humanoid frame all the more grotesque. Parts of it were dented, due to the violent exertions it had taken against us throughout the day. The right arm, as well, hung at a strange angle, as if semi-detached. Despite the small damages, the thing still moved, that much was clear, and the rolling roar of cannons and war emanated from within. How the thing had tracked us was nothing short of some awful mechanical miracle.

My companion was in the middle of asking me why I had stopped trying to figure out the motorized bicycle when he followed my gaze. His body went rigid, frozen in place.

"Jing," I whispered quietly, now wishing for my companion's ability to throw his voice, for it seemed moving my mouth inspired the brute to take a step toward us. "When I say 'now,' jump onto the back of the bicycle."

"What are you going to do," he hissed, "pedal away from it?"

This exchange seemed to be all it needed, since it picked up its pace and was now charging across the yard at us, roaring. Despite the ferocity of its approach, I kept my place, questioning my own sanity. Jing stood just beside the locked barn door and, hearing the commotion he cried, as if trying to break my paralysis, "Norwood!"

"Now!" I cried, certain that the beast's momentum was too great to stop. My furious pedalling, combined with the force of Jing's launch onto the bicycle seat, pushed us barely out of harm's way, and we heard a tremendous crash as if the barn had collapsed in on itself. However, with Jing's arms wrapped tightly around my waist, I did not spare the thing a single glance. By the time we heard a great roar rumbling from within the ruined barn, we were already on the road, zooming toward Newton Brook.

"Norwood," Jing cried over the air whistling by us as the village came into sight. "As much as I hate predicting our demise, even if we can keep ahead of it for a while, you can't keep this up all the way to the city."

I was already panting with the tremendous effort of pedalling the two of us. "I was… going to… make you… get off and… push," to which Jing cackled in disdain.

People in the village were poking their heads out of homes and businesses to see what the distant din was. The looks of concern on their faces turned to sheer terror when we heard Mr. Shackles crashing out of the forest directly behind us, obviously not bothering with the road as we were forced to. As if in a rage, the mechanical beast swiped its still functioning arm and effectively removed the corner of the closest, unlucky cabin.

The villagers scattered, some back inside and others, realizing walls would not stop this thing, simply as far out of the way as possible. Despite my best efforts as we shot through the village and past a road sign pointing southwards toward Toronto, Mr. Shackles was quickly catching up to us, and Jing was right in saying I couldn't maintain my frantic pedalling, for my legs were already seizing up from the effort.

"Norwood!" Jing screamed in my ear. "Duck!"

The bicycle wobbled in the ruts of the road as I put my forehead to the handles. Something—no doubt the same arm that had previously demolished a small home—brushed through my hair, almost grazing the back of my head. Jing was practically crushing my ribs with his arms wrapped tight around me as the bicycle swayed back and forth. My legs pinwheeled wildly in an attempt to regain balance, and when my foot caught on something that felt like the pedal, I pushed down hard.

The motor gave a deafening pop, and the bicycle lurched forward, now providing its own shocking momentum. At that point I didn't know what was more terrifying, the creature pursuing us with murderous intentions or the blur of scenery as we rocketed forward.

My feet finally found the pedals, now simply convenient footholds, and I gained control of our now self-propelled bicycle. We were keeping pace with the thing that, despite its massive strides, remained tromping a few feet shy of us, though this did not dissuade its lunging attacks.

Jing clung to me tightly as we survived another knock to the back tire. We shot down the farmland road, dipping up and down hills like a ship on turbulent seas. I couldn't help but wonder how much longer our luck would last.

A small brass blur leapt out of a bush beside us and pounced along down the road, somehow matching our speed. There came a barely audible crackling sound, and with a glance, I saw the addition to our manic race was the mechanical cat, Tickertape.

"—rton," came a thin but urgent voice from somewhere within the animal's structure, amplified by a radio, followed by a pop, "Norto—" The familiar voice cut out again, though it was slightly louder, and this time with another crackling it came through crystal clear, even over the din of our chase. It called, "Norton, can you hear me?"

"Norwood!" I cried back in outrage, then, realizing who I was speaking to through the mechanical cat speeding along, "Mr. Tinker?!"

The cat continued to bound alongside us, as if unaware that a voice emanated from its mechanics. "Damned device, I can barely hear you—" Another crackling pop. "A wireless two-way communication devic— ...—mething I've been fiddling with—" There was another pop and the voice cut out completely again.

"A wireless communication device!" Jing bellowed in indignation. "We're saved!"

I half-screamed, half-sobbed, "Mr. Tinker, that's very interesting, but we're currently being pursued by..."

There was another crackle, "Yes, yes, of course," Mr. Tinker could barely be heard over the roar of the machinated beast who's lunging arm barely missed our heads. "That's why I've had Tickertape following you. Same engine, different function."

"Of course," I replied, almost in hysterics.

"Now listen closel—" the voice cut out for a moment, "—important you find that out. It will only respond to certain command words and vocal tones. Consider—" with a loud pop the voice cut out again, and this time for good, because after a moment more alongside us Tickertape dove into the nearest field, disappearing.

Mr. Shackles was as close to our tail end as ever, and with an upswing of its massive arm, it managed to send the rear tire momentarily air-ward, threatening to turn us over. With a clever shifting by Jing, we righted ourselves, though Jing was squeezing me so tight I could feel the camera and parachute cords pressed between us jabbing painfully into my back.

Then it hit me—not the mechanical arm, but an idea.

"Take the parachute from the pack and let it go behind us," I called over my shoulder. I heard Jing open his mouth to protest, but I anticipated him. "Don't ask why, just do it!" I could feel Jing release his crushing hold on my waist with some reluctance. His hands plunged into the pack between us, scooping the folded fabric into his arms. I kept the bicycle as steady as I could as he turned, and heard a resounding snap, the parachute loosed, unfolding behind us.

I kicked the engine lever and it cut out, allowing me to swing the bicycle around into such a sharp stop, Jing was almost thrown off. He swore, then cried out over the dying engine, "We're *stopping*?!"

"No time," I called out, grabbing the pack from him as I jumped off the bicycle. "Impersonation of Mr. Willard. Do it!"

"What?!" he screeched. "What the hell are you talking about?!"

"The dastardly Englishman!" I cried right back at him, the slide case now in my hands, which were flipping through it with impossible speed. "Bowler hat, bad suit!"

Before us, Mr. Shackles was a dozen feet down the road fighting against the entrapping parachute. It roared and swung its arms wildly, tearing at the fabric. By the time I'd found the right slide it had liberated an arm and part of its torso, and as soon as it caught sight of us it began taking slow, deliberate steps, thrashing against the cloth and cord.

"Say..." I wracked my brain, "'Stop, would you, old chap,' in Willard's voice."

Jing trembled beside me before our encroaching mechanical attacker, cleared his throat, and managed to exclaim, in a slightly quavering voice that was no less a perfect impression of Archibald Willard, "Stop, would you, old chap."

And it did.

In mid-step, as if experiencing an onset of sudden paralysis, Mr. Shackles froze, and then fell over onto its side, stiff as a statue.

Jing and I obliged its sudden stillness with our own, our jaws hanging open. After a moment we both sagged to the ground, the strength in our legs giving out. "I... didn't know if that would actually work," I managed to mumble.

"Vocal tones..." Jing was shaking his head in disbelief. "So the command words were...?"

"'Would you, old chap,'" I replied. I managed to climb to my feet, which were still quite unsteady. "Can you make it get up?"

We kept our distance as Jing, in his perfect impersonation of Mr. Willard, commanded Mr. Shackles to its feet, though it had some trouble righting itself with just one functioning arm. I instructed Jing to relay a command and have the thing bend forward, and it followed his orders without issue, even reaching up, as if to remove its missing hat.

I approached the hulking beast with trepidation. Despite knowing it was in Jing's command, I was still terrified of it, and reasonably so given the relentless chase it had given. Up close the metallic monstrosity was even more smashed up, huge craters dinged into its frame, gears and tubing in the non-functional arm twisted out of shape. I found a catch on the back of the thing's chrome skull and managed the brass cranium open.

Within I easily recovered the glass slide of Jing, the photograph I had taken the previous night. I dropped it to the ground and crushed it with my heel, then held up the slide I wanted to replace it with. The picture I had taken even earlier yesterday, behind the Automaton House, of a scowling, disgruntled Archibald Willard.

Jing approached, smirking maliciously. "Find him and capture him, would you, old chap," Jing said in his Willard voice, then added, an afterthought: "Alive, if possible."

And the beast stalked across the field away from us, on a new hunt.

CHAPTER 7

IN WHICH NORWOOD AND JING RECEIVE
WELL DESERVED REST AND A RUDE AWAKENING

We were unable to engage the engine of the motorized bicycle after our close encounter with Mr. Shackles, so we resolved to, with the little strength we had remaining, pedal to our destination. Luckily we were only a little north of the city and I knew the roads fairly well, having spent much of my childhood gambolling about the countryside in my own lonesome fantasies.

The sun had begun to set, the sky beginning to darken, when we neared our destination, a large, beautiful, well-tended house surrounded by a wrought iron fence hemmed by abundant flower gardens and tangled, thorny hedges. The house was mostly in darkness except for a single room on the second floor, where a figure was bent over a desk, though I could make out no defining features. I hopped off the bicycle and Jing followed, our exhausted legs trembling from the exertions of the day. We snuck around the side of the enclosure and I revealed a place where a large, old willow tree broke up the fencing and provided a space to duck through.

We pushed our way through the vegetation and into the backyard, with enough space for two or three carriages, or a modest garden party—though it was empty this evening. We sidled up to the delivery door. Locked, I bid Jing conceal himself out of sight for a moment and was forced to knock.

There was a great ado from within; we could hear the occupant pound down the stairs and crash through the kitchen. The door was thrown open suddenly and without warning. The darkness permitted only a cry. "Norwood!"

The figure within launched against me, sobbing. "There, there, Mother. I am alive and mostly in one piece."

"Your father sent me away! He said I was hysterical!" she sobbed. "I just wanted you safe! And when I heard about what happened at the airship field—"

And I stood and comforted Dame Aveline Harper Quigley, my dear mother, on the threshold of my childhood home.

When Mother had calmed to what I hoped was a manageable point, I took her hands and looked her in the eye. "Now Mother," I began, looking on her face, wet with tears, "I'm fine, and I have someone I want you to meet, but you mustn't overreact…"

She assured me she was calm as could be, and so I turned toward the corner of the house. Jing loped out from the darkness, looking sheepish. "Hello, Mrs. Quigley…"

Mother let out an ungodly scream that reverberated through the countryside.

Mother had seen a picture of Jing in the evening paper, one of mine provided by the police, of course, and needed some convincing that he was a threat to neither my person nor our country. I pointed out that he'd had every opportunity to murder myself and several other more significant persons throughout the day, and had not taken any of them. A further complication arose when several armed neighbours from the surrounding countryside approached the property inquiring as to my mother's wellbeing.

Jing and I hid, holding our breaths. While my mother generally trusted me, I half expected her to reveal that Jing was within, but she assured our neighbours that she'd simply encountered a marauding raccoon and sent the neighbours on their way.

She walked into the kitchen where Jing and I sat with our hands folded in our laps, both of us as if awaiting a scolding. She crossed her arms and glowered at me.

"Well, my dear, I'm at a loss of words," she said, an edge in her voice; for my mother to be at a loss of words was perhaps the most frightening development of the day, as she was typically gifted with an abundance of them.

There was a moment of awkward silence as I withered at her glare before Jing spoke up. "From the pitch you hit outside, I would say you'd make an excellent dramatic soprano…"

My mother turned her gaze onto Jing and considered him for a moment. I feared the worst but caught a glimpse of amusement in her eyes. When asked later what won Jing her trust, she responded matter-of-factly that she always trusts a man who knows his vocal registers.

After I briefly outlined how we had been fleeing and protecting one another all day from such fearsome encounters as gargantuan automatons, Chinese thugs, the Queen's Royal Airship Navy and an excitable, gossiping French Canadian, she kissed his cheek and welcomed him into our home as if he was one of her own. Mother always was a woman of dramatic extremes.

In fact, as we recounted our day, and she hers, I realized some similarities in their manners. Both had a flair for the dramatic, a fluid, elegant movement, and sharp, often exhausting wit. After the initial awkwardness, they liked each other instantly.

Once she had sat us down for a hastily prepared meal of nonetheless delicious bread and cheese she, bolstered by our appearance, braved the dark, spider-infested wine cellar to liberate a bottle of red.

Jing and I summarized our day; escape from the station house, the dubious dumplings, the the terror stricken streetcar, our dockside deliverance, our meeting with Ms. Teston at the Exhibition and subsequent escape aboard the warship *Victoria*, the unceremonious ejection from that airship, and finally our sleuthing about Ms. Teston's secret workshop before a triumphant defeat of Willard's bloodhound machine.

"My, but you must be simply done in, you poor boys," she exclaimed. "And I won't keep you awake another minute, but I simply must tell you of the trying day I've had.

"Well, your father and I took a room at the Queen's Hotel last night so we needn't travel so far after the steamboat party, and how wonderful a party that was, aside from the murder, of course. I slept like a child, for that is the effect champagne has on me, but your father, that's Sir Hector..." she explained to Jing.

"We've met," he replied, neutral as possible, for Jing had a number of prejudices against my father's mistaken persecution against him.

"Of course," continued Aveline. "He was quite agitated about the murder, though he didn't tell me much about it."

I yawned and Mother waved her hand peevishly. "Yes, dear, I understand you're tired, one moment, I must tell you. Your father woke and went to the police station long before I was conscious enough to call for a meal. I broke my fast in the parlour with Mr. and Mrs. Egbert Ebbs, and some minor politician, I believe he's the Minister of Foreign Affairs. Terrible dullard.

"Well, Mr. Ebbs and the minister simply could not stop talking about the dreadful business of the murder. Mr. Ebbs has some rank with the Royal Navy, I believe. A rear admiral, something like that, he seemed to believe there was some sort of war brewing. He had been dealing with the Germans, or Austrians or what have you, their lot, informing some small group of dignitaries of the murder of..."

"Von Conrad," I offered, unable to stifle another yawn.

"Of course, Herr von Conrad, I'd met him at a gallery in Munich some time ago, beautiful artists, the Prussians. Marvellous beer, as well. Anyways, this didn't make the Prussians very happy, as you can imagine. Especially when it was revealed the murderer had been... well... you, darling," she nodded to Jing. "A... hmm..."

"Chinese," Jing mumbled, propping his head up on his arm leaning against the table, barely keeping himself upright.

"Chinese, beautiful land, China... or was that Japan? No, Sir Hector and I visited Shanghai and Hong Kong, looking to set up the business there. The Chinese have very... well, long operas. Anyways, apparently the Prussians took this as an open declaration of war from the Chinese, you know the way these kind of men are. It's always, 'What's for lunch? By the way, we're going to war this afternoon!' Well, of course, the Chinese, not to be outdone, openly proclaimed the Prussians to be liars and agitators interested only in the expansion of their empire, to which I would reply that this is a situation where a pot is calling the kettle black. Empires, you know.

"Well, the British military powers tried their best to smooth things over, but apparently there was some attack on a local Chinese restaurant. A young Chinaman set afire, or maybe just his shop, I didn't actually read much of the paper this evening. One thing has led to another and apparently the Prussians have promised to bring justice to their ambassador by any means necessary, and they stormed the Chinese Pavilion and are currently holding a number of Chinese dignitaries as prisoners within. The Chinese are inflamed, the British are apoplectic, troops have been mobilized... The things that can happen before dinnertime!"

I gave a somewhat more emphatic yawn, but mother ignored me.

"Your father sent me a note, outlining these events, and suggested I return home in case of any other hostilities in the city, so I hired a cab and went directly to him at the police station, of course, but he'd moved on to the airship field, so I followed. Another note followed, explaining there was some trouble involving the ambassador's murderer kidnapping you by hijacking a royal navy warship, although no one would tell me if it was by sky or water. All very confusing. Your father returned, anxious about your wellbeing but furious that I had not 'followed his command' and ordered me home. For my own safety, he said.

"Now, on any warm summer evening I would normally have been out of doors, either taking a glass of wine with my dear friends at one of the more fashionable establishments of the city, or at the very least walking the gardens of our home and watching the sunset over the valley, maybe with a good book. On a normal evening I would have been enjoying myself, but how could I enjoy the evening of my son's kidnapping by brigands unknown, or possibly his murder?

"Instead I sent the servants home or to their chambers. Away. An immediate mistake, for grief always brings on a thirst for a heady red wine, and I had never been into that awful wine cellar in my life, and though I am not too proud of a woman to make an attempt, the darkness and spiders returned me above ground."

As if in appreciation of her newfound bravery she downed a glass of wine and poured herself another. I shot Jing an exasperated look, but he simply smiled sleepily.

"In my chambers, I had mercifully been able to crack open a window to allow a little air, and was considering penning a note to your father, wherever he is, outlining my anger at being sent away when our family should be rallying together. Explain that a husband should not be without his wife in such dire circumstances... well...

"I readily admit, however, that I cried in earnest, and blotted the page. Angry, frustrated, helpless tears. Hector, both junior and senior, had sent messages in the late evening, both maddeningly brief, explaining they were doing all they could to find my darling baby Norwood, and for me to stay home for my own comfort and safety. I didn't want to be comfortable, and to hell with being safe! My apologies for the language, Jing, I am normally not so vulgar."

Jing's eyelids were drooping, and he mumbled, "I've heard worse."

My mother continued with barely a breath, "I wanted to be out with the rest, searching for Norwood and his murderous captor, though that the allegations have proved to be exaggerated against you, Jing, I am very glad. That you are not a murderer, that is. Your father is a decent man, Norwood, but he is traditional in his beliefs as to the limited capabilities of the female sex, a prejudice I was now confronted with.

"As I sat bent over my writing desk by the window, my eyes no doubt piteously puffy and red, I imagined myself a woman like Ms. Mave Teston. A previously distasteful idea which now seemed perfectly reasonable. Why should I not be able to don some sort of bicycle suit and stride confidently out of the house instead of counting on a carriage and driver? I cursed I didn't have the pattern to stitch together a fashionable woman's bicycle suit, and I cursed further that I didn't know how to sew, but I resolved to learn that as well, when there was a knock on the door.

"I couldn't imagine who would call at this hour, but could only imagine it was news of your death, Norwood. Such a terrible thing for a parent to imagine, but there you have it. I could only imagine that I was being summoned, finally, to grieve with your dear father and brother. Though as I listened, I realized the knock was coming from the delivery entrance, not the main door."

I downed the rest of my wine, exhausted at my darling mother's tirade, and she poured me another as I spoke. "We used to drive Mother mad by coming and going through the delivery entrance at all hours of the day and night." I turned to see why Jing had not responded. He had dozed off, and I was experiencing a sudden fit of yawns. It's not that we didn't care about my mother's woes or the imminent international crisis that was occurring around us. Far from it, the prospect of war between the three great nations of the world was quite distressing, but one can only be concerned about so many things when a comfortable bed is waiting.

"Look at me, blathering on!" Mother cried. "Why are you two not up in bed? Shall I summon Delilah from the servant's cottage and have her prepare the guest room? Delilah's always grumbling but she's quick as a cat when she gets a bit of steam built up."

"No, Mother, don't bother Delilah," I said, knowing full well our beleaguered housekeeper would complain to me—incomprehensibly, for her accent was opaque—about Mother until dawn if she was given any reason to. "Jing and I will just take my and Hector's old rooms."

I kissed her on the forehead and she put her arms around me in a more intimate hug than I was used to. Normally she was so proper, but she seemed desperate to hold onto me. "I am terribly glad you're not murdered, my dear," she murmured, tears in her eyes. I helped Jing up and directed the poor boy through the kitchen and toward the stairs.

As we began to climb the grand staircase, Aveline caught up to us and called with some urgency, "Oh, Norwood." I stopped, turning to her. She seemed to want to say something but was having some difficulty doing so. "I believe I will be joining the women's dress reform movement."

"Goodnight, Mother."

Jing seemed to rouse a little as I led him through the Quigley Residence, a modest manor seated on the cusp of the township east of Toronto, near the lakeside bluffs. I lit a lamp as I led him into my childhood room in the nursery wing, which had been added to the old house. A large bathroom connected the two rooms, which were across the hall from a small playroom that had become my studio as I had turned to the arts.

I brought Jing into Hector's room and showed him to the wardrobe; filled with some extra clothes we kept for last-minute visitors, of which I supposed he was one. "Here are some nightshirts, or some fresh undergarments, whatever you feel most at ease in..." I trailed off. Despite rubbing at the tired in his eyes, he was smiling at me with his signature sly smile. I left, bidding him make himself comfortable.

In my old room, the scents and sensations, the memories of the place, caused a great deal of emotion to well up inside and I slumped onto my bed, contented. I lazily kicked off my shoes and nudged at my socks until they were off, then began unbuttoning my shirt. After a moment the door to the bathroom opened and I glanced up. My jaw might as well have fallen clean off its hinges.

"Jing!" I stuttered, whispering urgently, "You're... not wearing any clothes!" Not a stitch save a necklace bearing a little bronze charm tied by a length of leather. In the hazy light of the lamp, his skin glowed golden-bronze, only marred by bruises and cuts. His eyes, beneath the fringe of dark hair, sparkled mischievously. After taking the sight in— my eyes admittedly lingering a little long on his slight, well-muscled body—I looked away.

"You told me to make myself comfortable," he said, but then shrugged. "I can leave if you want."

"Uh!" I exclaimed, looking up to find his backside facing me. I simply stared. He slowly turned around, a smile on his face, and made his way over to the bed. As he climbed up, straddling me, my stomach was doing sickening acrobatics, and my face was surely a flaming red. I couldn't dare to bring myself to gaze on his bare body, though I was fighting against a desire to study every inch of it with an artist's eye.

He leaned down, gently taking each side of my head in his hands. I allowed him to bring my gaze to meet his, he no longer looked impish; instead his face held a curious expression, not exactly sadness and certainly nothing sinister. Longing.

I made a study of his eyes, having not had the opportunity to see them this close. They were a rich earthy brown with flecks of coal in them, which reflected back dark silver in the lamplight. His lips, full and prettily formed, twitched nervously. He looked away.

"Sorry, I can go back into—" but I reached up and put both hands on his face.

I kissed him once, and then again. He kissed me back and let the weight of his smaller body lean onto mine.

And we lay together that night, and it was beautiful.

Despite our exhaustion, the nocturnal exertions gave us a renewed vigour, and after a time we lay side by side and spoke, our conversation languid and wandering.

He asked me a little about my life as a Quigley, and I told him a fair bit, though felt awkward, given the differences in our stations.

I asked him about his own, and as he told me a little, I picked up the end of his necklace and played with it in my fingers. The pendant was a small, circular bronze coin with a thick rim and a small square hole at the centre, around which were pressed four Chinese characters.

I inquired as to his wearing this trinket, and his face took on a sad, distant expression, one I would recognize whenever the subject of his origin or parents were inquired.

"I transferred to the Toronto Boys' Home when I was old enough, but I was left with the nuns as a baby. On the day I was moving over to the Home, I found this necklace on my bed with a note from one of the sisters, though she didn't leave her name. She wrote that this was found in my blanket and that she'd turned it into a necklace, as she believed my parents might want me to have it. The nuns were always trying to beat the foreignness out of some of the boys who weren't white-skinned, I thought they hated us... and the Native boys especially... so it surprised me, whoever she was. She didn't have to do that."

I asked what the pendant said, but he shrugged and repeated that he knew very little of the spoken language, and couldn't read it to save his life. "I did show it to Yaling. You remember, the dumpling lady?" he said with a sly smile. I remembered the woman well, though, as the rest of what we'd been through, speaking with her seemed so much longer ago than the morning previous. "She told me it was a coin stamped under the Tongzhi Emperor, but that that Emperor is long dead." He picked up the coin and studied it. "Yaling's an old harridan, but she's the closest thing I ever had to a mother. She gave me my real name, said it's what she would have named her son."

I was happy he felt comfortable enough to share this with me since speaking about it seemed to make him sad. I allowed us to lapse into a comfortable silence, and soon I realized he was breathing gently, having fallen asleep. I kissed him on his forehead, pulled my arm out from under him and was soon lost to the world as well.

I must admit, to sleep in another's arms was a joy I had not experienced before that night, but it was truly divine. I had enjoyed but never truly appreciated the love songs, sonnets and tales of desire that have pervaded the human species throughout history. Now, in Jing's arms and despite the fact he was a member of the male sex, all the operatic ballads I had ever heard were thundering triumphantly in my mind in time with his light snoring. True, our passions may not be the kind celebrated widely at this point in history, but it was the first time in my life I felt such an affinity to another.

I had not, to that point, imagined what two men could accomplish in an intimate matter—except perhaps in some of my more idle, distracted and solitary moments, late at night—but before we fell to exhaustion in each other's arms, Jing taught me that there are *many* things two men can achieve intimately, with a promise of many others.

I slept a deep sleep, untroubled by dreams or nightmares despite the trials of the previous day, no doubt due to my ability to hold close someone who had grown so dear to me. I awoke only once, very late, or very early, to relieve myself, and watched the bruised and battered but still exquisitely beautiful young man who slept beside me, his face serene in what little light filtered in through the curtains. I found his just barely audible snores enchanting, though they soon lulled me back into a happy sleep.

While our slumber may have been peaceful and untroubled, the manner in which we were awoken was the polar opposite.

Early the next morning, unbeknownst to any of us, someone less than an intruder but more than an unwelcome guest had let themselves onto the property via the same gap in the fencing through which Jing and I had slipped hours ago. This person, apparently skilled with a lockpick set, let themselves in through the delivery door and crept through the kitchen, up the stairs, making sure to avoid the creaky third step from the top. The invader made their way down the wing where my room was located, past my locked door and crept through the adjacent room, which had been left unlocked, through the adjoining washroom and took in the sight of Jing and I entwined in each other's arms.

I realized we were beset upon when I was awoken by a strangled yelp. My eyes fluttered open to take into the sight of two hands wrapped around Jing's neck, my companion's eyes wide with terror. The violent extremities terminated where they met the shoulders, which I followed up into the unshaven, dissipated, mad-eyed face of the attacker; my brother, Hector Daedalus Quigley, Junior.

Even in my undressed and discombobulated state, I lunged, throwing my full weight onto Hector, sending us tumbling off the bed onto the floor with Jing gasping for air above. Hector and I wrestled desperately for a few moments; he ended up on top, straddling me, and raised a fist, which quickly connected with my jaw and sent stars speeding across my vision.

Through my dizziness and pain, I heard a grunt and someone cry out in pain, and as my vision came back, I saw Jing standing over me. My brother had been sent sprawling backwards from a kick to the face and had crumpled on the ground next to the bathroom door, his nose bleeding profusely, sloshing over his shirt and the carpet in a sickening sight. He braced himself against the wall and managed to stand, then did the unthinkable. From the small of his back, perhaps from a holster hidden underneath his shirt, or from the waist of his pants, he drew a revolver and aimed it directly at Jing. I recognized it immediately as the eighteenth birthday present Hector had received from our father, recognition of his manhood or some such... I had received a camera for my own…

"I didn't want to do this," my brother spat at Jing, then called him a disgusting term I will not repeat on paper.

My body had gone completely tense, paralyzed with fear that I was about to see my beloved companion shot, point blank. Hector seemed intent, his fingers twitched on the trigger. Then we heard a mighty "thwack," like sledgehammer breaking apart stone. Hector lurched sideways and crashed into the door with an equally mighty crack before he collapsed in a heap onto my legs.

Behind him stood our mother, Aveline, who had entered through Hector's old room the same way he had come. She was holding an enormous tome of children's fairy tales she used to read to us that had since sat on a bookshelf and been mostly decorative before suddenly being employed as a defensive weapon.

I was stunned by the attack, and even more so by the state of undress of Jing and I in front of my mother, though she took in the scene without comment. I should have guessed my mother to be a worldly, broad-minded person.

Mother apologized for the discourtesy of the assault, explaining that Hector had snuck in, for she did not know he had returned until she heard the scuffle. Fortunately, as we quickly ascertained, my brother was not dead, simply struggling with consciousness, so as soon as Jing and I had dressed to an acceptable level of social decency, we attended to his sprawled body—though I did catch Jing tucking the revolver into the back of an old pair of my brother's pants he'd donned.

Hector stirred, which meant it would not be long until he

awakened. Jing and I, on each end of the body, carried him downstairs into the kitchen, perhaps a little intentionally clumsy on Jing's end, for he did not miss a chance to "accidentally" slam Hector into a wall corner, banister, piece of furniture or door frame, despite my protestations.

When we had him propped up in a kitchen chair in the pantry, a room that could be locked from the outside due to it containing some liquor—of which some of our childhood servants had taken to imbibing in between tasks—my mother brought forth some dining linens, and Jing went to work tying my brother securely to the chair. When pressed, he admitted to having much practice with the skill of ropework in his line of work, an admission that mystified me.

I protested, however, as Jing strapped Hector into the chair; he was my brother, after all. Mother seemed unbothered by Jing's attention, and she was attempting to stem the flow of blood from what was surely a broken nose. "You don't think he'd continue his assault," I muttered, apprehensive, as Jing tightened the last tablecloth the entire way around Hector's torso. He was unarmed. Jing scoffed at me, and Mother seemed to agree.

"We do not murder one another in this house," Aveline huffed, livid.

"Murder? Really, Mother, Hector would not have tried to kill me!"

Jing glared at me. "Didn't seem like that would stop him from killing me, Norwood." I acquiesced to his point.

Jing finished and stepped back, and Aveline cocked her head to the side, a concerned look on her face, understandable given the general household chaos before coffee had been served. "He may not have murdered you, Norwood, but... After you escaped yesterday aboard the airship, Ms. Teston was put under house arrest, and a call went out for the capture of... well you, my dear Jing. They're calling you a Chinese agent provocateur and an assassin. The warrant is dead or alive, I'm afraid."

Jing looked to her, his face going pale and he trembled a little. I understood. The frenetic energy of the fight coursing through our veins had dropped off and I was feeling fragile and helpless myself. I reached out a hand and took his, patting it, hoping to comfort him, though it's hard to imagine comforting someone with a country or two after him.

"You, Norwood," Mother continued, "are wanted for suspected treason, though your father is calling for you to be apprehended unharmed."

Angry tears filled Jing's eyes, and he turned to me. "Unharmed? So that mechanical monster they sent after us wasn't going to harm us, I take it?"

Aveline smiled. "You mean the bloodhound automaton?" I was surprised she knew immediately the machine we referred to, but she produced the morning paper, which had arrived moments before Hector's attack, from the dining room. Below a headline that read "Manhunt Continues for Chinese Assassin" with a full story and another photograph—credited to me, to my dismay—of Jing from the steamship two nights previous, were two other news stories. One described a related airship chase resulting in the arrest of Mave Teston and the grounding of Admiral Montgomery's vessel.

The third story on the front page described a mechanical malfunction in a piece of military grade automata resulting in the injury of a military leader.

> *Police are baffled by the attack of a security automaton against Archibald Willard, a royal military advisor visiting Toronto for the World's Fair opening ceremonies. Mr. Willard, an advocate for the use of the recently developed, military-grade automatons in urban police forces, has been demonstrating the Mr. Shackles unit, pictured above...*

Again, a picture I had taken on the first day of the Exhibition... the *Globe* seemed to have secured copies of my photographs from the police and were favouring my work...

> *The military advisor was attacked last night at a local station house by a malfunctioning prototype. Police say the mechanical giant crashed through the building and assaulted Mr. Willard, breaking the majority of the military advisor's limbs before confused and shaken officers smashed it to pieces. This comes after reports of an automaton of a similar description, or many, destroying city and private property in Toronto yesterday afternoon. Mr. Willard is now being treated at St. Michael's Hospital. The station's inspector is reconsidering his stance on the use of security automata in police investigations, "You should've seen the size of this f—*

Hector groaned from his chair, interrupting my reading. His front was covered in his blood and his eyes were bleary and unfocused as he came to. When he realized where he was, and that both Jing and myself now stood before him, he began to push against his restraints, though reliable rope work appeared to be yet another of Jing's many talents.

"Morning Hector," I said, a little more spite in my voice than I'd intended. "So glad you could drop in on us, though I don't recall ever having learned to awaken our guests so rudely."

Jing snorted, Hector swore at us, though at that moment, our mother swatted the back of his head.

"I made your father promise we would never raise a hand against our children," Aveline said apologetically, "but your behaviour is most atrocious, Hector!"

He seemed surprised and abashed to realize she was in the room with us, but still he scoffed, "Our father..." he muttered, but let himself trail off.

"Speak up, darling," Mother commanded, an edge of authority I had only heard her use among her belligerent society peers. "Your father what?"

"Why are you here, Hector?" I asked, trying a softer approach. "Threatening to murder someone who is completely innocent..."

He spat, blood speckling the pantry floor. "Innocent... ha. Father said this would happen," he hissed, nodding at where Jing and I stood together. "Seduced by a criminal, literally. My own brother a degenerate. Not that Father or I are surprised."

Jing made a move to apply further bodily harm to Hector, but I held him back. Mother smirked at her eldest son. "Don't assume you know what your father and I think of your brother... or you, for that matter. And accusing your brother of degeneracy, Hector? The stories I hear of your exploits... drinking substances of an illicit nature, gambling money that isn't yours, deflowering daughters, causing outrage among even the more liberal minded."

Hector paled but knew not to deny such accusations by our mother, a resourceful woman with socially frightening connections. While by no means a judgmental woman, Dame Aveline Quigley could never tolerate hypocrisy. Such words to her son stung.

I leaned in close and looked my brother in the eyes. I saw shame, malice, desperation, and exhaustion. He held my gaze a moment more, then spat, splattering my face with blood.

While I am not a violent person, at that I reached out and flicked his nose, sending him into a howl of pain. "I won't ask again Hector, why are you here? Mr. Willard would have little clue I might return here with Jing."

He spluttered, my administrations to his nose being a little overzealous, a fresh flow of blood dripped down over his mouth. Mother gently wiped away some of the blood with the hem of her robe without flinching.

"Willard?" Hector spat again. "That pompous idiot? It was Father. He didn't think you'd be stupid enough to return here, but he said we needed to make sure. To do what needs to be done." Hector glared at Jing. "I can't believe you, Norwood. Bringing that criminal, sodomite boy-whore into our childhood home..."

This time it was Jing's turn to restrain me, though he was too late.

I brought my fist against my brother's nose, which crunched sickeningly. My mother screamed and Jing cried for me to stop, but it took a moment's restraint against Jing's arms before I stopped struggling for further assault of Hector. Blood now cascaded out of his nose, and he sobbed in agony. Seeing his blood on my fist, I regretted my outburst the moment I had regained my composure; added to the pitiable sight of this abused, injured and stupid boy who was my older brother, nonetheless.

Jing handed my mother a napkin from one of the pantry drawers, and she was tender as she dabbed at his nose to staunch the blood. As my mother administered to him, Jing and I looking on the miserable sight, Hector muttered, in between gasping sobs, "Traitors... the likes of that Teston woman... Father trusted me... do what's right..."

Mother's napkin soaked through, I grabbed another and came forth, taking over. Hector flinched at my touch, at first, but then allowed me to clean some blood. I noticed tears of pain or shame streamed down his face, diluting the blood. "I'm sorry," I whispered, "for hitting you, but you have to believe me, Jing is innocent. We have reason to believe there was a plot against the murdered von Conrad and Jing was merely used to distract and inflame higher political powers."

Hector seemed like he was about to say something, but he instead looked down at his knees and muttered, "... traitors..."

I didn't know how to convince him, but something he had just said inspired a new train of thought. "Hector, why did you chase after Ms. Teston that night? She was on her way to meet von Conrad. Did you know something was going to happen?"

Hector's eyes went wide at the implication. "What? No! It was… It was business! Father thought she might be meeting with the Prussians and the Chinese during the Fair. He wanted to impress on her the importance of keeping business and industry within the power of the Empire… not hand it over to some bloody foreigners."

My mind was racing, and filled with questions. Did Father know about Mave Teston's plans? "The Prussian and Chinese workshops?" I asked.

Again, Hector's eyes went wide in terror. "How do you… Father had learned about it… he is a bloody Quigley, after all. He knew it would be bad for business… for the Empire. Trading secrets. He said she needed to be convinced she'd made a mistake."

"What did you tell her? Just before von Conrad was murdered?" I asked in a whisper, my face mere inches away from his.

"No one can be trusted," his muttered, terrified. "Father knew bad things would happen, and he was right, wasn't he? The Chinese sent a bloody assassin, afraid that the Prussians would get to Teston first."

There was no point in arguing further, but my thoughts were muddled; downright disturbed. Father was involved in making threats against Ms. Teston, and he'd involved Hector. Surely Sir Hector knew more of this bloody business than he'd first let on.

I resolved that I had to speak to my father, just he and I. Help him see reason, get his help to clear Jing's name. If I showed him some of the papers we had, he would understand, he would see that Ms. Teston's workshops were for the good of all. For peace. He was an intelligent and generous man, after all. Else I feared there was no hope for us. I would have to go alone, for Jing would be arrested on sight, even killed without provocation. I would have to find Hector Sr. by myself.

"Where is Father now?"

It was Mother who answered. "He's been too busy to run back and forth between town and here," she answered, taking over the job of administering to Hector Jr.'s injuries. "He's been staying aboard the steamship to run the bloody business of this Fair throughout the opening ceremonies."

And bloody business it was turning out to be.

Jing and I dressed completely, both sombre and lost in thought. He wore old play clothes of my brothers, an old cotton collared shirt, frayed knickerbockers and a cap pulled low over his head. We completed Jing's attire with an old costume wig of Mother's, dirty blond and shaggy, from when she'd attended a masque as a prince from *The Magic Flute*. The attire, combined with his height and the shaggy wig covering his face, gave the impression of a young boy out for a day's frolicking; it would be impossible to tell it was him unless you pushed the hair back and stared him straight in the face.

I dressed much the same, minus a wig, and pulled on an old coat of Father's. I gave Jing my own coat, which he'd been wearing the day prior, admittedly out of sentimental reasons, and I liked seeing him in it. He pulled the card Ms. Teston had given us out of the pocket, significantly more crumpled, and re-read her instructions. "Two rivers... We still haven't found the two rivers, whatever that means."

"Perhaps we can ask her," I said, distracted. "Although I suppose I'd have to break her out of incarceration..."

"After jumping out of an airship and battling a giant, evil automaton, I think we can handle that," Jing said sardonically, but he sensed my unease. "Norwood, what is it?"

"I'm going alone," I said, and he swore at me and began to protest, but I grabbed him in a tight hug and whispered, "It's too dangerous and I can't see you hurt or killed. I know we've only known each other a couple of days, and most of that was spent escaping one danger or another, but I've grown quite fond of you, Jing."

He scoffed, but I suspected it was to cover up a slight sniffle. "Where exactly are you taking me Norwood?" he asked quietly, still in my arms.

"Where you can hide, where you won't be found, where you'll be safe," I said, though I would say no more for the moment. We shared a kiss, so neither of us would have to explain ourselves further.

When I returned downstairs, my mother was spoon-feeding my brother a breakfast of porridge. She had cleaned him up as best she could, though bruises bloomed about his eyes and nose, and she'd left him tied up. I hoped now the worst pain he felt was to his ego.

"Don't get up," I said to Hector, whose glare turned into something approaching daggers. I turned to Mother. "Father's bound to send someone looking for Hector if he doesn't return to town soon. When they do, tell them it was all Jing's and my doing. Please don't disagree, just blame us. Say we tied him up and forced you to go along with it." I nodded at my brother. "He won't accuse you, will you Hector?"

Hector looked outraged. "Of course not! My own mother!"

"I'm going to take Jing someplace safe and go find Father and sort out this nasty business. He needs to know the truth."

"There's no place safe for that criminal sodo—" Hector began to say, but my mother gave him a withering glance, so he sank into a sullen silence.

Aveline followed me out into the foyer where Jing, bewigged and prepared as he could be, stood. She gave him a hug, warm and genuine, and they had a quick, whispered exchanged. She studied me appraisingly and smiled sadly. "So like a Quigley. Brave, headstrong, occasionally stupid. You get your bravado from your father... the intelligence and culture comes from my side of the family." She wrapped her arms around me for what I'm sure she believed was the last time, and she sobbed.

"Oh Mother," I sighed, attempting to stifle my own tears, "no need to be so melodramatic."

Despite the immediacy of the situation, we decided to spend a couple hours on a walk into town, hoping to appear like an older and younger brother passing an idle day, me with my camera bag slung over my shoulder, Jing carrying the notes we'd found in Ms. Teston's secret workshop in the metal canister. We managed to hitch a ride on a farm wagon, which shortened the trip, and we were soon cutting our way down through the city.

I was surprised, given the ongoing Exhibition events, that the streets were almost empty; just the occasional clump of men or women standing in alleys, whispering and glancing around nervously. Mounted police patrolled the streets in droves, outnumbering civilians. We made sure to keep our hats pulled low, but they didn't give us a second glance.

I stopped by one brave young newsy, no older than ten, selling the *Globe* on the corner of Yonge and Queen. There had been no further edition; the paper was the same I had seen at home. I asked him why the streets were so empty, and he grinned broadly, and whispered as if it were some grand secret, "War! They says there's fighting on the Exhibition grounds. Folks is scared it'll spread into the city." He seemed thrilled at this prospect. I thanked him for the information and we continued weaving through the city.

We came to the building I believed Jing would be safest in. Within the lobby of the Teston & Tinker workshop the same young man, now working on a different clock, waved us through; I did not even need to offer some fabricated excuse of why we were there. The workshops seemed deserted, though at the end of the hallway, through the same doors, beyond the same signs I had passed a week prior, Mr. Tinker's workshop was as dark and cluttered as ever. I caught sight of the emerald refractions from our mechanical feline companion,

Tickertape, who leapt up from the oil-stained floor and let out an unearthly screech, followed by a loud, fizzling pop.

"You infernal machine, I'm fixing your voice box now. You'll blow a condenser if you keep that up," came a thin though scolding voice from within. Jing looked at me, dubious, but we allowed the silenced clockwork cat to guide us through the gloom.

Mr. Tinker was further on, at his work table, hunched over a small component, using a complex system of refracted lantern light to see the intricate little materials within, along with a pair of glasses composed of multi-layered lenses atop his head. He looked, if possible, even more deranged than the day I had met him.

"A moment, please," he breathed, tweaking something with a minuscule tool. He didn't seem surprised or upset to have visitors. "Very delicate, these parts."

I shrugged at Jing, who sighed, but began gazing about at what was lit by the little light available to us. He picked up a pile of schematics and began to rifle through them. I bent down, nervous and impatient, and scratched at the crook of Tickertape's ear. The little automaton creature made a sparking noise followed by an expulsion of smoke in response, and I removed my hand.

Finally, Mr. Tinker seemed satisfied with his work and picked up the device, giving it a final look. He called the cat over and pulled open a series of metal clasps about Tickertape's neck. The cat's head fell backwards in a disturbing manner, though it didn't seem bothered, and he slid the device inside it. Once the head was returned it gave an indifferent, tinny "meow," and slunk off into the workshop.

"Precocious heap of scrap," Mr. Tinker stated affectionately. "Though there is some progress, the electric waves are unstable, must see to the power source, but workable, and promising. You did hear my voice, did you not, Harwood? We communicated through the device?"

I didn't realize he'd stopped speaking to himself, especially given the misnomer. Jing saved me, appearing at my side with a handful of plans. "Yes we did, Mr. Tinker," Tinker turned and scrawled some notes on a piece of paper seemingly unrelated to this two-way electric communication. "I think the problem may have been on this end as well," Jing continued after a moment of silence from Tinker. "If you had a proper transmission device, perhaps a tower, it would improve the range and quality of the transmission."

Mr. Tinker and I both turned and stared at Jing in amazement, my mouth hung open. He looked offended. "Why are you so surprised? I just looked at the schematics of your transmitter, and the equations. I studied hard enough when I could still put up with the nuns. I'm decent enough at math and sciences— What are you grinning at, Norwood Quigley?!"

"Young Mr. Quigley the photographer," Mr. Tinker said as if noticing I was there for the first time, though he didn't take his eyes off Jing. "And your companion is?"

"Oh. Uh, Mr. Tinker, this is my good friend... uh, John St. Andrew."

"Jing," he introduced himself, removing his hat and wig.

I jumped in before Mr. Tinker had time to accuse my dear friend of murder. "He's the reason the police are after us, why the Mr. Shackles machine was hounding us yesterday," I continued. "You see, I was on my way to see my father in one of the rooms on the uppermost deck of the *Hanlan's Pride* when Prussian Ambassador Herr von Conrad was murdered in the adjacent room. They think Jing murdered the man."

"But I didn't murder anyone," Jing stated, a signature air of defiance in his voice, he dumped the papers onto the desk, Exhibition schematics and correspondences scattering about.

"Murder? Who said anything about murder? I have too much to do without all this nonsense of nuns and police and murdered Prussians." Mr. Tinker waved his hands, dismissing us, turning to another machine on his workbench.

I put my hand on his shoulder and turned him to me, looking in his eyes, though he wouldn't meet mine, glancing away nervously. "There's something going on at the Exhibition, Mr. Tinker. The Chinese and the Prussians are at each other's throats over a murder they think Jing committed. There's talk of war."

The old inventor shook his head, dismissing the notion. "I have no mind for war... for politics."

"Ms. Teston's been arrested," Jing, now at my shoulder said, throwing the fact in Tinker's face like a challenge. "She's to be tried for treason for hijacking a royal military airship and helping me."

This gave Mr. Tinker pause. "Mave... she'll... be fine. She's perfectly capable."

"Not against the full force of military law," I answered, desperate. "Not in the face of a war that could span the entire world. We have evidence there was some plot against von Conrad—Mave was at least aware of its possibility—and I need to speak with my father. He'll be able to help."

Mr. Tinker turned away from us, rubbing his beard a moment, deep in thought. "I'll be no help to you, young Mr. Quigley," he muttered. "I... I cannot leave this building..."

Jing seemed ready with an insult both short and cutting, but I jumped in before he could say anything. "I need to go to the Exhibition grounds to talk to my father, but Jing needs somewhere to hide while I sort everything out."

Mr. Tinker seemed relieved this was all we were asking of him. "Of course. No one bothers me here, he'll be quite safe." He turned away, visibly taxed by the conversation. "Might as well make yourself useful, young Mr. Jing. Let us draw up this transmission device you speak of. I have a damned pencil about here somewhere..."

Mr. Tinker began to toss aside hulking heaps of machine parts, looking for paper and pencil. Jing raised an eyebrow at Tinker, bemused, then looked to me, pleading for me not to go. I could tell he was about to offer further protestation to follow me to the Exhibition grounds, so I joked, "You're too much trouble." I tried to keep my voice light, but it wavered.

Jing's arms enveloped me in a tight embrace. We kissed once. "Please be safe and come back quickly." He nodded at Tinker, who was now drawing madly, crumpling one piece of paper, starting on another, and then repeating the process.

I tried for an air of levity, though tears clouded my vision, "Simple enough, I just need to infiltrate a small, festive warzone and somehow sneak onto the ninth floor of an enormous steamship into the room of one of the most important men in Canada beside a recent scene of crime without raising suspicion."

Mr. Tinker, at his mad drawings, almost inaudibly muttered, "You could try the inter-suite door."

His sentence hung in the air for a moment, not quite sinking in. He continued rambling to himself about steam-powered transmission devices and faulty electrical outlets.

"Mr. Tinker... inter-suite doors?" I asked, still unsure about his meaning.

He crumpled another piece of paper, tossed it aside, and then turned to the stack of Mave Teston's letters and schematics we had brought into his workshop. He flipped through and brought out a floor plan of the *Hanlan's Pride*, the enormous steamship, and circled a section of the drawing before turning back to his own stack of papers.

Jing and I approached the *Hanlan's Pride* plans. As I gazed on the section Mr. Tinker had circled, my stomach dropped and I felt ill; a dark, terrible truth speeding toward me.

Unlike the bottom floors of the ship, the hold, the engine room, the crew quarters, the mid-levels of the ship were passenger rooms, giving the floating hotel its reputation. The upper floors, especially, were larger suites, most connected by a single panel door between them, including 902B, von Conrad's room, and 902A... my father's.

I became conscious of Jing's eyes on me. "Norwood..." he said cautiously.

"I have to go." I turned away from him, crashing into a stack of automaton limbs. I kicked at them and sent one flying to crash against the far wall, spooking Tickertape, concealed somewhere in the gloom, which let out a mechanical approximation of a hiss in response. "I have to go speak to my father. Now." I stalked through the dark, out of the workshop. Jing called something after me, but I kept going, out through the building and on to whatever would come next.

I pushed the thoughts of this revelation out of my mind as I walked south along Spadina—no streetcars were currently running down to the Exhibition. I needed to feel like I was moving fast, purposeful, feel the ground pounding beneath my feet, propel myself forward, machine-like. I couldn't think about the connecting door at the moment. I hadn't even seen it, so I couldn't know it existed in the final construction of the *Hanlan's Pride*.

I pushed the thought further down as I rounded the corner at Front Street, following the shoreline westward toward the fairgrounds, past Fort York, the city prison looming in the distance.

The closer I got to the New World's Exhibition grounds the more deserted the city became, and I soon realized why. I could hear the distant pop and echo of gunfire. British military airships hovered overhead as if taking in the spectacle of whatever was unfolding on the fairgrounds. At the Exhibition's extremities, cordons of mounted police patrolled the streets, although their attention seemed focused on containing the activity on the festival grounds and I was able to sneak by unbothered.

While the grounds were empty of visitors, I could see a number of boats and ships dockside on the waterfront, including the towering *Hanlan's Pride* where I hoped I'd find my father. I would need to navigate the fair's avenues quickly. Beyond the occasional airship, the sky was otherwise clear and blue, the buildings of the Exhibition grounds as I passed through the Eastern gate were palatial, resplendent, abandoned, banners flapping gaily in the gentle breeze. Sounds of gunfire exchanges grew louder the further I pushed into the fairgrounds. The world seemed to have abandoned Exhibition mania to take up a madness of an entirely different sort.

CHAPTER 8

IN WHICH THERE IS AN INTERNATIONAL CRISIS
AND THREE KIDNAPPINGS

As I approached Victoria Circle at the centre of the fair, signs of small battles were clear; the occasional pockmark of bullets, a splatter of blood, an overturned and charred stagecoach. As I passed the central monument to the Empress, I looked up to see the Union Jack flying from the statue... well, it had been loosened by unclear means from its original flagpole and, tattered, ridden with bullet holes, had got caught on the royal matriarch's head and crown, covering her eyes to the sight of the war-torn fair she presided over.

I was jogging at this point, *Hanlan's Pride* ever closer, though I feared with so many passengers sheltered on board she would depart for safer waters before I reached her. I turned a corner to make for the waterfront and found myself confronted with a chilling sight: two battalions of men in the path before me. On one side of the road, I was faced by a cluster of men in the deep navy-blue uniform of the Prussian Army, all carrying pistols, rifles or unsheathed sabres. I ducked back behind the corner before I was noticed since I was within spitting distance from the other group closest to me, but peaked around to watch the situation unfold.

On the other side was a coterie of Chinese nationals and guards, led by the ambassador I had spotted in the opening ceremonies, enraged and storming out of the police station the previous day and at the airship field. His thugs who'd assaulted Jing and I were thankfully nowhere to be seen. His severe face was ever graver, mirrored by his compatriots, a couple of whom had drawn their weapons and seemed ready to open fire on the Prussians.

"We did not murder your ambassador," the leader of the Chinese group, whose name I had since learned is Cheying Chen, stated with gravity. "We were promised safe passage by the British to negotiate the release of my people from our pavilion, stand aside."

The Prussians chortled or growled threats in reply. One stepped forward, a little unsteady on his feet—perhaps intoxicated? "Ve are not saying *you* deed," he called out, casually waving a pistol before him. "Ve simply beleef you are hiding ze von who deed. Ve heard zat he vas contracted by a Chinaman, and so here ve are, ve find many!"

He waved his gun in the direction of the ambassador, and one of the Chinese guards shouted something I could not translate, but Chen held up his hand and the man stood down, though the tension was palpable. "And you think we are the only Chinese in the city?" the ambassador called back, unflinching in the face of the Prussian thugs who were clearly just looking for a fight.

Another Prussian soldier muttered something and spat, and their apparent leader nodded. "You are ze only Chinese with ze airpower to kidnap ze Queen."

The Queen? Kidnapped?! What fresh hell?!

"I am zinking ze Engleesh vill not be happy vith you over zat."

Ambassador Chen scowled, and barked at the other man, "Further lies we do not have to answer to. Out of my way or we will kill every single one of you without hesitation, I was promised—"

Perhaps the stand-off would have lasted a little longer but for the clumsy trigger finger of one of the Prussian soldiers as he shifted his stance from the back of the group. A gunshot rang out, someone swore, but this was all it took for the defending Chinese to open fire.

I crouched and took quick glances, hoping each group would back off and flee. Instead, both took defensive positions behind walls or buildings. I watched as the Chinese ambassador took in the battle scene surrounding him, an emotionless expression on his face, before turning and walking for cover, as if taking a ponderous stroll through the garden, even as bullets flew around him, kicking up dirt around his feet.

That was, until a stray bullet—from whichever side, I couldn't tell—grazed the ambassador's leg, causing him to tumble to the ground.

What idiocy possessed me to involve myself I cannot say, but I saw that his countrymen were pinned under cover and engaged in the intensifying firefight. I could not watch a man cut down so needless before me, so I leapt from my safe position and, ducking low, cursing myself for such brazen behaviour, crab-walked to the ambassador. I had never felt so vulnerable in my life, but the man was attempting to stand, so I was able to half-help, half-drag Ambassador Chen between two buildings where we were out of the line of fire.

He studied me, the same severe, neutral expression on his face.

"You have my thanks," he said, as if I had brought him a cup of tea, though he also spat back in the direction of the fighting, which seemed to be ebbing somewhat with shouts from the Prussian side. "Guns… there is no honour and no skill to simply point at someone and kill them."

I tore off a section of my shirt and wrapped it around his leg to help staunch the flow of blood. "Mr. Chen… I know Jing… John St. Andrew, the man they say killed von Conrad." I winced as a bullet exploded the corner we had taken cover behind seconds before, raining splinters down on us. "He didn't do it, he's a pawn in some larger scheme."

The Chinese ambassador considered me a moment. "Who are you?"

"Norwood Quigley, sir. I'm the son of—" but Chen's eyes bulged.

"Your father. We have spoken. He is not a good man." This stung, but I let him continue. "He cares not for China or Prussia, or even England. He cares only for money. Money and power."

My stomach twisted at the accusation, and I was about to protest when someone threw themselves around the corner, a Chinese guard, followed by two more. They seemed mostly intact, though one held a spot on his shoulder that was bleeding through his coat. The other two continued to exchange fire with the Prussians while the injured man consulted with Chen. It was a quick exchange and the man called an order to the others while the Chinese ambassador asked me to help him stand.

"We retreat to Exhibition Station," he explained as he braced himself against the other injured man's good shoulder. "Think on what I have told you, and beware of warmongering men, young

Quigley."

The bulk of the Chinese group retreated through the alley, ducking through a building, a couple left behind giving covering fire as they retreated. I followed them out through a store selling French trinkets and parted ways with them as they cut across the Canadian Pacific Plaza for the main station. I resolved that whatever the ambassador said, however grave things appeared, I had to get to my father.

Making my way across the Exhibition grounds proved perilous and impossible. Small battalions of Prussian and Chinese soldiers clashed at every turn. The Prussians were no longer drunk agitators but organized squads of soldiers. The Chinese, for their part, seemed to be sending every guard and soldier they had, and not just to retake their captured buildings.

And it seemed the English and Canadian forces were moving in as well. While some were certainly concentrating their energies on evacuating any unlucky Exhibition staff that had come to work that day or aiding wounded combatants on either side, a number of trigger-happy British soldiers seemed intent on engaging any Chinese forces in sight.

This I found the most vexing; unless the Prussian thug spoke true and the Chinese had somehow kidnapped the Queen, which seemed sure to lead to an international war. I ducked in and out of abandoned shops and restaurants but stopped when I heard groaning behind the counter of an information kiosk. An injured English soldier had taken refuge, and I called for help from some of his compatriots exchanging fire with Prussians across the street.

"The Queen's been kidnapped," he confirmed when I asked him why the English had joined the battle. "No one's sayin' nothin' 'bout who did it, but we all know it's the damned Chinee." I shook my heed as another soldier threw himself behind the desk and began tending to his friend's wound, a shot to the stomach that did not seem to stop gushing blood and viscera. "Kill 'em all, the buggers!" he deliriously called after me as I ducked out of the kiosk.

From there I hopped a fence and ducked between the columns of the Woman's building. A troop of Chinese guards moved through the street in front of the structure, so I huddled out of sight near the wide-open entrance.

The building, dedicated to achievements of female artists, scientists and inventors, was a palatial edifice with an enormous mural just inside the foyer. Painted by an American artist, the piece was titled "The New Woman Mural," three panels, the centre depicting women in an Edenic field, the others showing a set of female scientists in a medical laboratory attending to patients, the third a familiar fiery-haired woman, a wrench held aloft aboard an airship in flight.

So focused was I on the mutterings of the Chinese soldiers, and praying to these New Woman that the men would pass me by without notice, that I did not see someone walking out of the shadows of the abandoned building until he stood in the centre of the foyer.

It was the Ojibwe man I'd seen time and time again, still dressed in a dark suit. The bowler hat was atop his head, although he removed it as he saw me spy him.

"Quigley," he said at a normal volume, his voice deep and calm, and my eyes went wide.

At that moment there came shouting from the street and I slunk further down the column, prepared to be captured or fired upon by Chinese troops, although their attention seemed to be directed elsewhere, so I sprinted along past the building, away from the troops and the man in the shadows. If the mysterious Ojibwe man attempted to get my attention further, his calls were lost in the cacophony of the battle around us. That he was tailing me there was no doubt, as I'd seen him again and again over the past two days. This simply added to the feeling of anxiety and oppression welling up inside of me, and I wondered to whose side he belonged, and what his malevolent purposes for me were.

I wove in and out of more buildings, consternated that I was forced by the fighting closer and closer to the airship field, which put me further from the *Hanlan's Pride*.

Beyond the fence and the temporary—now empty—audience stands from the Royal Airship Navy demonstration the previous day loomed a handful of landed airships. I recognized what I believed to be the grounded *Victoria* down on the far end, near the military hangars.

I was following the fence toward the water when I saw a group of intoxicated Prussian Army soldiers in my path. They must have taken shelter around the Lighter-Than-Air Pavilion. I cursed to myself, unwilling to put myself in harm's way, my only other option to hop the fence and continue through the structures on the airship field, ever further away from my destination—I had been forced to completely circumnavigate the entire Exhibition like a fool, though I supposed I was unscathed to this point, so that was something.

I crept behind the audience stands, scouting for the best route to remain unseen when I saw a heartening sight. Two airships hovered nearby in front of the Quigley Airships hangars; one of them an older, rickety-looking model, unnoticeable among the dozen other airships moored in the field. The other was the *Halcyon*, my father's personal transport airship.

I crept closer, my heart rising. I hadn't even thought my father might land the *Halcyon* here, but what safer way to travel given the impassable ground route. I moved between two of the Quigley Airships hangars and heard some voices up ahead, though I couldn't make out what was being said.

As I neared the front of the hangars, I recognized two of the men, the thugs who had been tailing Ambassador Chen; the wiry Chinese man, Jiao-Long, who wore trousers and a simple overshirt, his arms revealed to be covered in tattoos and his imposing companion, Qiang Li the Ox, though they were now out of uniform. They were listening to a third man barking orders in Mandarin from within the hangar.

The two men were scowling in concentration at whoever was talking, a Chinese crew working aboard the rickety airship behind them preparing for takeoff. I crept closer to listen. At first, I didn't know what compelled me forward, since these brutes would block my way to the *Halcyon*, but the speaker's voice was deep and growling, like rolling thunder, and he spoke in fast and fluid Mandarin, yet it was still familiar, somehow.

Two of the men, following a command, pulled an old woman from within the hangar, dressed in regal black clothing, save for the sack pulled tight over her head. She harrumphed at the rough treatment but couldn't speak, apparently gagged.

I realized from her shape and her signature mourning dress that this was the Empress. The Royal Dowager. The British Empire's Queen. I couldn't begin to fathom what to think, except to inwardly employ every swear word within my vocabulary, a few I'd learned from Jing over the past day.

Two of the airmen pulled and prodded her onto the older airship beside the *Halcyon,* and I prayed my father or one of his airmen might notice and intervene, but there was no one in sight. With a final, punctuating command, the enormous, brutish Chinese man and his compatriot nodded and followed behind them, pulling the bay door up and closed behind them, and the older airship's engines buzzed to life.

My mind was racing. An international crisis; the Queen of England kidnapped; the New World Exhibition a war zone; Ms. Teston, one of my few allies, was under house arrest; my brother a pawn in the murder of an ambassador; my intimate friend, however briefly I had known Jing, was the target of an international manhunt. The world seemed to me, at that moment, utter madness. I needed to speak with the only man who could do anything about the situation. I needed to find my father.

Although, as it happened, I needn't look very far; as the older airship carrying the Queen lifted off the ground and drifted

Westward, following the lakeshore, the man who had been speaking Mandarin to the Chinese thugs walked out of one of the Quigley Airships hangars, approaching his airship. His walk was brisk, confident, strong, military. I watched as my father climbed aboard the *Halcyon*, and my world came crashing down.

My vision had gone black, my breath lost, but after a few moments, I found myself staring at the place the *Halcyon* had been moments before. I could barely breathe, air came in deep, heaving breaths, but had little effect calming me.

My father had been giving orders to the kidnappers of the Queen... in fact, he likely was the kidnapper. Of course, the events of the previous few days all made sense. My father, posing as a mysterious Chinese man behind a screen, had arranged for Jing, a petty criminal and prostitute, to offer companionship to von Conrad. My father had somehow arranged a means to sneak through a hidden panel door connecting his room to von Conrad's. He had been among those who condemned Jing before any investigation, and although he seemed concerned enough for my safety, he had wasted no opportunity to recapture the two of us, in one piece or otherwise. He had even sent my brother to the place he knew I might seek refuge... our childhood home.

Thinking about the matter logically, which seemed a mad thing to do, there really was no one better connected to instigate a murder and an international crisis than Sir Hector Daedalus Quigley. Everyone in the Empire trusted him; everyone in the English court knew him, he and mother had even shared tea with the Queen on a few occasions. He had an intimate knowledge of English military affairs and royal security. All looked on the kindness and generosity of Sir Quigley with the same reverence that I'd had for him my entire life.

I snapped out of my trance and looked up to see the *Halcyon* turning over the lake, heading back toward the city, toward whatever fresh evils the crew and my father had in store.

There was no other thought in my mind, but I must have looked a sight to the airmen near the Royal Airship Navy hangar. Bruised, cut up, spattered with blood, harried from the excessive trials of the past day, the airmen sitting about near the *Victoria* looked up, bemused as I flailed my way down the airship field toward them. The airmen, who'd been sitting around looking glum perked up, curious of my panting, anxious, unintelligible cries of "Deeds most foul!" and "Royalty! Betrayal! Plots! Murder!"

I was almost sobbing with relief when I recognized the navigator and a couple of the airmen from my brief time aboard the *Victoria*, and they quickly summoned Admiral Montgomery, then did their best to calm my panic-induced raving. By the time the admiral arrived, I was able to tell him an abbreviation of my story: the Queen's kidnapping not a mile away from where they stood by Chinese men not under Chinese control but by my father who was, as far as I could tell, the root cause of the hostilities consuming the Exhibition grounds.

Admiral Montgomery motioned to his men who looked startled, but stood at attention. He motioned over to two airmen, Livingston and Hornby. "You are to go to her home and demand Ms. Teston released on my orders. She'll be under house arrest in her lodgings near the workshop. Tell her guards it is a matter of international security. Bribe them, beat them down with your fists if you must. I don't care how you do it, but if what young Mr. Quigley has said about her involvement in this is true we need Mave Teston. Bring her to this very spot. Go, now." The men, surprised at the order, nodded and made for the northern exit of the airship field.

"The rest of you, prepare for departure immediately," he barked. There was some hesitation; one of the men even questioned his order. They'd been grounded by orders of the fleet admiral. To disobey that order was treason. Montgomery nodded. "This is an unsanctioned mission, volunteers only. I will not reprimand any man who stays on the ground, but at the moment we are the only ship in the Royal Navy who knows the truth about the Queen's abduction, and every minute puts Her Royal Majesty another click away from the ship given her namesake. I'd like to close that distance, immediately."

We were all aboard the airship in seconds.

Montgomery motioned I follow him as we felt the gentle lurch of the *Victoria* lifting from the ground. "Well, Mr. Quigley, this is the second time in the span of a single day I am expressly disobeying orders for your sake." We walked together out onto the deck and took in the sight of the Exhibition ground below still teeming with battle. "We were grounded yesterday pending an inquiry into my loyalties. Mave is the most capable woman... the most capable person in the world. She is the only one I would do such a thing for, and it's clear to me you are just as noble as she."

I smiled at the gruff admiral, though I considered his compliment; it was unfortunate such a nobility only became apparent in times of adversity, against a backdrop of dark deeds.

"Come," he led me into the bridge, "let us save our queen."

However unfortunate the circumstances, it was thrilling to be part of such a well-oiled machine. We were quick to determine the course of the abductor-flown airship, likely following the shore of Lake Ontario southwest over the small, booming port town of Hamilton, then cut in landwards heading west, cutting over the States to Seattle or Vancouver if the old airship could make it.

I joined the men on deck with a spyglass, keeping an eye out on the horizon to spot the rogue airship.

The *Victoria* was an outstanding airship and it wasn't long before I helped confirm sighting of the small, outdated, decrepit merchant class vessel. The captors' airship chugged along following the course as we had suspected, although as they spotted us, the other vessel did its best to catch the wind and outmaneuver us. I was glad to be on the better ship.

I followed Admiral Montgomery down into the launch bay below the bridge. A dozen small double-seaters, stealth-class and fighter-class airships sat waiting to deploy, and most of the crew stood about at attention.

"Alright men, we're boarding the hostiles. Six Sparrows—" I took this to mean the stealth-class ships, "—one pilot, one boarder, just the way we trained. Her Royal Majesty is aboard. You are to neutralize the captors, take control of the airship and secure Her Majesty's safety at any cost, understood?"

"Aye, Admiral!" the men cried in unison, and I joined in... a little late, to my embarrassment.

Admiral Montgomery's smile was grave. "If you can leave any of these men alive, they will answer for their crimes, but otherwise..." he patted the pistol on his hip. "You have your orders. Good hunting, men."

The men dispersed, most climbing into the small compartments with the deck crew preparing to launch six of the Sparrows. One young man a little older than myself approached the admiral and I. He had dark brown skin, lively, sparkling eyes and a smile that seemed electric. He was immaculately dressed, his uniform spotless and exquisitely pressed.

"Yes, what is it Daley?" asked the admiral.

"Sir," the young man saluted, a faint Caribbean accent in his voice, "I believe you sent Hornby, my boarder, on ground duty."

The admiral nodded. "To retrieve Ms. Teston, that's correct, Daley."

The pilot's face dropped. "I was hoping, sir, to be part of the rescue."

The admiral smiled as if to a child excited to join in a sports game. "My apologies, Airman, but you'll have to assist from the deck this time. Damn shame," the admiral turned to me, "Daley is one of the best young pilots in the fleet."

"I'll do it," I said without hesitation. The admiral offered a polite but brief protest, and relented faster than I would have thought, given his rank. Daley was practically dancing with excitement. "Just don't get yourself killed. Aveline would kill me," the admiral tossed back over his shoulder as he walked back up onto the bridge.

"Airman Laurence Daley," the young man shook my hand vigorously. "But most just call me 'Lady'."

I was a little taken aback by his admission as he led me to his craft, for he did have an elegant, effeminate air about him that he didn't, like other young men I know, attempt to hide in machismo. The craft afforded most room to the pilot, with little more than enough space for another person to crouch positioned behind them. He handed me a pair of goggles and donned a pair himself.

"Lady, you say?" I asked, attempting to hide the surprise in my voice with an equal amount of genuine interest.

He grinned and clicked his heels together, then gave a theatrical shrug. "If the boot fits. Now let's fly!"

The deck crew, through a series of pulleys and guides, were able to line up each small airship by twos, with Lady and I at the back, behind two other small, stealth-class airships. A bay door was opened behind us, to my surprise, and the small airship lurched backwards.

"Hold onto your knickers, Quigley!" he crowed as we zoomed backwards out of the *Victoria*.

There was a sickening moment of free fall and I could hear Lady laughing with joy before the engine kicked in and the Sparrow shot forward and up. A glass dome protected the pilot's seat, but the back portion where I sat was open to the wind, which whipped through my hair with a speed I'd never felt before. The Sparrows flew as quick as their namesakes. I glanced up to see the five other airships following suit, but we shot ahead, leading the small flock in formation.

Lady seemed excited, but agitated. "Let's see if we can kick this into high gear and get there first." Lady slapped a few switches and pulled a lever. Our Sparrow lurched and then dipped before zooming ahead at a breakneck speed, catching an air current.

As we neared the rogue airship, some pops registered over the wind roaring in our ears.

Lady cackled, "Good luck hitting this!" The Sparrow zoomed up, then did a sickening plummet which Lady followed with a loop in the air before shooting forward. I was screaming my protestations, to no avail. "Don't worry! We present such a small target at this range and speed we're near impossible to hit!"

At that moment there was a pop from the left envelope, and the Sparrow veered sharply in that direction, the small vessel giving a mighty shudder. A bullet had torn through. Lady swore and flipped some levers, managing to right the Sparrow, though it seemed to resist the compensation of its damaged left ballast.

"I'm going to get you on board, and then I'm going to have to land

and make repairs!" Lady called over the roaring wind and the whine of the Sparrow's engine. The rifle fire had ceased; the captors were either reloading or preparing to be boarded, for with our slowed vessel a few other Sparrows had overtaken us and begun to board.

"Five other airmen on board, and you." I watched as one of the boarders leapt four feet and clambered over the side, only to be immediately shot and crumple to the deck. "Okay, four other airmen and you. Looks like they have five, and their pilot. I'm bringing it up on our port side. Try not to fall, Quigley!"

I crouched, positioning myself in preparation to make my jump. I had done the occasional unsafe inter-airship leap before, to my mother's horror, but onto a vessel full of hostile thugs was quite another thing altogether.

Lady brought the Sparrow in a sharp but well-executed swoop and we were close enough to the captor airship that I could see the scowls of the fighting men aboard. One man mere feet away from me could see me just as well and rose a rifle aimed directly at my face.

Lady twisted the Sparrow and I leapt with the sudden momentum of the motion, thrown directly at our attacker. By some miracle the bullet missed me and I was flung into the man, knocking him with a nauseating crack onto the deck. His bullet, however, blasted through the Sparrow and punctured the right envelope, and the small airship disappeared from the side of the larger one, hissing steam behind it. I prayed to whatever deity might be above that Lady could save himself.

However, there was no time to dwell on his plummet. I raised myself from the man I had knocked unconscious, realizing we were evenly matched. Lady was right, I counted five attackers, including the one I had sent sprawling, and five of the boarders had made it, including the man who'd been shot and myself.

The Chinese thugs were fighting, either hand-to-hand with the boarders or ducking behind cargo on the deck to reload their weapons or exchange fire. The final Sparrow zoomed to the side of the airship but was shot down by rifle fire before the boarder could make the jump. More poor souls lost to the sky...

It was at that moment I realized I had undergone this venture unarmed, beyond my fists, and little knowledge of firearms or marksmanship... A folly for someone boarding a hostile airship, I supposed.

One of the Chinese men without a gun advanced on me, a dagger shining in his hand. I reached for the closest weapon available to me, the fallen man's rifle and held it up by the barrel. My attacker sneered at the way I had grabbed the weapon and advanced, lunging at me with the blade. I jumped backwards, away from the blade, and the scoundrel chuckled maliciously.

Not well acquainted with the finer points and workings of the rifle, I brought the butt of the rifle about, like a cricket paddle, crashing into the side of his face. He spun about with the unexpected blow and stumbled, dropping his blade and threatened to go tumbling over the rail of the ship. As a mercy, I grabbed his collar, threw him backwards onto his crewmate and administered a *coup de grace* with the butt of the rifle, for good measure, apologizing as I did so.

The other airmen were engaged in combat with the rogues, all weapons tossed aside because of proximity or lack of ammunition. I moved in to help them, but one airman saw me approach and cried, "Search below! Make sure there are no others! Find—" but his duelling partner had swung a fist. It was Qiang Li the Ox, one of the brutish men from the previous day, one who had been taking orders from my father.

But no time for that. I had my orders, like the others. I was very familiar with merchant vessels, so I found the stairs to the lower deck without issue. The bow of the ship, where there was less room and cramped crew quarters, was empty which left only one other area: the airship's hold.

I walked in with the rifle raised. The wiry man with arms covered in tattoos, Jiao-Long, stood behind the same lump of regal fabric I'd seen escorted on board earlier. She was seated in a rickety chair, still hooded. He looked concerned for a moment until he saw my face, and a knowing smile crept across his.

"Young Mister Quigley," he called out in greeting, a heavy accent flavouring his words. He bowed in mock respect. "I thought you your brother."

"The ship is ours," I called out, though he no doubt heard the quaver in my voice and saw the rifle tremble in my hand.

"You look like brother, but not father. No beast in eye, no fire in veins," he said, somehow sliding a dagger from his sleeve. "You think this is it," he waved the blade about, motioning at the airship around him. The blade glimmered and danced in the lantern light. "You think this important? This trick. You fooled. You not like father."

He tossed the blade in the air, caught it by the blade end, then threw it. I wasn't able to dodge it, and it cut through the top of my left shoulder. My finger twitched and the rifle, still loaded, unbeknownst to me, fired. He took it in his left breast and went sprawling to the wood planks of the airship.

After I'd dropped the rifle and thrown up the little contents in my stomach, I managed to stagger over to where the captive sat, doing my best to avoid looking at the lifeless body, doing my best not to think about what I had just done. I pulled off the hood and there she was, the Empress. Dressed in all black, a ruffled veil pushed back over her hair, her face, dark featured and lined with age, looked more bored and annoyed than concerned. I had seen her this close in person once before when I was very little, and she seemed an imposing figure. It struck me as odd how in her current state she seemed little more than a small, exhausted old woman.

She raised an eyebrow at me and I jumped to action, gently pulling the cloth gag out of her mouth. She gave me a thin smile. "I must say, this is the most excitement I have seen in a while."

We glanced together at the dead man beside us. I felt the colour further drained from my face and my nausea return in force, but the Dowager shrugged, then looked back to me. "Quigley, was it? I wonder if you might untie my hands," she said, her voice filled with calm, quiet dignity.

"Of course, Your Majesty!" I retrieved the blade of the man I had killed and then carefully cut the ropes that bound the Queen's wrists behind her in the chair, my hands shaking ferociously.

"There's a dear." She rubbed her hands, grimacing in pain. "I am, admittedly, old, and have the pleasure of suffering from rheumatism, very uncomfortable. I thank you."

By that point two of the airmen entered the hold and bowed to the Queen who waved their propriety off, indifferent.

The men seemed unharmed, but after making sure the Chinese man was indeed dead turned their attention on me. Blood had soaked through my shirt and coat, and they made me hold my sleeve to the wound to staunch the flow, one of them swearing about the fight, but then he turned to the Queen. "Pardon the indelicacy, Your Highness."

She smiled and rolled her eyes. "I am a mother, good sir, and was a wife, and have therefore suffered all the indelicacies one could imagine. But I wonder if there may be a more comfortable room aboard this vessel to which we may retire. Warmer? Better lit, even? Oh, thank you. Lead the way. Too kind of you."

The airship was indeed ours, the Chinese thugs either dead or incapacitated. As best we could, we converted the unkempt captain's quarters into a room befitting royalty, though we missed some distasteful postcards that seemed to perversely amuse Her Royal Majesty when she pointed them out. "How the times change! So much variety!"

She seemed in good spirits, despite her capture by brigands, and even requested I pour her a drink from the captain's personal store "to calm the nerves."

Back on deck, I found the *Victoria* flying beside us and one of the airmen was corresponding with the warship by waving flags. The surviving Chinese men were bound together, their injuries tended, but minimally. For our part, all but the shot airmen, my cut and those downed in their Sparrows, we had suffered little harm. In the cabin, one of the airmen had turned the airship about and we were soon in sight of the Exhibition airfield on a slow descent.

The two airships, the *Victoria* dwarfing the captured vessel, touched down simultaneously, although the second we felt the ground beneath us, Admiral Montgomery had quit his vessel and was striding across the field to ours. We lowered a crude gangway for him, and he was greeted at the top by myself, one of his airmen, and the Queen of England. He gave a deep bow and the Queen smiled warmly. "Ah, Elijah. Still taking to the air, I see."

"Your Majesty, I have failed you." His terse, gruff voice sounded repentant as he extended his hand to her. She took it and waved his statement away as he helped her down the gangway.

"Pish posh Elijah, you are apparently the only man of action among this whole navy. Any of those other dullards would have sat on their haunches and waited for orders, but I expect nothing less of you than a vigorous chase." She nodded at the gathered airmen on the ground, who each bowed, but stared at the Queen in stuporous awe. "And your men have taken such good care of me."

Admiral Montgomery nodded. "It was young Norwood Quigley who first alerted us that you'd been taken, Your Majesty."

She turned to me, appraising me. "Ah, yes, the Quigley boy. Son of Sir Hector? I see your family has a habit of collecting knighthoods.

Deservingly so, I suppose." My stomach flopped at this thought. Sir Norwood? But Her Majesty didn't know... "So who was it this time, Elijah? Crazed radicals? Indian mercenaries? I suppose one does make so many enemies running an empire."

"Chinese, Your Majesty, though Quigley says..."

The two turned to me and words failed me. To confess that my father, the knighted Sir Hector, had devised to capture the Queen— I looked up from a study of my feet and opened my mouth to describe the events to Her Majesty, but at that moment saw Ms. Teston striding across the field with the two airmen, Livingston and Hornby, struggling to keep up.

"My eyes must fail me, is that Mave Teston?" the Queen cried with delight. Though Ms. Teston barely greeted the monarch as she approached, and it was the first time I had ever seen her look visibly distressed.

"They got them," she spat. "The bastards took Darius... Mr. Tinker. And Norwood, they got Jing."

My stomach dropped out. Admiral Montgomery stuttered, "Who, Mave?"

But it was I who was able to provide the answer. "My father."

CHAPTER 9

IN WHICH NORWOOD SPEAKS TO HIS FATHER,
PERHAPS FOR THE FIRST TIME

Ms. Teston explained what had happened as we secured the Queen in the Lighter-Than-Air Pavilion, liberated by the British during our airship sojourn. There was still a war going on throughout the Exhibition grounds and, even safe within, rifle fire could be heard outside; though the Queen promised she'd speak to "the dullards," her chief military leaders, and do what little she could to cease hostilities. "At this point in my life, I have had more than enough of war."

Ms. Teston had heard Admiral Montgomery's men, Livingston and Hornby, at the door, attempting to persuade the two guards posted they were to release their prisoner on the orders of Admiral Montgomery. Ms. Teston located a revolver she had stashed away in case of such a situation and blew the lock off, surprising all present. Ever a persistent woman, the guards were disarmed and Ms. Teston made away with the two airmen in tow.

The inventor kept lodgings just around the corner from the T&T workshop, and at her insistence, the trio first made their way there as Ms. Teston wished to make sure Mr. Tinker was safe and sound. Her anxieties were well founded, for just as they turned the corner onto Adelaide, they saw a medium size merchant-class airship preparing to take off from the roof of the building.

"It was the *Halcyon*, Norwood," Ms. Teston explained to me in the Quigley Airships Room. "I watched as your father and some brutish men in his employ were hauling Mr. Tinker and Jing aboard. My inventors told me how they'd stormed the building, demanding, with the Queen's capture, Mr. Tinker be relinquished into their custody for the safety of the Empire."

"A trick..." I muttered. "The Queen was a distraction, another transgression to pin on the Chinese, and so was the fighting. He was after Mr. Tinker the whole time... But why?" I could scarcely imagine what would motivate my father to organize such a thing simply to abduct an eccentric old inventor.

Ms. Teston shook her head, anticipating my thoughts; "You don't know him like I do, Norwood. Darius is the greater genius, more brains and imagination than the combined minds of myself and every inventor in our workshop. Before we met, Darius had been developing weaponry for the American army... devices that would sicken the hardiest of souls. The work... broke him, in a way, and he was looking to escape and turn his attention to inventions that would help rather than harm. If your father and whoever he is working with want Darius for malevolent purposes, to complete his early inventions, I fear the worst."

I was astounded at the thought of Mr. Tinker, the creator of a fantastical mechanical beast like Tickertape the automaton cat, creating such dire weaponry. "And Jing?!"

She shook her head, her face twisted in anger, mirroring my thoughts. "The others said a small Chinese adolescent was taken with Mr. Tinker, and from the street I saw someone struggling against capture. By the time we had gotten to the rooftop, the *Halcyon* had taken off. A perfect prize for the great Sir Hector Quigley, to capture the murderer of von Conrad, likely to turn Jing over to the Prussians himself to curry favour."

"We need to go after them," I insisted. Montgomery and Teston nodded in agreement, to my relief.

"I would offer the services of the *Victoria*," Montgomery jerked his head toward the gargantuan warship behind us, "but my first duty is to protect the Queen until we can get these hostilities under control. Plus, this is the *Halcyon* we'd be going after. A warship would be no match against the fastest airship on the planet."

Ms. Teston grinned, a shrewd look on her face. "Well, perhaps the second fastest... Follow me gentlemen."

We left the Queen under ample guard. She wished us luck, but admitted the exertions of being kidnapped had taken their toll and that it was time for a nap. Flanked by a few of Montgomery's airmen, Ms. Teston led us to one of the smaller Quigley airships hangars on the field, completely closed and locked up, unlike the others. She tore a panel off of the lower section of the hangar door and reached inside, jigged with some of the mechanics and the large automatic hangar door began to slide open. She flicked a lever within and a number of electric lights inside twinkled to life, a sight that never ceased to amaze me.

What we found confused me for a moment. The airship appeared to be my father's, the *Halcyon*, but I soon noticed subtle differences in the design. I could even see an updated navigation system on the underbelly of the airship. The hull was a rich, sturdy cedar, the alloys and materials used in the structure holding the ballonets was all coloured a beautiful, metallic gold.

"The *Halcyon II*," Ms. Teston smiled, gesturing at the new airship as she led us aboard. "The first in a new generation of airships. A feat of engineering wonder—maximized aerodynamic design. A little project by myself and some of the top engineers at the workshop, commissioned by your father last year. We were going to unveil it at the end of the first week's celebrations, but given the circumstances..." Ms. Teston smirked, "I think we can push the maiden voyage ahead of schedule."

Admiral Montgomery, the two airmen—Livingston and Hornby— and I marvelled at the sleek design and gorgeous detailing of the *Halcyon II*. With a nod from Montgomery, the airmen set about fully opening the hangar door. Meanwhile, Ms. Teston went below deck to prepare the engine, and I followed her to help however I could.

"The only problem," she called over the engines sighing to life, "is we need a pilot. I understand the mechanics and could manage, but I've only ever piloted a larger airship on a handful of less urgent occasions."

Admiral Montgomery scratched his beard. "I specialize in warship-class vessels, myself, and I'm rarely piloting those on my own." His airmen as well were mostly trained in piloting small fighter or stealth-class airships or working together aboard larger vessels. We had the airship almost ready to depart and were deliberating over who would attempt to pilot this advanced vessel when we heard a great crash from the airship field.

Outside, the mangled wreck of the Sparrow was a horror to observe. Steam poured out of the machine in a great rush, the envelopes on the sides flapping in their death throes; one was completely deflated, the other following suit. The body was obscured in the mist shooting out of the small engine... None could have survived such a wreck, I thought to myself, when a figure rose from the steamy veil, staggering slightly on the wreckage. The four of us ran forward to help this poor soul, but out from the steam jumped a grinning, slightly dishevelled Laurence Daley, Lady of the *Victoria*. He dusted his hands off, grease staining the pristine material of his coat. When he noticed the admiral, he came to attention.

"At ease, Airman," Admiral Montgomery commanded, undisguised awe in his voice.

"Nice flying weather," Lady exclaimed, his grin as bright as the sunshine. "I had to land and make emergency repairs, Admiral. Apologies for the damage to the Sparrow, sir."

Admiral Montgomery waved this off. "How would you like an upgrade, Daley?" He motioned for the young airman to follow him, and we all returned into the hangar. "I've been told you flew with a Caribbean smuggler vessel in your youth. You must be used to merchant class airships, like this one."

The admiral motioned at the *Halcyon II*, gleaming gold from the rays of sunshine that streamed into the hangar. Lady walked a little nearer to the new airship, appraising it. He padded over to the starboard side, looking it up and down, before he turned to the four of us and gave a dramatic shrug. "Well, she doesn't look like much, but I suppose we can get her into the air."

And so, in a matter of seconds and with little ceremony, I became Captain Norwood Quigley of the *Halcyon II*. I suppose this made sense as my experience aboard airships was matched only by Lady's, who'd been flying with his family's own (illicit) Caribbean-based business since he was a child. While everyone seemed to defer to me without question, I assumed this was because the vessel was Quigley property and so, in an indirect way, belonged to me.

What a strange position to be in. As we prepared for takeoff, Admiral Montgomery entrusted Livingston, Hornby and Daley into my service—I protested, but they had all volunteered—while he went and sorted out this mess at the Exhibition before bidding us adieu with: "Good hunting."

With his departure I now had Ms. Teston, Lady and the two airmen before me, awaiting orders. My very own crew.

"Oh!" I scratched my chin. "Lady, to the bridge and prepare for takeoff. Livingston... Oh, you're Hornby, uh, secure the rigging! Make sure everything is... rigged. Livingston, yes? Good! Release and secure the spring lines and retract the gangway, then stand by the bridge for further commands. Um... Ms. Teston?"

"Mave, please" she smirked. "I believe we're beyond formalities."

"Mave then, would you be so kind as to see to the engine and make sure everything is prepared for takeoff?"

"Aye, Captain!" she gave a grinning salute. My four crew members went about their tasks, so I boarded the ship to prepare myself for her maiden voyage.

I was at once immediately familiar with the vessel but found much had changed. I'd travelled on the *Halcyon* times beyond counting in my childhood, throughout the New World and even one voyage across the Atlantic. In a way, I had served as a crew member with Hector Sr. as captain. I found that much of the improvements for the *Halcyon II* were in material and design, and probably in an improved differential steam-powered engine as Mave had hinted at. I could tell just by looking at her the *Halcyon II* would give the older sister, as the saying goes, a run for her money.

Lady had made himself comfortable in the bridge on the bow of the upper deck. The bridge's design was much improved and streamlined and would have increased visibility when we were up in the sky, in addition to a modern navigating system, a vast improvement over the decades-old *Halcyon*, which still used point men. Lady flipped switches and pulled levers as if he'd been flying it his entire life, easing the airship to life.

The large control board seemed overwhelming, and I said as much, but Lady snorted at my ignorance. "Maybe if it's your first time on anything other than a bicycle... Look, this is the onboard point-to-point system. pretty smart if the weather's clear. It reflects the light from whatever's below us and projects it onto the scrim here."

He flipped a switch and a beam of light shot out of the panel onto a piece of canvas stretched over the console. I realized it was the dirt ground beneath the ship. "Means the pilot can navigate without point men. Makes things a bit more efficient than shouting out a window. All of these gauges show wind speed and direction, air pressure, engine power." He pointed to a number of strange apparatuses on the board.

"Wow!" I exclaimed. "Still seems... complicated!"

"If anything, it makes things less fun," Lady scoffed just as one of the airmen—was it Livingston, or Hornby?—walked into the bridge.

"Yes, Hornby? Sorry, Livingston... all the spring lines are retracted? Very good, I will let everyone know we are casting off."

I moved toward the door, but Lady cleared his throat. "Captain? Why not just make the announcement here?" He pointed to a brass apparatus on the board, a sort of tube fitted with an electrical device, a number of switches below. He instructed me to flip a switch and speak.

"Hello?" My voice resonated through the airship with an electric crackle, loud enough to make me squeak a little in surprise, which was in turn amplified. Lady and Livingston chuckled at my expense, though I took it in stride, grumbling, "Prepare for take-off."

Despite the excitement of the maiden voyage, there was a sense of urgency to our preparations and take-off. We slid smoothly out of the hangar and were underway in a matter of moments. Mave, who appeared above deck, assuring me all was well in the engine room, mirrored my own emotions. She and I stood together on the bow deck outside the bridge, gazing into the horizon.

Mave had observed the *Halcyon* fly eastward, the direction we would follow. "My guess," I said, my eyes scanning the horizon for our sister airship, "is they're making for the Quigley Airships depot in Montreal to prepare for a cross-Atlantic flight."

Mave nodded. "You think they mean to make for England?"

"The *Halcyon* doesn't carry the navigational equipment for the journey, and it's either Montreal or St. John's where they could get one quickly. Plus, the direction... follow the St. Lawrence River up to Newfoundland and be on their way." We consulted with Lady, who adjusted our course to cut across Lake Ontario, keeping land in sight on our left, hoping to shave off a bit of the lost distance if they were following the shoreline.

The maiden voyage of the *Halcyon II* was a wonder. The speed of the vessel, the way it cut through the air, left one almost breathless. Even Lady was impressed, saying how in spite of her size, the *Halcyon II* was almost as fast as a Sparrow.

It was about an hour before we spotted another airship on the same course as us, and a tense hour it was. The airship was closer to land

and a little higher than us. The speed and course of the *Halcyon II*, for indeed we were cutting off the other ship, meant that we were catching up, though the superior piloting of the other craft by Sir Hector kept her just out of reach.

Mave, the two airmen and I stood on the port side of the main deck, ready to board, as we were moments away from being neck and neck with the *Halcyon* thanks to Lady's genius maneuvering. Lady had explained the builds of the ships were so similar, the *Halcyon II* only slightly slimmer, that he would be able to get them side-by-side.

"We board," I called out over the roaring wind. Mave and the two men nodded in response. "They have two of our very dear friends, one an innocent man condemned to die without our intervention, the other abducted for dark purposes. While the airmen under his command likely don't know what they're tangled up in, my father, Sir Hector, will do whatever he can to keep his captives. Be wary and... well, thank you."

The *Halcyon* managed to stay just ahead of us, so while we consulted on the deck about what to do, Lady, without warning, used a similar trick from the Sparrow but with the agile *Halcyon II*. We felt a sudden dip and a sickening moment of plummet before the pilot found a stronger air current. This, plus the momentum of the dip had us inching closer into formation beside the pursued airship.

As we glided up alongside the *Halcyon*, we could hear shouts from her deck. I motioned for everyone to take cover.

I poked my head out from around the corner of the rear cabin and a rifle shot rang out. The corner of the structure by my head exploded, showering the deck with splinters. Livingston and Hornby took the opportunity to throw themselves from where they were concealed and leap onto the deck of the *Halcyon* without a moment's hesitation. As I gathered my wits and rounded the corner, I saw one of the men wrestle the rifle from the hands of the marksman who'd shot at me, while the other airman traded blows with one of the hostile crew members on deck.

The *Halcyon* veered portside, pulling down and away from our vessel. This took some maneuvering on the part of Lady to bring the ships side-by-side again.

In the meantime, Mave had pulled herself up to stand on our vessel's railing, bracing herself against some rigging line with one hand, her revolver in the other. As we again closed the distance, I watched as the inventor, quite a crack shot, felled another airman who had come out from the lower deck. Mave and I threw ourselves onto the deck of the *Halcyon* when a jump seemed possible. As we did, the *Halcyon* slammed into the sister ship, gave a mighty shudder, and began to descend further.

Mave and the two airmen engaged with our aggressors, about a half dozen airmen of my father's employ, men who would have once greeted me familiarly, although a few were already downed or seemed hesitant to attack. They were, after all, labourers, not soldiers. I had to make a quick decision, my father would be on the bridge, Jing and Mr. Tinker below decks, or I could stay and fight the airmen.

I, of course, chose the coward's route. Dodging the fighting on deck, I ducked through the door to the lower decks. I took the steps three at a time and, through some extraordinary strength that couldn't have been my own, kicked open the door to the hold. What I found there shocked me.

One of the airmen was keeled over on the floor, clutching his delicates, his face bloodied. The other younger airman kneeled, a look of distress and embarrassment plain on his face, and fear as well for the pistol pressed against his temple. Over his shoulder the weapon was held at arm's length by Jing, who nursed a split lip and a swollen eye.

"The door wasn't locked, you idiot," he stated, a smile of relief and affection spreading across his face.

As I closed the space, Jing quickly explained the men had been playing a little rough, though became distracted when the shouts and combat began above. He had taken advantage of their inattention. I should have known my dear friend would be no damsel in distress. I wished we had even a moment that I could take him in my arms.

"I know this man." I looked on Jing's prisoner, a young, swarthy, dark-haired boy no older than us; a gentle, if not dull, airman. "Mr. Perry, isn't it?"

He scowled. "Can't believe I was taken by a bloody catamite," Perry muttered, avoiding my eyes. Jing smirked and the young airman continued. "I was just following Sir Quigley—your father's—orders, Mr. Quigley... Norwood... sir."

"Did he come readily?" I nodded at Jing, speaking to the lad. "Did he not protest? Can't you tell abduction when you see it? See to your colleague." Perry looked ashamed and stood tentatively, scowling at Jing, who returned the look, pistol still at the ready. The young airman dragged his friend to the corner of the hold and began to clean the man's wounds.

"Mr. Tinker?" I asked, and Jing nodded into the far corner of the room, a concerned expression clouding his face.

The genius inventor was a pitiable sight. He was hunched in the corner, between two stacks of crates, two machine components clenched so tight in his hands the skin of his palms were raw and bleeding. His face was like a corpse's, his eyes sunken and empty.

Jing came over and examined the inventor as well. "He's been like that since we got to the roof of the workshop. We were working on plans for an electrical radio transmitter when your father came in and demanded he follow, 'for his own safety.' Mr. Tinker refused, and your father set his men on me until the inventor relented, but every step out of the workshop seemed an agony, and he wouldn't budge when we came to the stairs to the roof. When one of the men lifted him, he fainted clean away. He's been like this ever since."

I could hear that Mr. Tinker muttering something and I leaned in. I couldn't make it out at first, it sounded like gibberish, "England fragile mister crow thirty-three high street London England fragile mister crow..."

I leaned down and, gentle as I could be, pulled the machine parts out of his bleeding hands. Jing tore strips of cloth off of his shirt and I wrapped Mr. Tinker's hands. That would at least staunch the bleeding for now, but the cuts would need cleaning later. He offered no complaint; in fact, he didn't seem to register my presence.

"Mr. Tinker?" I whispered. He didn't speak but gave a slight nod. "I wonder if you'd like to go up onto the deck and get some air."

The older man gave a disturbed shudder. "No," he said, his voice little more than a weak exhale. "I expect I wouldn't."

Jing gave me a worried glance. I continued, "Ms. Teston... Mave is here. Would you like to see her?"

He nodded. "Mave's here. That would be lovely."

I turned to run and find Mave, however, Jing caught my arm. We locked eyes and then embraced, his lips finding mine. One of our captured airmen scoffed at the sight, but we paid him no mind. For a moment I held him in my arms, and this braced me for any war and ruin to come.

After a tender moment shared, we turned our attention back to Mr. Tinker, who continued to mutter his strange gibberish. I leaned in and followed his eyes to a label on one of the crates beside him.

> *Mr. Crowe,*
> *33 High St.*
> *London, England*
> *FRAGILE*

I stood and wrenched the crate top open. Within were a number of light bulbs and electrical components of strange designs, packed in hay, stacked carefully. If there was some meaning, it eluded me.

"You should stay with him while I go and see if Ms. Teston is... available." I went to move, but Jing grabbed me and pulled me in for a final quick kiss.

"Had no idea we were on the love boat," I heard Perry mutter as I moved to the door. Jing advanced on him, pistol in hand, but I turned back and looked down on Perry.

"Show him the mercy he wouldn't have shown us," I proffered.

Perry appeared freshly shamed, although Jing shot me a gloomy look. "You're no fun, Norwood."

Above deck I found Hornby standing over the incapacitated, injured or dead crew members of the *Halcyon*. We were victorious in capturing the *Halcyon*, although my father was conspicuously missing from the crew.

I found Mave and Livingston at the door to the bridge at the bow of the airship. They were throwing their weight against the door but gave up their efforts as I approached.

"Locked up tighter than a nun in a convent," Mave roared over the wind. "Won't budge an inch. We even tried shooting it off. He must have reinforced it as if he was expecting to defend himself from within."

I pointed above to the inches of crawl space between the semi-rigid structure keeping the ship aloft and the roof of the bridge cabin. "I'm just small enough, I'll crawl through the front and smash my way in through a window. Swing in, easy enough."

"Like hell, you'll fall to your death," Mave cried. "We're flying on an incline at top speed."

"Give me a boost, that's an order," I commanded, not even sure of the idea myself, but there was little else we could do. "Mave, Mr. Tinker is below with Jing, unharmed but out of sorts."

Mave frowned as she and Livingston linked their hands for me to use as a foothold. "He can't abide being outside the workshop... His nerves."

"See to him," I grunted as I hauled myself up, wriggling into the precious few inches of space I had, though the whistling wind drowned out any reply.

My brother and I used to scramble up the sides of the *Halcyon*'s cabins to hide in the crawl spaces, driving our minders and our mother batty, though even then the spaces were a tight fit. Now I was crushed beneath the thick canvas envelope of the structure and the bridge roof, wriggling along. I inched my way to the front of the ship, my eyes watering from the freezing air I was exposed to. I could see we were on an incline, a rather steep one at that, and for some reason, the *Halcyon* had ended up far from shore over Lake Ontario and seemed intent on testing her nautical capabilities as she was on a steady course into the water.

I squirmed myself sideways so I was parallel with the front windows of the bridge, the windows that peer over the bow of the airship. With a quick prayer to whatever unfair deities were above, I reached up and clawed at some rigging on the envelope for dear life. I swung a leg out, then another, and my body followed. I kicked off of the bridge's roof and, with the most powerful swing I could manage given the awkward positioning, I threw myself off the roof of the *Halcyon* and hung in the whipping wind for what felt like an eternity before I crashed through the window and tumbled over the control panel, onto the floor of the bridge.

A moment of blackness before the realization hit me. My reckless airborne gymnastics had been successful, and my arms and legs seemed to work. I had not, against all odds, been sliced to ribbons.

I opened my eyes to find my father standing over me.

"Norwood," he said in an unreadable tone, holding his hand out to me, but I recoiled and crawled away, attempting to right myself against the control panel, small glass shards sticking into my hands. Now that I could control my limbs, for the most part, I realized I had a number of cuts, and my legs shook violently as I managed to stand before him, bracing myself against the panel, brushing glass off myself.

Father smiled, though the kindness I was used to in his face was gone, in its place something cold, automaton. "I'm impressed, Norwood. Impressed and relieved, of course. Here I was thinking you and your brother were completely incapable of dauntlessness and athletic skill. I suppose a little of me rubbed off on you after all."

There was a tone of jest in his voice, but the dig came off instead as cruel; it stung, despite my anger boiling up at my father. Hector and I had always tried to prove ourselves to Father, though we both failed in our own, unique ways—my creativity and non-competitive nature, Hector's licentiousness and sensual indulgences.

"You didn't seem to mind including Hector in your scheming," I replied, snarling like a cornered animal. I had never spoken to my father like this, but something had snapped in me after my near-death experience hanging off the bow of the *Halcyon*, and his treatment of

Jing and Mr. Tinker.

His lip curled in amusement. "Ah, so Hector ended up finding you after all. I figured he'd gone off to drink his life away in some beer hall. Yes, Hector played his part. I almost had you as a cog in the grand workings, but I never anticipated you'd be so challenging. I just assumed you'd be content fiddling with your camera."

"Well, we managed to get the Queen, and catch up with you to free Mr. Tinker and Jing, camera and all," I threw the accomplishments at his feet like a gauntlet, my face flushing with anger.

Father nodded. "The Queen too! I figured after a few hours someone would notice she was gone and send the entire airship navy after her. Maybe even find her in Vancouver or Shanghai. That would have made an amusing headline for your paper."

"While you slink away with Mr. Tinker, unnoticed," I completed the thought.

He smiled the same, chilling smile. "And here you are. No, I shouldn't be moderate in my praise. You've shown extraordinary skill and resourcefulness to do what you've done and to get where you are. Norwood, my son, you're a true Quigley. I'm proud of you."

I was stunned. Words failed me. My parents had always supported me in my endeavours; my mother especially had been enthusiastic about my artistic pursuits. My father, on the other hand, had been more reticent. I had always feared he was secretly disappointed in what I'd made of my life. Hector Jr. and I both had always striven to make my father proud, it was what we wanted most—to impress the man who impressed us above all else.

And now that he offered it to me, I found I didn't want it. I knew who he was and what he was capable of. His pride in me meant nothing; it even repulsed me.

"I never thought this moment would come," he continued, "but I'm so proud that it has. Norwood, together we can accomplish great things. We can change the world."

"How?!" I snarled. "By manipulating nationalists and soldiers of every stripe to shoot up the Exhibition grounds? To start a war?"

"Indeed," he said in a tone he would use when lecturing Hector and I. "As a writer, you know better than anyone how well fear and war capture the minds of people. How well they'll pay for it. They gave you the life you've enjoyed, you know. Weapons, warriors, warships. Now think of that on a global scale. The vain Prussians, the proud Chinese, the noble British," he spat each as if it were the ultimate insult. "Now imagine if Quigley Airships, or at least companies owned by Quigley Airships, supplied them all, flying ammunition and uniforms and rations to all the corners of the world. And all that money would flow between armament suppliers, the military, engineers of weaponry like Ms. Teston and Mr. Tinker."

I was sickened, aghast. "War for profit. That's what this is all about."

He scoffed, taking a step toward the door. Someone was pounding on the other side. He couldn't expect his men had freed themselves, could he? "War has always been about profit of one kind or another, Norwood. Don't be a fool. But no, that is not what this entire business is about. As one who is uninitiated, I wouldn't expect you to understand that this is about more than just petty cash, stupid boys playing soldier with their guns and old men carving up maps. That there is something bigger than all of us... Ah, but I'm saying too much, and we have so little time and an eager guest.

"Your choice, Norwood. Abandon the misfits on the other side of this door and come with me. Contribute to something greater. This is your chance to truly shape the world."

I couldn't fathom what he meant. He must have seen the rage in my eyes, for he merely sighed, took a deep breath and then whirled about. We both moved at once.

Father threw the door open, and as I lunged for him, I saw the face of a confused Jing falling into the room. I, by some miracle, knocked my father off balance, pushing him with some force against the remaining glass of bridge windows. They cracked behind him. My goal: to liberate the pistol he had drawn from within his coat. I wrestled against my father and heard Jing behind me cry out my name. Then two gunshots rang out.

Jing's cry of pain was distraction enough for my father to throw me off of him, and I dropped down beside my companion, clambering to shield him from further harm. He was holding a smoking revolver—Hector Jr.'s, liberated from my brother that morning—in his hand that had gone off simultaneous with my father's pistol. Jing had fallen prone, a great deal of blood welling up from a wound, though I couldn't tell where it was in the chaos.

I looked up and saw my father had moved to sit on the window ledge I had crashed through moments before, clutching his side, a bloom of blood welling up through the material of his coat under his hand. He had dropped the pistol and sat, calm, wind whipping about his hair and scarf. He considered me with a curious look on his face.

"A pity," he said, neutral, as if making an observation about a news item, unaffected by whatever pain he felt, "to kill a son with so much unrealized potential..."

With that, he leaned over backwards and tumbled out of the *Halcyon*. Gone.

Livingston, or Hornby, ran into the cabin and, when I waved him away from us, he went to the controls to right the ship's course. By this point, Jing had recovered from the initial shock of being shot—he had not died, a promising sign, despite all the blood.

He managed to sit up and we found the wound, a nasty looking chunk of flesh missing from his upper left arm. I pulled off my coat and used it to staunch the blood as best we could.

Mave emerged from the lower deck with her arm around Mr. Tinker, who looked prepared to faint, and he kept repeating the muttered address as if it was some delirious incantation. Mave consulted with Hornby (or Livingston) at the control panel, and I attended to Jing's wound, perhaps offering a kiss or two for his comfort as he swore in pain and fear.

"I hate to interrupt," Mave growled from the control panel, sending Livingston (or Hornby) out of the cabin to check something, "but we've got an issue."

My father, it seems, had changed course drastically. He had started us on a slow but eventual descent into Lake Ontario, then had torn out essential steering mechanisms, locking us onto our course. Repairs were impossible without tools, parts and time, none of which we had.

Hornby (or Livingston) returned, reporting the *Halcyon II* was on our tail, but we had a good head start into the lake and were steadily picking up speed. Our watery demise seemed certain.

"Boat boat boat," we heard from the corner. The four of us turned to see Mr. Tinker, his eyes clenched shut, muttering and rubbing his brow.

I left Jing propped up and went to the other man. "There are no boats as far as we can see, Mr. Tinker," I said gently as I could though an edge of fear was plain in my voice.

He grabbed me violently by the collar, his eyes still clenched shut, and shook me like mad. "BOAT!" he screamed. "BOAT BOAT BOAT CUT BOAT!"

Ms. Teston rushed over and pulled her colleague off of me, but the shaking and screaming had done it. "Turn it into a boat!" I cried out, and everyone looked at me as if Tinker had shaken the sense out of me. "Cut the aft lines first, allow the aft of the *Halcyon* to hit the water, then cut the mid and bowlines. The upper structure will fall off and the airship will be turned into a water-ship!"

Ms. Teston nodded, though still looked at me as if I was mad. "Airships—least of all one this old—aren't built for water landings. She'll take on water and sink."

"All we need is a few minutes," I said, standing, preparing for action. "Maybe even less. Lady can bring the *Halcyon II* in close enough and open the loading door and we can get everyone off. We're going to do it." I moved to the door asking, or, rather like a captain, commanding Ms. Teston to prepare the injured or incapacitated for a speedy disembarking.

I leaned down and kissed Jing on the forehead on my way out of the bridge. He grabbed my hand and held me there a moment, looking into my eyes, then nodded and I was off to save us, come hell or high water—one seemed just as likely as the next.

"Listen up men," I called out on the deck, standing beside my airmen, Livingston and Hornby. The conscious members of the *Halcyon*'s crew were gathered in the centre of the deck, looking equal parts sullen and battered. "We have moments to act before the *Halcyon* completes its final voyage to the bottom of Lake Ontario with us on it." I outlined my plan and the fashion it would be carried out, and commanded five of the more unscathed of the surviving *Halcyon* crew—including young Airman Perry—to help me cut the aft and midlines, while Livingston and Hornby would take care of the bowlines.

Perry agreed immediately, perhaps some desire to atone for his part in my father's plans apparent, though one of his compatriots grumbled, "What of Sir Hector?"

"My father..." I swallowed, almost unable to admit it to the men who had flown with him, some of them for as long as a Quigley had owned an airship, "has abandoned ship. And abandoned us to oblivion." The airmen before me seemed dubious, and there were some further mutinous grumblings. "There are those of us who followed him, believing him a great and honourable man... myself chiefly among them. He was no more than a scheming con man. A lying, deceitful opportunist. I offer you the chance to make up for the damage you've done working with him..." I looked to each man, who seemed to consider this opportunity. "And save your own skins in the process, as well."

They looked to one another, before Perry jumped up at attention, "I'm with you Norwood," and others joined him.

We distributed daggers, blades and saws between the six of us, and I directed them to their posts, as there were six main lines to cut. I ran to the port bowline with Perry taking the line opposite to me on starboard. I peaked my head around the back cabin; we were coming up on the water fast, at an increasingly perilous angle. I glanced back beyond the aft of the ship, the *Halcyon II* speeding after us, though still a distance behind. I prayed Lady would make haste, take our cue and save our forsaken souls.

As we neared the surface, enormous waves lapping at the underside of the *Halcyon*, whipping up a cold, chilling spray off the water, I bellowed as loud as I could muster, "Brace yourselves! Aft! Cut the lines!"

Perry and I slid our blades through the ropes and ducked as the aft lines and ancillary rigging snapped. The deck gave a violent lurch, swinging down from the back of the airship. The thrusters uncoupled from the engine lines with a hissing pop. There was a terrible shudder as the aft splashed in the water. We clung for our lives. I attempted to stagger forward, toward the others, screaming, "Midlines! Cut!"

More snapping and the *Halcyon*'s envelope began to drift, the rear thrusters no longer tethered as they should be. The body of the ship was lurching with each swell of the lake and I fell to my knees, clutching the railing. "Bow lines!" I shrieked, my voice going hoarse, "CUT!"

There was a final twang as the envelope shot away from the body of the *Halcyon*, which listed off to the starboard side and crashed into the water, the thrusters hissing steam as they slammed into the murk. With a great groan, the body of the airship, suspended until now below the envelope, was supported only by water and the loose structure of the airship's body, buffeted by the Great Lake. Terrible waves crashed over the deck, and it was clear from the angle of the *Halcyon*'s deck that we were already taking on water.

"Group up at the pilot's cabin!" I cried out over the roar of wind, water and the terrible roar of our failing engine below deck. The airmen and I scrambled across the slippery deck, listening to the pops and cracks below us as the airship's hull began to come apart. Mave cradled a now unconscious Mr. Tinker in her arms, and Livingston (or Hornby, possibly) supported Jing, who looked pale from his injury, and concerned for my safety as I clambered forward over the deck, which rocked violently with each swell of the water.

As we clung to the railings and were splashed with icy water, we glanced upwards at a shadow that blotted out the sun. The *Halcyon II* descended, passing over us once, before skimming the waves and turning about by the skill of Lady's incredible airborne dexterity. Just as I'd hoped, the pilot lowered the loading door into the hold.

"On!" I screamed at the group who huddled together down the deck from me as I continued to pull myself along by the railing, still not close enough. Ms. Teston went first, leaping onto the extended platform and scrambling up with Tinker slung over her shoulder. Livingston and Hornby hauled Jing and another of the injured airmen up, and the others climbed in ones and pairs.

Soon only Perry and I remained aboard the *Halcyon*, the aft dipping below the water at a perilous angle, waves lapping at our ankles. I looked back over my shoulder to him as I neared the lowered door and saw him scrambling across the soaked deck when a mighty crack split between his feet, and he slipped sideways as the deck of the *Halcyon* was rent apart beneath him and a cloud of steam erupted from this hellish maw.

"Help!" he sobbed as he clawed at the deck, his legs dangling in the air with nothing but the submerged lower deck beneath him. If he didn't slip and fall in and get dragged under with the floundering airship, a wave would swell and send the jags of the split deck back at him, through his midsection.

I crawled across the deck toward him, more groans and cracks coming from under us. I grabbed one arm and hauled with all my strength, and we managed to get all his limbs back on the solid but ever disintegrating deck. I pushed him ahead of me crying, "Go!" over and over with a few swear words thrown in for good measure. I watched as he made the leap onto the *Halcyon II*, but just as I reached the railing, about to throw myself aboard behind him, there came a terrible snapping beneath my feet, and my world suddenly went sideways as I slammed into the now vertical deck before sliding into the frigid waters of Lake Ontario.

I thrashed about the freezing waters, battered about by debris that I attempted to cling to all the same. I managed to flail my arms above water but was knocked below by a wave, or perhaps a section of the sinking ship. The water was so cold it was a shock to my system, now flooding my mouth and nose. I could feel the pull of the sinking airship beneath me as sure as if I was shackled to its wreckage. Then, a pull from above, two arms around me. Then, blackness.

CHAPTER 10

IN WHICH THERE IS AN END
TO THE ADVENTURE AT THE NEW WORLD EXHIBITION

The world around me was all in darkness, though occasionally a strange light would flicker by, blinding me a moment and gone as fast as it had appeared. Sound came back next, hushed whispers, a child crying somewhere else, though everything was distorted. I wondered if this was my final resting place below Lake Ontario. Some watery hell.

Next, my body began to return to me, less pleasant than sight or sound. I was lying in a bed, but even still I ached everywhere. I started bawling from the pain, crying out for my mother, and a woman appeared dressed all in white with one of the blinding lights. She whispered to me, told me to say a prayer to God above, all was well and I was alive, as she helped me to drink a bitter substance. Whatever it was worked wonders because I sunk back into the darkness.

I entered the world again, barely surfacing above the effects of the narcotic, though feeling a little better. With the pain dulled, I could at least stand to move my head about.

A private hospital room. A man stood at the foot of my bed, looking down on me, shrouded in darkness. At first I feared it was my father come to finish the job of killing me; one can still drown a man on land, given enough water. He spoke and, while his voice was familiar, it was not that of Sir Hector Quigley.

"Rest, Mr. Quigley," he said in little more than a whisper. "You are safe and all is taken care of, for now. You have righted a good many wrongs."

"J... Jing?" I asked him, but the narcotic, whatever the nurse had given me, seemed to grip at my mind once again, and I sunk back down into the black.

Mother visited daily, as did Mave, along with Lady. Even my sheepish and haggard looking brother, Hector Jr., stopped in to see me once, though he did little more than mutter, "Sorry Norwood, get well soon," before scurrying off. Young Perry, the dark-haired airman from the *Halcyon* was also my routine visitor, and the young man could scarcely talk to me, he was so in awe of the way I had come to his rescue, but he promised he would make it up to me one day.

Their company—even the brief visit from my brother—was a great comfort, for they each knew what Jing meant to me.

Now that we had some time and privacy, and her dear friend Mr. Tinker was safe and secure, Mave—as she continued to insist I call her—and I had time to talk. She explained to me, while I recovered in St. Michael's Hospital, how she had been corresponding on plans with von Conrad and Ambassador Chen for the first three international

Teston & Tinker workshops and apprenticeship programs—in London, Munich and Peking—sharing science and engineering skills between the three nations. They would trade ideas, experiments and designs, fostering relations between great minds spanning the globe, and then set up more workshops as the program expanded. She believed someone had overheard of the plans somewhere during their formulation, as they soon suspected their correspondences were being intercepted.

"Even when we brought the proposals through official channels, we met with resistance on all sides," she explained, sitting next to my bed in a sky-blue bicycle suit, gazing out the window at a rainy, early summer day. "The Chinese military isn't fond of sharing their engineers. The Prussians feared further erosion of their tenuous empire if they loosened a hold on their geniuses and trade secrets. Worst of all, though, were the British. They spoke of treason, of undermining the Empire, the influence of foreign powers. Bah!"

Though the Chinese were suspicious of the Prussians, and vice versa, Mave thought she'd tackle both the diplomats in person during the opening ceremonies, first with von Conrad—a liberal, anti-militaristic, open-minded ambassador. She thought their meeting had been kept a secret, but then Hector Jr. had caught up with her on the *Hanlan's Pride* that night.

"He asked if he could speak with me about a business proposition," she recounted, scowling. "He was rather intoxicated, and I dismissed him, saying I was on my way to an appointment. He inquired after von Conrad's health, and I threatened to throw the little sot overboard, but he said, 'the British Empire protects their own and not those who betray her.' He told me if I had my dear friend's best interests at heart, I would look after British interests, exclusively."

She shook her head. "He could have been reading a script prepared by Willard himself, that man is a terrible propagandist. Though he struck a nerve. I don't have many people in this world. My family is dead, there are only two people they could threaten whose lives I hold above my own. One is safe in New York…"

"The other is Mr. Tinker," I finished her thought, and she smiled, though her eyes were sad. After an anxious and sleepless night in the hospital, a night where he begged without ending to return to his workshop, Mave had escorted him back the next morning. She reported once within he was back to work, contented. He had apparently been mumbling about designing an airship that could land in the water, stabilize itself and be turned into a boat. The workshop had returned to work much as before, though they engaged private security agents—human, not automaton—to guard against further intrusions or kidnappings, at least for the time being.

"I told your brother what he could do with his threats, but of course the plan to delay me had worked and things had already been set in motion. Von Conrad dead, and Jing…"

"Framed, set to die," I said, unable to keep the melancholy from my voice, though I did not want her to soften discussion of my dear companion to me. I'd had Ms. Teston confirm that, yes, the panel doors on the *Pride* did exist, hidden behind armoires used to block the doors to split the suites up and allow for more individual rooms during the opening ceremonies. The backs of the armoires in 902A and 902B had been removed then replaced at some point, and so my father had slunk through, murdered von Conrad, and slunk back and out the door to meet me before Jing had even exited the water closet. How, after all, could anyone suspect one man murdered another from his own room?

"Of course nothing Jing said would convince the authorities he was anything but a Chinese agent," she paused for a moment as the nurse came in with my lunch. "The suspicion was already there, your father just made sure it was confirmed. And then you saved him..."

"He saved me enough times," I said, thinking of the way Jing's arms had wrapped around me beneath the waves of Lake Ontario.

"He was the first to realize what had happened as the *Halcyon* sunk," she went on. "After we got Perry aboard, we all rushed to the side to see the *Halcyon* splitting apart, to see you struggling to stay above the water and debris. Then Jing leapt from the loading door. He had secured some rope around his waist, the genius. By some miracle, he missed the wreckage. There was a moment where he disappeared and I was sure you were both lost. Then, we saw him pulling at the end of the rope, his uninjured arm wrapped around you. We hauled with all our might. He had just enough strength to get you up onto the airship but by then... he'd already lost so much blood... It was incredible, the way that boy flew, you'd think he was born with wings." Mave shook her head.

I had tears in my eyes, but somehow managed to return her astonishment with a smile. "I suppose he conquered his fear of heights. To think the day before he'd never even been on an airship."

We sat in sad contemplation of the events of the past week. A fragile peace had been struck between England, Prussia and China, mostly thanks to Ambassador Chen and Admiral Montgomery, though the Queen apparently had some cutting words for her generals and admirals at an afternoon tea following her safe return. The city had closed down the Exhibition so they could fix most of the bullet holes and mop up some of the blood but had gotten back underway, more popular for the battle that had raged over Toronto's fairgrounds.

Most amazing, and despite Ms. Teston's public protestations, the official story was that a group of independent Chinese radicals—with no affiliation to the Chinese government or military, the papers stressed—had taken advantage of the Queen's visit and lax security to kidnap her and demand ransom. This did not explain how a half-dozen of the Queen's personal guards had simply vanished without a trace at the hands of petty sky pirates. We suspected collusion with my father and whoever else was involved in the plot.

Admiral Montgomery, for his part, was praised for his heroism but admonished by the fleet admiral for disobeying direct orders and flying a grounded airship. While the circumstances were extraordinary, he and his men were to be investigated by an independent military commission—it appeared as if someone with ties to the airship navy was out for blood.

In an uncharacteristic bout of extreme disorganization, Admiral Montgomery had given his entire surviving crew shore leave all at once, and they had disappeared from Toronto... Everyone except Lady, who had taken up residence on the *Halcyon II*—Lady apparently referred to it as "my ship" now. Mave asserted that someone involved wished to tarnish the spotless reputation of Montgomery's career for his interference in the Queen's kidnapping and ceasing hostilities.

I couldn't will myself to care much about the happenings beyond the hospital. I missed Jing. As I recovered under the dictatorial care of the St. Michael's nurses from my accumulated injuries, all I could think about was Jing's smiling face, his lacerating wit, his arms around me.

During my recovery, I had the pleasure of visiting a fellow patient at St. Michael's, a military secretary to the British Crown of some influence. He'd been injured by the mechanical monster, Mr. Shackles, when I'd had the idea to sic his own bloodhound on him after harassing Jing and I for the better part of the day. He had yet to recover sufficiently to be transported back to England. I made sure we had some time alone.

The man was in a pathetic state. His four limbs were splinted and mummified in casts in various places, his jaw was wired shut in a particularly uncomfortable looking device, his neck held in place in a similar fashion. His suit had been switched out for a grimy hospital smock, his golden hair limp and oily, handsome face gaunt and bruised, eyes sunken—I assumed he had not slept well since his injury—though they went wide with fear and hatred the moment I appeared in the doorway.

"Are you well, Mr. Willard?" I asked, limping into the room, closing the door behind me. I myself had hardly recovered, but when I had heard from Mave that he was healing down the hall, I'd decided to pay Willard a visit to give him my best.

He began to grunt in an unseemly manner. I grinned, feeling a sense of power that matched the rage in the pit of my stomach.

"Don't worry, sir, I just have a few questions for you," I said, hobbling over to his bed. I stood at the corner, my hand resting lightly on the lower portion of his cast-wrapped left leg. He twitched but was unable to move beyond that. "I promise, I'll only use my lighter methods of interrogation, as you were so kind to do to Jing... John St. Andrews, as you know him. You seem to have lost your words, and I don't think nodding is an option, but blink once for 'no' and twice for 'yes,' understood?"

He scowled at me and grunted as if calling for someone. I pressed some of my weight into his cast until he howled in pain through clenched teeth, and started blinking with fervour. I nodded and eased up.

"Were you working for my father?" I asked. The man's eyebrows knitted, but no response of blinks came, so I leaned onto his cast again. After a moment of muted howling, he blinked twice.

"Did you know about the murder? Were you a part of it?" I made a motion to lean again, but he blinked once, his eyes otherwise wide with fear.

"Was it my father who ordered Mr. Shackles loosed on Jing... John St. Andrews, the Chinese boy?" I asked, his eyes went even wider, but after a moment he blinked once. No, of course not, that was just

Willard looking to test his machine on his own initiative. My face flushed, thinking of all the pain and fear that creature had caused to Jing and myself and the havoc it had caused across the greater Toronto region.

"Was my father working for the British Crown?" I growled. Willard blinked once. "Was he working for anyone in the military?" Another single blink. "Do you know who he was working for?" Another. My temper rose in spite of myself. "You're lying!" I spat, I raised my fist and slammed it on the man's cast with all my might. Something cracked—his cast? The splint? Something beneath?—and the man screeched through his wired shut teeth, shuddering in his bed. "Tell me! Who was he working for?!"

I felt something warm in my palm and looked down to see my hand was bleeding, cut by splinters of the plaster cast where I'd been clenching my hand onto the cracked material. Shaken out of my rage at the sight of blood, I looked up to see Willard's eyes rolling into the back of his head, tears streaming down his face.

I stumbled backward, and then rushed out of the room. I am normally a gentle soul, perturbed by violence, but something my father had said to me at the start of this entire bloody business came back to me, about not knowing the darkness in men's hearts. Perhaps this week had been my first real glimpse at the true darkness in the hearts of others, and in my own. I had caused pain in others, I had taken a man's life, something I could never forgive myself for. I did not visit Willard again.

On the third day of my convalescence, while the nurses discussed my possible release into Mother's care, I was sitting with Lady in the garden, enjoying a mild summer afternoon, though it did little to improve my mood. Lady's company, however, was welcome, for I had grown fond of the foppish, theatrical dandy. He had even managed to shoo away my imperious nurse.

"Livingston and Hornby showed up yesterday," he said after we'd shared an embrace and made ourselves comfortable on a bench, watching a crone berate an irate nurse across the garden. "Along with the little Native boy... Algernon."

"Perry?"

"Yes, Algernon Perry. He met them in a hotel frequented by airmen. They fear the railways are being watched for our crew. A couple of the others have already been picked up by the military police."

"I'm sorry to hear that," I said, and meant it. Montgomery's men had been brave to a fault, and we all feared they faced unwarranted punishment for their interference in the Queen's kidnapping. Someone was on the hunt. My mother, inside making arrangements with the nurses, had explained to me moments ago how a couple of men in plain dark suits, whom she suspected as federal agents of some kind, had shown up at the hospital asking about the accused murderer and his accomplice; Jing and me.

The head nurse, an iron-fisted Scottish woman, had explained she'd heard of no such nonsense, and would they please not waste her time. However long they were put off, we needed to prepare for their eventual return.

"Livingston, Hornby and Perry were hoping they could join our crew," Lady continued.

"Our crew?" I raised an eyebrow, and Lady nodded, undaunted by my incredulity.

"Figure they can get a ride out of town," he continued, "serve a while, maybe hop off in Montreal or somewhere in the States if our travels take us there."

"What makes you think I have plans to do any travelling?" I asked. I was still deeply disturbed at the ultimate betrayal of my father, and at the thought that I had killed the Chinese pirate, Jiao-Long. I felt broken hearted without Jing. I had fallen into an uncharacteristic melancholy at the confluence of these sentiments. The thought of getting up and leaving town on some fresh adventure seemed impossible without Jing at my side.

"Norwood..." Lady was trying to think of some way to persuade me when we heard a great deal of clattering from above. A window had been thrown open and most of my mother's torso was leaned out over the garden, flailing indelicately. She screamed, "He's awake! He's awake!"

Lady and I looked at one another, our mouths hanging open. We exploded from the garden bench and crashed through the hospital doors, flying up the stairs with my nurse screeching after us that I was supposed to be resting.

We thundered down to the end of the emergency ward and wrenched the curtain aside. Flanked by a scowling nurse on one side, and Mave and my mother grinning and sobbing, respectively, lay Jing, looking irritated. He was still pale and gaunt as he'd been for the past three days, lying unconscious, feverish, on the brink of death, but he was alive and eyeing Lady and I.

"Do you all have to make such a racket?" he asked, his voice weak and dry.

"I quite agree!" his attending nurse began to protest, but I threw myself onto Jing in a passionate, perhaps improper embrace.

The nurses, his and my own, who had followed us upstairs into the ward, began to offer fresh protestations as Jing groaned with the pain of moving his injured arm, but the combined efforts of Lady, Mave and my mother ushering them away, suggesting they fetch some hot soup for their patients allowed Jing and I to remain together, and I kissed him once or twice (or five times) in our moment of privacy. "I'm very glad you're alive," I whispered.

He snorted. "Me too," but he held tight to me with his good arm.

The others returned, assuring us we all had a few moments to talk in private without the nurses descending with their orders of forced bed rest.

"What were you doing in here, Mother?" I asked.

"Mave and I were making sure Jing was being properly cared for and given every attention of the nurses, though all the details had been sorted and the nurses had been paid in advance for his treatment. We don't know by who," she gave a dramatic shrug. "While unnecessary, I thought at the very least the names Quigley and Teston still carry some weight, however diminished our reputations."

"Diminished?" Jing asked, incredulous. We explained about the freezing of Quigley fortunes given my father's undeniable involvement in the kidnapping of Mr. Tinker, though he was pegged as an anti-British, colonial radical rather than orchestrator of von Conrad's murder and the entire international incident. This put Mother in a somewhat awkward social position, though she had a modest inheritance of her own to keep her life going for the time being.

Details of the Teston & Tinker international initiative had been released to the papers by someone—we suspected Willard, though how he had accomplished this trapped in a bed down the hall was frustrating and astounding—and Ms. Teston, ever a contentious individual, however genius, was being smeared and attacked by nationalists as a traitor in the papers.

"Not that it matters," she said, indifferent. "I plan to go ahead, calls of traitor or not. Her Majesty and I are old chums, and she owes me a couple of favours."

"Though a sojourn out of the city is advisable!" my mother added. "Mave has a couple of friends from the States, a Ms. Cohen Kopchovsky and a Ms. Hart. We are planning a woman's only bicycle tour around the world... a novel endeavour."

I was shocked. "Mother, have you ever even been on a bicycle?"

She sniffed at me. "I should think it's dreadfully simple and that I can manage, though perhaps you think it's not suitable for a woman."

I thought nothing of the sort, especially under the intimidating glare of the two women before me. I let the matter drop.

Quigley Airships, Mother explained, would be in flux as neither she, Hector Jr. nor myself had any desire to run the company, however lucrative an endeavour it might be, nor did we have any sentimental ties to it given Father's use of its power in such dreadful pursuits. Mr. Lightly would execute a breaking up of the various properties and assets after an investigation was completed.

Eventually, we would all benefit from the sales of it. She intended to split the proceeds between the three of us, and donate her own to any charity or cause she saw suiting along her global journey. What Hector Jr. and I made of our fortunes, in both a literal and figurative sense, was up to us.

I nodded, now resolute with Jing beside me, alive and almost well. "I'll use mine to pay my crew," I stated to everyone's surprise. "As part of my portion, I will take the *Halcyon II* and follow Father's trail."

Jing and Lady nodded—Lady, especially, looked pleased he'd be flying the *Halcyon II* once again—but Mother and Mave looked uncomfortable. "Norwood," Mother said, her voice all gentleness, "I am furious at him, perhaps more than you. But whatever secret deeds and evils your father may have committed while living... however many deaths he was responsible for, he's gone."

I was blunt with my question: "Have they found a body?" Mave and Mother shared another glance, we'd already had this conversation. I crossed my arms. "Gone, not dead. Even if I can't find him, I at least intend to find out who he was working with in the murder of von Conrad, and his attempt to start a world-wide war."

I frowned to myself. Since the conversation with my father on the bridge of the doomed *Halcyon*, I kept thinking about the way he'd hinted at being part of something bigger, more than a greedy businessman looking to profit from war. I looked up from my thoughts and found everyone studying me, anxious looks on their faces. I grinned sheepishly. "Though I must admit, I have no idea where to start my investigation."

"What about England?" Jing asked, and everyone's attention turned to him. He thought a moment, recalling something, then recited: "33 High Street, London, England. Was it Mr. Crowe?"

"Fragile!" I recalled in excitement, squeezing Jing's hand, and he nodded. I turned to the others. "It was the name on the crates in the *Halcyon*'s hold. Father must have been flying to England, and deemed these crates important enough to deliver to this Mr. Crowe."

"Could be a place to start," Lady warranted, "although we'll need some equipment and upgrades before the *Halcyon*'s ready for a cross-Atlantic flight."

At that moment a monstrous, scowling nurse returned with two bowls of soup for Jing and I, grumbling all the while. Something in her muttering caught my attention, and I, summoning up politeness from the deepest wells within, asked her to repeat. She fixed me with a glare. "Running through my ward all pell-mell! Ordering soup like we was your housemaids! And then those pushy men in the suits show up again and harass the head nurse all talk of murderers and fugitives, and they've got a warrant to search the place! Maybe they'll arrest the lot of you and leave us in peace," she grunted and stomped away.

We were dismayed, least of all at the slights by our caregivers. The return of the agents my mother had mentioned, with Jing still a suspect of murder and conspiracy, Lady and crew under investigation by the Royal Airship Navy and neither myself, Mave nor Mother in particularly good graces of whatever malevolent forces were responsible for the intrigues at the New World Exhibition, we figured a conversation with these visitors would not be productive.

Jing struggled to his feet, but in his weakened and injured state, he could barely be expected to make a great escape by foot.

Some of the past week's events had taken hold of me, however, and I was quick to devise a plan that required dropping Lady out of a window and asking my mother to disrobe. My friends and loved ones set about to my scheme without hesitation.

We went in pairs, first Mave and my mother, though Aveline, for her part, had received a costume change. Ahead of Jing and I by a dozen feet my mother walked at Mave's side, the latter in her signature bicycle suit, the former in the clothing Jing had worn into the hospital, so technically old clothes of Hector and I—shirtsleeves and a pair of trousers, somewhat tattered and torn by the excitement of the week.

Jing, as well, had been changed from his patient's smock into my mother's travelling gown. We had furthered the disguise by wrapping his head and hands in bandages and plopping him into a wheelchair. He resembled nothing more than a tragic, though stylish, female victim of some horrendous accident.

When I asked him, while wrapping his head up, if he was well enough for the endeavour, he smiled, exhausted at the effort of dressing. "I'm just glad that, unlike the night we met, I'm actually wearing something this time someone's trying to arrest me."

We were wheeling along a short distance behind Mother and Mave when I saw the two tall, broad-shouldered, dark-suited, grim-looking men of European stock stalking down the corridor in our direction, chased after by the hospital matron and Jing's nurse. The head nurse, a dour-looking older woman, kept pace with the men, berating them with a steady stream of "Really now!" and "Hardly regulation, sirs! I'll have you reported!"

The men were dumbstruck by Mother and Mave, who they neared in proximity. A woman in a bicycle suit was one thing, but another in little more than rags...

The head nurse looked beyond and we locked eyes. She seemed to be considering if she recognized me.

"Hope you're up to a bit of a jaunt, my dear," I muttered as casual as I could while looking for another route of escape. There was a laundry room through a door nearby, though Jing's nurse was pointing at me. With the agents intent on us, there was no means of getting through the door undetected.

"My love! Come to me!" I heard my mother cry out in a passionate manner. I glanced up from Jing to see her reach for Mave's hand and pull her into a stiff but distracting kiss. This did the trick. The jaws of the nurses and agents, as well as my own, all dropped at the sight, and my mother, getting into the act, dipped Mave expertly. The nurses screeched at the impropriety in their halls, and one of the men scowled, though the other seemed intent on the sight.

"Quick, in here," a quiet voice came from the door, now open. A woman held it ajar, though it was not a woman's voice, but I took advantage of the opportunity and wheeled Jing through. Inside we found a stout laundress of a swarthy complexion, though she smiled a thin smile at us as she pulled the door closed, and I recognized the face beneath the long hair that hung over her eyes and ears.

"You!" I almost screamed in surprise and terror. It was the slight Ojibwe man who had been at the scene of von Conrad's murder and at the airship unveiling the next day. This same man had attempted to speak with me during the battle of the Exhibition, and I realized it was he who'd stood over my bed three nights ago, when I was under the influence of the nurse's anodyne, assuring me all was well. He'd been correct up to a point, I supposed.

He motioned for me to be quiet and led us over to an enormous laundry cart filled with linens, sitting on a steam-powered service lift. He lifted the sheets and smocks and nodded for us to get in. Jing looked at me, shrugged, then stood and let himself fall into the soft cradle of sheets. The mysterious Ojibwe man took the wheelchair from me and wheeled it into the corner with some others, then looked to me. "Hurry, they'll check in here. I promise I'll explain what I can in a moment. Please trust me, Mr. Quigley."

I climbed into the laundry cart with Jing, and the man pulled layers of cloth over us. After a moment we heard the door slam open. "You!" a gruff voice called out. "Washerwoman!"

"Aye?" the mysterious Ojibwe man shot back in a high, feminine voice, impressive given he was more of a *basso profondo*.

"Two people just come through this door?"

255

"Aye sonny," the man grunted in his feminine voice. Jing and I tensed. "They're still standing in it, interrupting my rounds." There was a moment where this sunk in and the "washerwoman" let out a cackle as one of the men swore at her.

"Come on, maybe they got back into the ward," the other man growled at his companion and the door slammed behind them. We heard the disguised Ojibwe man step onto the lift and hit the lever, and the thing shuddered to life, lowering.

Jing and I looked to each other beneath the weight of the sheets, unsure of what to do. The lift shuddered to a stop and the linens were thrown aside. The Ojibwe man stood in his dark suit and bowler hat—he'd somehow changed in the little time it took the lift to reach the first floor.

I climbed out, and the Ojibwe man and I helped Jing out, who wobbled as he stood. The man walked over to a shelf of linens and drew aside a stack of sheets, revealing clothes folded within—a shirt, trousers, suspenders, a cap and a pair of boots. "Put these on, they may be a bit more comfortable," he nodded at Jing, who went to the task of stripping out of my mother's travelling gown and changing into the waiting clothing with my help, without a shred of modesty.

"Who are you?" I asked, wary, as I helped Jing climb into the trousers.

The expression on the man's face was inscrutable, but there was warmth, kindness, amusement that played about his eyes as they met mine. "I am many things, we are many things. We are so often nameless, but I suppose you can call me Benjamin Two-Rivers."

"Two-Rivers!" Jing and I cried out in unison. Mave's instructions were not to find two rivers, but this man of the same name!

"You were at the exhibit, during the battle... on the airship field... on the steamship!" I pointed out, and he nodded.

"Watching, waiting," Two-Rivers explained. "Against all the oaths of my people I approached you during the battle at the Exhibition. I was going to tell you Mr. Tinker was to be kidnapped. I would have ruined everything... stopped you from saving the Queen, and I feel the battle would have raged on." His smile was sad. "I suppose even we who think ourselves wise make mistakes, but fortunately mine did not interfere with your excellent work, Mr. Quigley."

Jing winced in pain as I helped him pull on the shirt, but he turned his gaze on the man as Two-Rivers went to the door and peaked out. "We... your people?"

"You aren't... working with my father, are you?" I asked, though the question seemed stupid after I said it, given his aid.

Two-Rivers turned, and the warmth had faded from his eyes, replaced with a slight steely scowl. "I can say little. We are not working with your father but in direct opposition. We are nameless. We are the sentinels. Where others strive for domination and power, we strive for harmony and balance. We strive for peace... but I say too much. We would like to help you, Mr. Quigley, Mr. Jing. I can say little more, but we would like to help you."

"Oh," I said, looking to Jing for an appraisal. He shot me a dubious look and shrugged as much as he could manage. "Alright?"

"The corridor is clear," Two-Rivers continued, after checking once again. He opened the door and, with Jing propped against me, we hobbled our way out into the empty lower hallway, which seemed reserved for service and supply. "You seek information about your father. We can help you and your crew get to where you need to go and may be of further use in your goals. We cannot reveal our work, but we will be in contact."

The thrum of a familiar engine came from without, and Jing and I were temporarily distracted as we watched the *Halcyon II* touch down carefully in the middle of Shuter Street, to the amazement of those walking by, and the surprise and chagrin of several carriage drivers. We would need to hurry before it attracted the notice of the suited men searching for us.

I looked back to the door where Two-Rivers had been standing moments before, but he had disappeared. Jing hurried me onward, and there was little I could do but brace him against me and propel us forward.

Mother and Mave awaited us outside of the Shuter Street entrance. Red-faced, casting nervous glances at my mother, Mave helped me walk a weakened Jing toward the cargo door of the *Halcyon II*. Perry, Livingston and Hornby stood inside, frantically gesturing us to board. Mother's face was flushed with the excitement of the morning, and kissed Jing and me on our foreheads before Mave helped my companion aboard.

This gave me a moment alone with my mother, a woman who, until a few days ago, was secure in her life and fortunes. Now all was changed. Her husband had been revealed to be behind malevolent machinations and was now presumed dead. One son had been duped in the endeavour and seemed consumed by shame and failure. The other son, myself... well, I was triumphant in many ways but feared what the future held for my dear mother, and myself, but I could see a new edge of defiance and daring in her.

She threw her arms around me in a tight embrace, all her old habits of propriety lost. "I am so proud of you, Norwood," she whispered before pulling back from the hug and appraising me a moment. "I would ask you to write, but I fear our little bicycle gang will not have a fixed address for the time being."

"I shall follow your exploits in the papers, I'm sure," I said smiling. "That will be a sight to see, Dame Aveline Quigley astride a Starley Rover on some road abroad. A change from the society pages, at the very least."

Mother kissed my cheek, squeezed my hand. I turned away toward the airship; I didn't want her to see the tears in my eyes and inspire the same in her own. She always was the melodramatic type.

Mave shook my hand as I approached the *Halcyon II*'s hold door. "Two-Rivers?" I asked, and a shadow passed over her face. "Is he good or bad?"

She pondered this a moment, then shrugged. "I don't know if good or bad is the right way to look at it."

"You were to meet him?" I asked, remembering the initials "BTR" in her notes. "With von Conrad."

Mave nodded. "And in my meeting with Ambassador Chen. It was Two-Rivers who approached me and advised me that our letters were being read. He asked if he could be part of my negotiations to protect me, and my interests. You asked if he's good or bad... I think he's more of a meddler. However..."

She nodded over my shoulder. I turned to see the two men in dark suits hurtling forth from the hospital entrance toward the waiting vessel.

"Take your time," Lady's voice crackled over the airship's electrical announcement system, sounding bored. "Just a couple of crackers we're trying to get away from. Might as well invite them aboard."

"Perhaps you should take your leave," Mave winked as I climbed past her, up into the *Halcyon II*. "Good hunting, Norwood. Give 'em hell!"

I'd barely climbed up the loading door of the *Halcyon II* when the airship bobbed upwards, between the hospital and buildings opposite of St. Michael's. I turned back to wave, but Mother and Mave had already disappeared into the nearby alley, dismaying our pursuers. Being a Quigley no longer held the safety and security it once did by any member of the family, it seemed.

One of the men drew a pistol and aimed it at the *Halcyon II* to fire, but I watched as the hold door closed behind me. His compatriot pushed the man's hand down, stopping the attempt.

By the time the door closed fully, we were well above the roofs of Toronto. When I walked onto the main deck, I glanced back over the aft to see the city sinking back into the horizon. Or, rather, we were speeding forward, on to whatever may come

EPILOGUE

IN WHICH THERE IS THE BEGINNINGS
OF ANOTHER ADVENTURE

My crew got us to the city of Montreal by the next morning, easy enough. Lady directed the *Halcyon II* to an illicit airship yard outside of the city proper, though we could see the small, bustling riverside city just over a hill and across the river to the south, smudged by the smoke of hundreds of chimneys.

The yard was a riot of cargo and airships in no particular arrangement or order. The vessels were made up of all different sizes, models and qualities, though they skewed toward older and ramshackle merchant class vessels.

The crews of the vessels matched the mix of airships to the tee. The pristine, gold-accented *Halcyon II* stood out like a gay Catholic lass among stern Protestant preachers. To my relief, Lady was well acquainted with the procedure of haggling for decent mooring by process of trading threats, witticisms and—what seemed to me—far too much money with a dour, slouching Frenchman.

We were surprised soon after mooring by a visit from a woman; a respectable looking Jewess in a dark shall and head wrapping, though young, perhaps a few years older than myself. She conversed with Jing and Lady in French—my understanding of the language being rudimentary on a good day—and she handed us a shipping manifesto for a ship called the *Athena*.

"That would be us!" Lady showed me with a grin after the woman had departed, disappearing into the chaos of the illegal airship yard. "For now, at least, to avoid attention while we get some work done... we're to pick up some supplies tomorrow and deliver them someplace north of the Kawarthas."

"Oh." The unexpected work struck me as dubious. "Did she... say why? Or who she is?"

Jing smirked, leaning against the hull of the *Halcyon II*. He could now walk, unassisted for the most part, and I was glad of his improvement. "'J'suis anonyme. J'suis une sentinelle,'" he quoted, and I raised my eyebrows to a roll of his eyes. "Nameless. A sentinel. Sound familiar?"

Two-Rivers... or at least someone working with him? I admitted it did, and that we would pick up the work. I at least owed Two-Rivers that much for his help. And the work paid, so there was that as well.

Lady was thrilled at the prospect of shore leave in Montreal, and threw his arms around Livingston and Hornby, promising he'd get them drunk and find them women or men, whatever their fancy, as a celebration of their new posts. At the prospect of a night of debauchery, the two men, in the proper English fashion, gave ample, gentlemanly protests that did not seem especially genuine.

Algernon Perry, my new airman formerly of the original *Halcyon*, volunteered to stay behind with me to guard the airship. The lad seemed quite in worship of me, to the delight of the crew and my horror—while I'd saved his life, I was hardly a hero, and I had seen enough of the deeds of men I once thought heroes that left me wishing to avoid their company.

I ordered him on shore leave, promising that if we were picking up work where we could find it to afford equipment for a cross-Atlantic flight, it might be some time before we had a full evening's rest. The boy seemed disappointed to be ordered away but slunk off into the crowd as Lady regaled his crewmates with tales of bold, unclothed daring in brothels from St. Kitts to St. John's. I scoffed at the motley crew I had assembled, and the depravity Lady planned for them at the top of his voice.

Jing and I retired to the captain's quarters. I had to tend to his wounds and thoroughly observe the healing of his bruised body, as we had no doctor aboard. We were poor guards that evening. That is all I will write on the matter.

A news story must convey the facts, navigating the perilous waters of bias to approach something resembling the truth. It must find some order to events and have a beginning, middle and end, though the world does not follow this form.

A news story is simpler to write than one documenting life beyond the borders of a broadsheet. Life is rarely as ordered, prejudice seeps in, and every ending feels rather like a new beginning. I have attempted to recount the events of the New World Exhibition and its many intrigues as faithfully as possible, though I find an ending difficult to approach for these reasons.

I pen this from my writing desk in the captain's quarters aboard the *Halcyon II*... I suppose I can call it the *Halcyon* and spare myself the ink, given the original is far from airworthy in its current state. I can also call the captain's quarters my own, as this is my ship, though I share the cabin with Jing.

My crew has proved themselves intelligent and resourceful, if a little unconventional. Lady had a hammock from the cramped crew quarters installed in the *Halcyon*'s bridge—one has to duck under it to consult with him—and he rarely leaves even when he's relieved of duty. I don't discourage this. He's the greatest airship pilot to take to the skies, in my reckoning, and I am happy to have him aboard and as close to the control panel as possible.

Livingston and Hornby keep to themselves for the most part, though they are unfailing in their duties as airmen. However, if we ever make it to Old Britannia, they expressed a desire to return home to their families, although I can't imagine them parting each other's side for an instant.

Algernon Perry dogs me about the *Halcyon* like a pup, wide-eyed and full of indelicate questions about the companionship between Jing and I. Jing jests that the young airman is sweet on me and that he'd most likely join us in our quarters if we invited him. Jing also mocks my bulging eyes and spluttering at the thought but points out that I have never said "no" to the suggestion. Despite the somewhat awkward circumstances, he's a loyal airman and is training under Lady's sharp eye and bawdy humour, and I believe he'll make an excellent pilot someday soon.

For his part, Jing has almost overcome his fear of heights, although he prefers to be inside out of the violent tugging of air currents. Outside of my cabin, he has made himself quite useful in the engine room. I feel he has a special affinity toward machinery and could be an inventor who'd make the Teston & Tinker workshop proud, given enough time and study. Inside our cabin, he warms my bed after a long day of flying, for the skies can be cold even at the height of summer. I try to take his jesting and arcane references in stride... although I admit I've learned a great deal from him in exchange for making him a good airman.

And myself: Norwood Quigley, novice journalist, photographer, captain of the *Halcyon*, also known as the *Athena*? I was reunited with my precious camera aboard the airship, and plan to set up a darkroom in the *Halcyon*'s store when supplies can be found, but in the meantime, I have been documenting our journey with the little film I have left, helped along by Mr. Tinker's fabulous and frightening flash explosion device.

As an airship captain, my anxieties recede and my confidence grows with each order I give, and I enjoy my role as a captain more every day, though I find myself feeling for my crew as a mother duck feels for her accident-prone ducklings. I worry about them constantly, as they are the types who find trouble without fail—enough to fill another book no matter where we land, and even among each other aboard the *Halcyon*.

In any case, we delivered our first shipment to a small, independent

Cree tribe in the Kawarthas, only to be given another missive by a spotty, gangly Cree adolescent—another nameless "sentinel"—to deliver enormous wood carvings to a scholar in Vancouver, our current heading. The purpose of the work eludes me, but our delivery to the Cree community turned out to be much needed medical supplies, and each job has promised to pay better than the last so I cannot complain. We may eschew authorities and the law under a false name, but I am proud of my crew and my ship.

I am also proud to stand close by Jing's side on the deck of my airship, as we did early in the morning after my crew's debaucheries in Montreal. Lady, nursing a headache and complaining of the early departure and a lack of sleep, eased the *Halcyon* skyward, and Jing and I watched as the sun broke the horizon in the east.

Despite the trials of the preceding week, we couldn't help but grin at each other, myself dazzled by the beautiful sight of the sunrise lighting the face of the person I had come to love so dearly. Arms around one another, I felt a surge of hope as we continued our ascent into the cloudless sky, matching the sun's rise.

Jing and I shared an embrace; we were together, come what may, and I whispered in his ear, "Come, let's have an adventure."

-N.I.Q. II
May 12, 1893

ACKNOWLEDGEMENTS

I would first like to acknowledge that the land on which I live, where much of the story was written—and, in fact, where the story takes place—is the traditional lands of the Mississaugas of the New Credit First Nation, the Haudenosaunee, the Anishinaabe and the Huron-Wyndat. I wish to acknowledge them as the past, present and future caretakers of this land, traditional territory named Tkaronto, "Where The Trees Meet The Water," "The Gathering Place." Furthermore, I was born and raised on traditional territory of the Passamaquoddy and the Wabanaki Confederacy, and I'd like to thank the Elders and current communities of the land I call my home. I strive to combat colonial forces that undermine, distort or erase the vital role of Indigenous people in our world through my writing and practice.

I'd like to thank some generous early readers. Jeremy Willard, this book should have been dedicated to you. Steve Berman, your support and encouragement are the only reason I got through draft one; I also took out an adverb or two, begrudgingly. Matt Bright, your feedback, after sitting down and reading that first draft in a single evening, shaped what the story has become.

This book is a Glad Day Bookshop success story. When I read a snippet of a half finished draft at the Naked Heart LGBTQ Literary Festival in 2015, the encouragement of attendees and the coven of the sci-fi, fantasy and horror authors was the catalyst to overcome my imposter syndrome and finish the damn thing. Special thanks for the friendship and support of James K. Moran and Stephen Graham King. Much love to the staff, owners and board of Glad Day, especially Michael Erickson. I have a job that doesn't feel like work and enables me to write; I live a charmed life.

Finally, thanks to Kenny and Bruce, my boys.

ABOUT THE AUTHOR

MJ Lyons (@queer_mikey) is a writer, bookstore professional and game maker. He has written for dozens of publications, including a five-year-long column with a colleague on lesser known LGBT history, History Boys. He also published his short story, "To kill in a god," in *Clockwork Cairo: Steampunk Tales of Egypt*, and a chapbook of speculative fiction short stories, *Temple of Cats*. His game writing includes *LongStory*, a LGBT-positive dating sim for young people, *The Last Taxi*, a dystopian resource management VR game, and *Later Daters*, a dating game set in a retirement community. He lives in Toronto with his goblin of a cat

Renaissance
Diverse Canadian Voices

Renaissance was founded in May 2013 by a group of friends who wanted to publish and market those stories which don't always fit neatly in a genre, or a niche, or a demographic. We weren't sure what we wanted to publish exactly, so like the happy panbibliophiles that we are, we opened our submissions, with no other personal guideline than finding a Canadian book we would fall in love with enough that we would want to publish and sell.

Five years later, this is still very true; however, we've also noticed an interesting trend in what we tended to publish. It turns out that we are naturally drawn to the voices of those who are members of a marginalized group (especially people with disabilities and LGBTQIAPP2+ people), and these are the voices we want to continue to uplift.

To us, Renaissance isn't just a business; it's a family. Being authors and artists ourselves, we are always careful to center the experience of the author above all else. We involve our authors in every step of the process, and trust that they know how to best market their labour of love, though devoted committees take on the difficult tasks of copy editing, designing and marketing to achieve professional results.

At Renaissance, we do things differently. We are passionate about books, and we care as much about our authors enjoying the publishing process as we do about our readers enjoying a great, professional quality and affordable product on the platform they prefer.

renaissancebookpress.com
info@renaissancebookpress.com

If you enjoyed this book, you will love these other Renaissance titles!

Find them all (and more!) at
renaissancebookpress.com

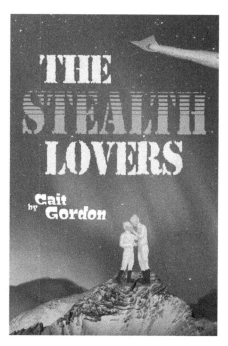

LGBT/Science-Fiction

MANY YEARS BEFORE THEY LANDED ON CINNEH, TWO YOUNG MEN STARTED BASIC TRAINING, ALSO KNOWN AS "VACAY IN HAY."

Xaxall Dwyer Knightly might only be a private, but his sergeant is fascinated by him. During a combat exercise, Private Knightly wins the distinction of being the first-ever trainee to throw an opponent through a supporting wall. The teen has the strength of five Draga put together.

Vivoxx Nathan Tirowen, son of General Tirowen, stands tall with a naturally commanding presence. A young man of a royal clan, the private has an uncanny talent with weaponry. The sarge is convinced that Private Tirowen could "trim the pits of a rodent without nicking the skin."

When the two recruits meet, Vivoxx smiles warmly and Xaxall speaks in backwards phonetics. Little do they know the bond they immediately feel for each other will morph into a military pairing no one in Dragal history has ever seen.

THIS IS THE STORY OF THE STEALTH— LEGENDARY, FORMIDABLE, AND FABULOUS.

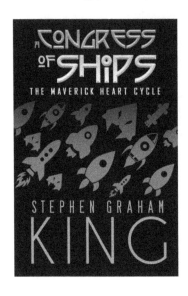

A CONGRESS OF SHIPS

BY STEPHEN GRAHAM-KING

Science-Fiction

In a desolate system on the outer edge of Pan Galactum, the skin of the universe has ruptured, tearing open a portal to an alternate reality. Witnessed only by the sentient science vessel N'Dea, a massive, battered ship falls through, housing a community of refugees fleeing an enemy that has pursued them across the cold reaches of space for decades.

But have they come alone?

Summoned by N'Dea while en route from a reunion with dear friends on the Galactum's capital, the mystery is a lure that fellow Artificial Sentience, the Maverick Heart, cannot resist. It's now up to Vrick, along with humans Keene, Lexa-Blue and Ember, and allies old and new, to come to the aid of this ship of lost souls. Together they must find a way to seal the breach for good, before a ravening hunger can spill through and rip the Galactum apart.

THE FACE IN THE MARSH

BY ELIZABETH HIRST

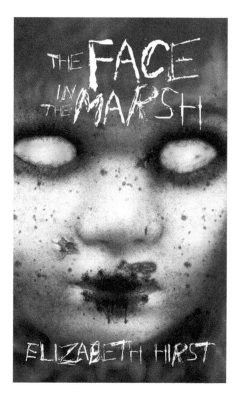

"Terrifying and
wonderfully queer."
Nathan Fréchette, author of
Blood Matters

Kenzie is twenty-five, with two degrees and no job prospects. When her parents offer her a job curating their museum, Ettenby's Log Palace, she accepts out of desperation, despite their history of family conflict. She arrives praying that her secrets will stay buried, and her hard-won mental health won't relapse.

Once at the Log Palace, Kenzie is fascinated by an unsettling collection of junk dolls found on the property. As she follows the thread left by the collection, she discovers a history of poltergeist activity, witchcraft and death on the small island housing the museum.

CPSIA information can be obtained
at www.ICGtesting.com
Printed in the USA
LVHW091706300719

625872LV00008B/956/P